Happy

Happy

Happy

Happy Happy Happy

NICOLA MASTERS

LAKE UNION

PUBLISHING

Text copyright © 2022 by Nicola Masters

Published by Lake Union Publishing, Seattle

www.apub.com

Amazon, the Amazon logo, and Lake Union Publishing are trademarks of Amazon.com, Inc., or its affiliates.

ISBN-13: 9781542039000
ISBN-10: 1542039002

Cover design by Emma Rogers

Printed in the United States of America

For my family

CHAPTER ONE

I'd forgotten how many stars you can see in the arse end of nowhere. And the moonlight here is so bright it might as well be full-on daytime. There are twelve knockers nailed to the front door now. Two of the ones I remember from The Bad Old Days have been reduced to nothing more than lumps of rust, a track of reddish brown highlighting the course of the all-too-frequent rain to the front step. I brush one lightly with my fingertips. It flakes under my touch.

I stand on the doorstep of the house I've actively avoided for thirteen years, unable to believe quite how much has changed. London has turned me into a completely different person, unrecognisable, totally transformed from—

'Charlie Trewin! I can't believe my eyes. It's been years! How the hell are you?'

In a thousand years I didn't expect Lowenna Murphy to still be with us. My curmudgeonly neighbour had seemed to be at least a hundred and fifty years old ever since I was born. And yet here she is, leaning out of her bedroom window in her nightie. I've never seen her in her nightie before. I probably could have lived without it.

'I thought I heard someone sneaking around outside,' she continues. I suppose it's good that her hearing hasn't deteriorated.

'How's your father?' she asks me, solemnly. 'He didn't look good when they took him away.'

I open my mouth to reply but nothing comes out. I actually don't think I've spoken aloud since I told the taxi driver where I wanted to go when it was all over. He was a mercifully quiet man, and I couldn't have persuaded my thoughts to sit still even if he had wanted to chat. I clear my throat.

'He died, Lowenna,' I tell her. Might as well keep it simple.

Lowenna raises a hand to her mouth. Her wedding ring gleams in the moonlight. I never met her husband. He died before I was born.

'Oh, love. I am so sorry to hear that. Let me pop on some clothes and I'll be right over to make us a tea.'

'No!' I answer a little too quickly. She looks offended, despite it being past midnight, so I add, 'I think I'm just going to go straight to sleep, if that's OK. I had a long day.'

She nods.

'Of course, lovely. But you let me know if you need anything. Absolutely anything at all.'

Her offer catches me in the chest somewhere. It's been a long time since I've even known the name of a next-door neighbour, let alone had the kind of relationship where you'd do things for one another. I've forgotten what it feels like. Lowenna pulls her curtains closed and after a couple of minutes the light goes out, leaving me standing like a lemon in front of my old front door. If there were a bar open past midnight, I'd be there in a heartbeat. Unfortunately, I have no choice but to go inside.

◆ ◆ ◆

It's worth noting that my dad was a collector of absolute shit. He didn't like to let go of things. When it first started he told me he was going to put it all on eBay. It seemed optimistic, because he barely knew how to check the email I'd set up for him, but I didn't question it. I was probably too self-absorbed, to be honest. And then, eventually, the first stuff he brought into the house was buried by more recent additions, and suddenly I had to dodge old shop dummies when I went to the loo in the middle of the night.

Towers of tins teetered in every corner of the kitchen, many of their sell-by dates a distant memory. The garden was littered with toys, even though the only child who'd ever lived there (hi) had grown too old for them many years previously.

My mum would be rolling in her grave if her ashes weren't somewhere in amongst the chaos. The poor woman. She used to say she wanted to be scattered at sea and instead she was swallowed by a tide of junk.

◆ ◆ ◆

I never came back. When I left for university I left for good. I couldn't deal with the memories or the pitying looks our neighbours gave me as they squeezed my hand and told me how proud she would have been. I always wanted to point out that she couldn't have been that proud or she wouldn't have done what she did, but I was too scared of making things awkward. It was true, though. Nothing good ever happened in Carncarrow, so I swapped the seagull cries and sandy shoes for sirens and air that felt weirdly thick until I stopped noticing.

I thought I'd love the anonymity in London. Nobody knew me, so nobody looked at me like the very idea of me made them sad. I didn't even have to live in fear of Lowenna banging on the wall if I happened to play music a fraction of a decibel too loudly. And I did kind of think I'd be like the students you see on TV. I'd collect a gang of ride-or-die friends who I'd know for the rest of my life. I'd wear short skirts, maybe have a couple of one-night stands, always be throwing parties. But, big shocker, none of that happened. I soon discovered I wasn't outgoing enough for any of those things. I'd love to play the 'dead mum' card (it has to have its uses) but I suspect I just wasn't built that way. So, I settled into obscurity, chipping in my quid for the tea kitty and spending my nights in my room, telling myself over and over again that I wasn't lonely, it was a choice.

I moved into a flatshare after university, 2:1 in hand, and worked in a bar to make ends meet. Socially, it was very much the same situation, and I kept telling myself it was fine. Eventually, I found a sensible career in HR, and the rest is history. Don't get me wrong, it's *boring* history, but there's fizzy water on tap and the office moves fast enough that you never really have to think about whether you actually want to be there, so it'll do.

I met my fiancé, James, at the gym. He was doing actual exercise, and I was walking as slowly as possible on the treadmill while watching *The Chase*. At our age, the world and his (soon to be) wife are getting married, so now we are too.

Dad and I never really knew how to deal with what Mum did. You just don't. I think the sight of me must have reminded him of everything he'd lost and all the things that were too painful to think about. I think that because I *know* that seeing him did the same for me. So, we did what any normal family would do and pretended the feelings we couldn't even begin to handle didn't exist. He'd text me every few weeks to ask how I was, and I'd lie and say I was fine. Great! Everything all good at work, and I definitely don't regret moving away at *all*. So. Good.

And then suddenly the phone rang. A nice lady was telling me gently but firmly that I needed to come and say my goodbyes, and I was on the next train. It was all over too quickly but I made it by the skin of my teeth.

◆　◆　◆

I turn the key in the lock and push, then meet resistance as I try to open the door wide enough for me to actually fit through. After a few attempts at shoulder-barging (which would perhaps have been

4

more effective had I applied myself more at the gym) something gives way, and I'm able to peer around the door to see what the problem is.

A stack of newspapers, or what I assume must have been a stack before it toppled over, is heaped on the doormat. I squeeze my arm through the gap and flap my hand around, hoping to make some room without dislocating my shoulder. I can imagine the faces of the firefighters if I end up stuck in this position and Lowenna has to send for help. It doesn't bear thinking about. I probably went to school with some of them.

'Fucking come on, you piece of shit,' I hiss.

There is a small chance that the stresses of the day are starting to get the better of me, but I try to keep the swearing quiet in case Lowenna hears me. I'm thirty-one years old and she'd definitely still scold me, even though she always used to have one of the foulest mouths I've ever heard. The papers eventually give way enough to allow me to squeeze myself inside, albeit with some danger to the buttons on the blouse I put on this morning in London before everything caved in. I shut the door behind me with a click.

I pause for a moment with my back to the hallway and take in the smell. It smells like a childhood spent running into the house with seaweed in my hair, Dad hot on my heels, laughing my head off. It smells like the day everything changed. It smells like so much happiness and sadness all rolled into one that I might throw up. I take a couple of huge breaths and snap on the light. Then I turn around and trip over the papers I'd already forgotten were there.

'Fuck!'

The hallway itself is exactly as chaotic as I expected it to be. All of the pictures I remember are still on the walls: happy faces from my childhood, drawings I did as a kid, a couple of oil paintings Dad took off Dave in the village because apparently there was a chance they were Turner studies. They were not Turner studies. They were crap.

'Someone worked really hard on these,' Dad used to protest when I said we should throw them out. 'All that effort gone to waste. No, we can't.'

The shelf that runs along one wall is stacked with odds and ends. There are cracked vases and chipped ornaments next to grimy glassware and a few floral pillboxes. He always said he was waiting for the day *Antiques Roadshow* came to town, but I never believed him. He just couldn't bear to let anything go after Mum. So, I'd smile and nod and help him find space for the next box of stuff, because what else can you do? He's . . . was my dad.

I sink into the chair by the door and remove my shoes because old habits die hard, then I switch the light back off again. The darkness is complete for a couple of seconds, until my eyes adjust to the shafts of moonlight on the piles of junk. I weave my way through the hall and up the stairs, navigating by the moon and by touch. I don't have the energy to get reacquainted with the house tonight. I could sleep for a week.

I expected my old room to have been taken over with rambling piles of junk, but when I switch on the light I see that it's exactly how I left it. It's almost aggressively neat. Where Dad responded to Mum's death by hanging on to everything he possibly could, I've found it easier never to get attached to anything. What's the point when it can all be ripped away from you in a second?

What few posters I stuck up are neatly tacked to the wall at perfect right angles. Johnny Depp smiles down haughtily (I know, I know, I was young). There's a fine layer of dust over everything, but it's all exactly where I left it. There's even a calendar pinned to the back of the door with the date I was due to leave for university circled so emphatically it obscures almost the whole of September. I feel a twinge of guilt for leaving it up.

The bedding gives me a chill of recognition. The splashy floral pattern is burned into my brain from lying under it, too ill to move, shortly after I started junior school.

I was supposed to get up so that Dad could take me to school on the way to work. But it turned out I'd been struck down with what I can only describe as an earth-shattering, fevery stomach thing (I have no medical qualifications, I don't know if you can tell). All I did was lie there and shiver, or lie there and complain about being too hot. I'd occasionally mix it up by puking in the mop bucket.

I slept a lot. My dreams were weird. But whenever I woke up my face felt lovely and cool, and Dad was there. He'd brought one of the dining chairs up, and he sat in it, holding a flannel to my forehead. He was supposed to be at work.

'Alright, monkey?' he asked softly when I opened my eyes again. I nodded.

The next time my eyes fluttered open he was stroking my hair. A giant glass of orange squash had appeared on the nightstand.

'Dinner's ready.' Mum poked her head around the door. 'How's the patient?'

'Still under the weather, aren't you?' Dad gave me a small smile, and I nodded weakly before I shut my eyes again.

'Are you coming down?'

'I think I'll stay here for a bit, keep an eye on things.'

'Yes, Matron,' Mum teased, and I could hear the smile in her voice. I forced my heavy eyelids open for a second, just in time to see her plant a kiss on the top of Dad's head, and then I heard her go downstairs.

The next time I opened my eyes it was dark and something wasn't normal. The room seemed to be rumbling. It took a minute before I realised it was the sound of Dad snoring. I lifted my head a fraction and could make out his shape still filling the uncomfortable chair by my bed.

As my eyes adjusted to the glow of the nightlight I saw his head drooping backwards, his mouth wide open. A guaranteed crick in the neck.

I sat up, suddenly aware of how thirsty I was, my only thought being that glass of orange squash. When I went to pick it up I noticed there was an empty dinner plate on the nightstand now as well. He hadn't left me once.

I settled back down and fell asleep again, lulled by the sound of his snoring.

I close the lilac curtains and get undressed. I find some old pyjamas that haven't seen the light of day in thirteen years, and I pull them on. Honestly, years and years of trying to make something of myself upcountry and I still end up back in Carncarrow wearing Forever Friends PJs. It's *almost* as if none of it was worth it. As I climb into bed my phone buzzes on the nightstand.

Everything OK? reads the text.

I'll deal with that in the morning.

◆ ◆ ◆

I'm woken at least three times in the night by the seagulls shrieking. The first time it happens I leap out of bed, absolutely convinced there's somebody screaming outside. Then the memory of the past twelve hours or so washes over me and I sink back onto the mattress, pulling the covers over my head. The second time it happens, I put a pillow over my ears like people do in films, but it feels like a very impractical solution, and also like one that might suffocate me. The third time, I yell the c-word at the seagulls because it's, like, 3 a.m. and I'm mad. I get a sharp tap on the wall from Lowenna for that one.

The next time I wake up, it's daylight and I have no idea what time it is. The curtains are sunlit from behind, giving everything in the room a pinkish hue, so it's definitely not early.

My phone vibrates on the bedside table. It briefly stops, then it carries on. I flip it over.

James.

My thumb hovers over 'Answer' for a second as my mind races. I should answer and tell him . . . Actually, that's where I fall down. I don't know what I want to say. I change my mind and hold my thumb on the off button so hard that the tip turns white. The screen goes black, and I throw the phone into the drawer next to the bed. It lands amongst some manky old sweets, a sheet of stickers, a mini troll doll, some pens, and a handful of old coins. Teenage me had to keep her small amount of clutter somewhere. Although if she'd understood how much everything was going to cost when she got to London, she might not have been so blasé about leaving those coins behind.

There's an old school photo on the nightstand. I look really gawky, and my heart could break for that sad teenager if it wasn't quite so pre-occupied with recent events. I stare at the girl in the silver frame. She has flyaway hair and wears a blue blazer. She has acne sprayed across her forehead, and her too-small school blouse strains over the chest she was always worried people would tease her about. I remember being too embarrassed to tell Dad I needed a new shirt, but also burning with humiliation every time I walked down the corridors.

I've never understood the people who look back at their school-days with fondness. I guess I just like to leave depressing things in the past. Move on, clean slate.

The girl in the frame was so excited to leave forever. She had such high hopes for an exciting new life. I pick up the photo for a closer look. She'd be so unimpressed with me now.

CHAPTER TWO

Without even thinking about it I sit up and search the floor with my toes until I find my slippers. I haven't done that for thirteen years and the instinct is still there. As are the slippers.

Johnny Depp smirks down at me from the opposite wall. A seagull cries on the roof. I pull myself to my feet and throw on my old pink dressing gown. There's a tissue in the pocket, probably last used circa 2006. I guess even teenage neat freaks can be disgusting sometimes.

I pad down the stairs in my slippers. There are piles of books at the end of each step. Frankly, it's a miracle I made it up in the dark last night without incident. The little stained-glass window in the front door splashes jewel-coloured light across the heap of newspapers still lying on the doormat. It almost looks artistic. It's probably the first time anyone's ever thought a pile of tatty old tabloids looked beautiful.

The kitchen has acquired at least double the amount of clutter since I've been away. It's fascinating, really, because in a thousand years I wouldn't have thought there was space. Most of the tins and packets are years past their sell-by dates. It looks like Dad was preparing for something terrible to happen, when he was really trying to claw back control after it already had.

The entire room is full of him. Which is not even a cheap shot about all the stuff in here. I see him everywhere I turn. In the corner by the larder is the spot where my play kitchen used to stand. Dad would sit at the table for hours as I served him something like a fifteen-course taster menu of the finest, artisanal, Michelin-starred air. The sink is where he used to let me stand on a chair and 'help' with the washing-up, which mainly involved him crowning me with bubbles and occasionally handing me a teaspoon to dry because it was all I could be trusted with. The worktop is where he once spent a rainy afternoon showing me how to make a giant mess with bicarbonate of soda and vinegar. I think he tried to imply we were doing chemistry. I swallow the lump in my throat.

◆ ◆ ◆

Through the window I can see that the back garden is littered with bits of old bikes and a rusty metal frame that must once have been the swing. The sun is shining and, upcountry, this might be what July looks like. But this is September. Some of the leaves are just beginning to turn. I try to ignore the splatter of seagull shit on the window.

I open the cupboard I always used to make a beeline for in the mornings and, sure enough, find a box of cereal. It could still be thirteen years ago apart from the fact that Snap, Crackle, and Pop have aged. As I crunch my way through a bowl of what could honestly be cardboard for all the attention I'm paying to it, I survey the room. The same old photos and drawings still decorate the fridge, although they've faded a lot and the magnet collection has expanded. I feel a stab of something unpleasant. I need coffee.

I boil the kettle and spoon some terrible instant coffee into a cup while I finish my cereal. I pick up an old paper from the hallway and lean against the counter as I sip, reading about a footballer who did something sexually heinous a few years ago. Even though he's the one on trial I feel as if he's judging me for taking my time over breakfast on a day like today. My chest starts to flutter. I need to get to work.

Except, I mean, what am I supposed to do now? Do I go back to the hospital? Do I start contacting funeral companies? Do you just call them, or do they call you? Do I have to get quotes? Won't that be weird? Should I be making other phone calls? Something about banks, maybe? Do I have to see the body? Will it still look like him? Will I have to identify him? I surely did that last night when I spent an hour holding his hand until he slipped away.

My knees feel weak and I slide onto the lino, resting my head against the cupboard under the sink which I know for a fact holds the dregs of every bottle of cleaning product that has ever entered this house. My hands are cold and I place one against my forehead. I don't even know what I'm doing here. It actually feels presumptuous to think I'd be required to organise anything. People manage fine without me.

I can't believe this time yesterday I was just sitting at work. I would have been absentmindedly doodling in my notebook and trying to ignore the meeting happening around me. I didn't think my life was about to get worse. I suppose I didn't realise it could.

Nope. Stop it. This is not OK. I have a very nice life, and a very secure life, and I'm happy. I'm happy, I'm happy, I'm happy. Apart from this, obviously, but this is *very* new and aside from this I'm happy.

I was leaving a conference room feeling thoroughly hopeless when my phone rang. I can't even remember what the meeting was about now – some 'streamlining' exercise or other, which basically means firing a load of people at once and somehow never stopping to think about the number of families whose lives you're shattering at the same time. I'm unlikely to ever be senior enough to be asked for my opinions. So, I would have nodded for ninety minutes until my neck got sore, and tried to agree with whichever designer-suited director was telling us the company needed to cut jobs to save less money than his Mercedes was probably worth.

I don't usually answer my phone at work but I'd forgotten to put it on silent, and I thought my Beyoncé ringtone might not be in keeping with the professionalism I spent so long pretending to have. So I made an exception just to shut the thing up. I was actually quite thankful for the reminder that real life was carrying on somewhere in the outside world. Even if it turned out to be in an insurance-scam office in some far-flung country. I walked in circles around the shiny foyer of my office, my ballet flats making barely any sound on the marble floor, while the high-powered women around me tapped authoritatively through their workdays in Louboutins and amazing suits.

'Is that Charlotte?'

'Charlie, yeah.' I held a hand up to my free ear as if that was going to help with the noise on the other end of the line. I also squinted, which was equally useless, really.

'Hi, Charlie. Um . . . Oh God, I don't really know how to say this.'

The stranger on the other end of the line sounded so upset and flustered it brought me to a halt. A man from a different floor collided with me.

'Watch where you're going,' he barked. I gestured apologetically as the woman on the phone drew a shaky breath.

'I'm sorry. My name's Pauline. I'm a friend – a good friend – of your father's and I'm with him at St Joseph's Hospital, and . . . could you come and see him? He's asked for you. I'm afraid it's not looking good.'

'I . . .'

13

Something cold that wasn't really there trickled all the way down my body and everything tipped a little bit sideways.

'Charlie?' the lady on the other end of the phone pressed after a few seconds of dead silence.

'Charlie?' Magdalena, my boss, said as I perched on the edge of a decorative planter that was definitely not designed to support the weight of a human. 'Quick, get her a chair!'

'Charlie, can you hear me?'

I guess I let out a noise because the woman on the phone seemed to know she could continue. I was aware of somebody trying to press a glass into my hand.

'I don't want to frighten you, but I really think it's important that you come and see your father as soon as possible. Where are you now?'

I looked around the glass atrium with the indoor water feature and the rainforest plants you could only manage by hiring a company to come in and tend to them for you. People in expensive suits and shiny shoes bustled every which way, seemingly filled with a sense of purpose I could never even imagine. Like really happy ants.

'London.'

And then I ran away.

I mean, I didn't literally run. Nobody really runs. I'm not a monster. But I walked very quickly to the tube station without saying anything to anybody I worked with, and without making eye contact with any of the fancy heels and occasional briefcases coming the other way as I passed. And then I was crammed onto a packed carriage – honestly, why so packed in the middle of the day? Did nobody have jobs? – and the rails were screaming through the open window. We rattled away from the minutes that needed typing up, and the yoghurt I'd left in the fridge for a mid-morning snack.

And then I was at Paddington. And then I was on a train, and never once through any of this did I think I might need to phone James. I finally remembered him just as we were leaving Devon: a rush to the head, a gasp, and a very nice old man over the table from me asking if I was OK. I staggered out of the carriage and stood by the doors, rocking with the motion of the train. There was a chalk horse carved into a hillside in the distance.

'Where are you? I'm making tagine.'

'Sorry, I . . .'

Honestly, where could I even start? He only needed the facts, but it was difficult to tell where the facts were going to lead to questions I couldn't answer right then.

'Charlie?'

'Right. Yes. Sorry. I'm on the train. I have to go home. To Cornwall, I mean. My dad – I don't know. I had a call. He's in hospital.'

I happened to glance up and catch the eye of the nice old man I was sharing a table with. He smiled and gave me a cheery wave. I pulled my face into something like a smile and raised a hand in return.

'Shit, do you need—'

'I don't need anything,' I snapped, before I could remember not to be a bitch. I took a breath. 'Sorry, I just . . . I just need to get down there, see what's what. Could you tell Magdalena I won't be in tomorrow? Tell her I'll let her know.'

'OK, and I could—'

'Thanks. I think I'm about to go through a tunnel,' I lied. 'I should go.'

'But, Charlie, I—'

'Thanks, love you, bye!'

The feeling fluttering in my chest morphs into actual pain and I let a sound escape. I don't know if it's a sob, or a cringe, or the start of a panic attack. What the hell am I meant to do now? I'm not prepared for this. They should teach this kind of thing in school. You could sack off all of geography and use the time for Tragedy

Management. Who needs to know what an oxbow lake is anyway? I know *that*, but I haven't learned the ins and outs of what you're supposed to do when somebody dies and you're in charge of the situation. Because I guess I *am* supposed to be in charge of the situation.

I try to shake the sudden-onset pins and needles out of my hands. I spend a couple of minutes trying to do breathing exercises like they taught us in the mindfulness class I went to half of once before deciding it was a waste of time. It doesn't really work (shocker), but a frantic knocking on the window snaps me out of it.

I jump to my feet and see Dad's old mate Reg standing in the back garden, peering through the glass. He and Dad used to take me to the pub, ply me with pineapple juice and lemonade, and let me win at travel Snakes & Ladders when it was all getting A Bit Much at home. Now, he recoils as I pop up from behind the sink, which I would take great exception to if I hadn't just smeared yesterday's mascara all over my face. He's in his mid-sixties with a receding hairline and broken capillaries tracing their way across his bulbous nose. But I'm big enough to admit that he probably looks more attractive than me at the moment.

I give him a weak smile, motion for him to wait where he is, and then scrabble around for the key. There are three lidded pots on the windowsill and not one of them holds what I'm after. I swing around and eye up the worktops, moving tins at random.

'What are you looking for?' Reg asks as he simply pushes the door open and walks into my dad's kitchen.

'The key, Reg.'

He laughs.

'Have you forgotten where you are, young lady? Nobody's seen a key for donkey's years, you know that.'

It's a fair point. I don't think I'd locked a door until I moved to London, and even then it was only because Felicity from the room next door in halls used to sleepwalk.

'Now. Let me look at you.'

Reg steers me into the light from the kitchen window and stares at me. I wonder what I look like to a man who hasn't seen me since I left home at eighteen. I definitely expected that one day I'd come back to show everybody that I was a Fabulous (capital F) city girl with a Fabulous (also capital F) life. Now that the moment is here I think I'd settle for Not Completely Depressing.

I know I've lost weight, that's always at the forefront of my mind, even though I hate myself for constantly thinking about it. My hair has been cut and grown out probably a thousand times but it remains resolutely boring on account of the fact that I won't keep it up if I try anything fun. There are a few strands of white working their way through now, which I'm in very strong denial about. I imagine my eyes must have shadows under them, and they obviously remain the same old basic shade of brown. I can feel the patch of eczema on my neck flaring up. It's like it's flaking away even as Reg watches.

The least I could do if I was going to disown everything and everybody I'd ever known would be to come back looking interesting. Or, dare I even suggest it, good? Or maybe like I'd seen and done amazing things. At least get a hair braid and an anklet, you know? But I'm still just me. Not that Reg lets on if he feels any disappointment. His eyes briefly alight on my ring, and I instinctively put my hand behind my back. I suddenly feel twitchy, as if Reg's gaze might dig into the part of my brain where I've buried everything I never want to think about.

'It's nice to see you,' I say to distract him. I actually don't think I'm lying, either. There's something about him arriving just as I was

17

about to fall to pieces. I feel safer all of a sudden. He'll know what to do. I open my mouth to ask and he immediately shushes me.

'Here.' He hands me a business card.

'But you don't even know—'

'Tell me you weren't going to ask me about the funeral.'

I mean, I wasn't technically going to ask *that*, but I did want to know what to do next. And if Reg thinks it would be natural for me to ask about the funeral this morning then I guess I have my answer, in a roundabout way.

'Go and see my mate Trelawney on the high street. He'll talk you through everything,' Reg continues, as I turn the card over and over in my fingers.

He glances around the kitchen, taking in the detritus – the box full of folded-down cereal boxes in one corner, with a pile of tablecloths on top and a cat bed on top of that. I really hope there isn't actually a cat around here somewhere because if there is, I have forgotten to feed the cat.

'You'll have your hands full getting this place tidied up. I loved your dad but God knows he was a dirty article.'

Perfect. That means to-do list item number two is sorted as well. I'm going to clean up.

I have a game plan and I never even had to admit I didn't know what I was doing. Reg is a magician.

He pulls me into a gruff hug which is over too quickly, and then leaves, tripping over a stack of old washing baskets on his way to the door. He swears, and then salutes, and is gone. He never was one for small talk, was Reg.

As soon as he's out of the door I wrench my ring from my finger. I don't know why, and I don't know what to do with it now. I pull open a cupboard crammed with half-filled food packets. Then I change my mind, hurry out of the kitchen, and bound up the stairs. I brush against something as I go and I hear a crash behind me, but I don't stop. In my old bedroom, I wrench open the drawer I hid my phone in and consign my ring to the pile of Things I Don't Want To Think About©. I instantly feel free. It's as if removing that little band from my finger has lightened my entire body. I close the drawer, stand up a little straighter, and glance at the corner of the room I used to curl into when I had something on my mind. It's more tempting than ever today.

Honest to God, who would ever want to be a thirteen-year-old girl? I thought my mum was going to knock my bedroom door down after I stormed into the house after school, threw – not dropped, actually threw – my bag on the floor, and raced upstairs. The sturdy shoes she bought me to last made one hell of a racket on the steps.

'Charlie?' she called, as she banged on the door. 'I'm obviously going to come in anyway so you might as well just—'

'Fine!' I huffed, wiping away tears because again, and I cannot emphasise this enough, who would ever want to be a thirteen-year-old girl?

I sat on the floor with arms around my knees, leaning against the side of the bed. Mum opened the door slowly, peering around the gap. When she saw me on the floor she came and sat next to me, adopting the same position. We sat there in silence for a while, punctuated only by an occasional sniff from me. She actually seemed at ease, and if I hadn't been so wrapped up in myself I probably would have thought it was nice. It hadn't happened much lately.

'So, what have you got the arse for?'

'I haven't got the arse!' I snapped, because I definitely had the arse. Mum didn't say anything.

'Adam,' I eventually said into my knees so it came out all muffled. Mum sighed, and shifted so that she faced me.

'What's he done?'

'Nothing. He's got a girlfriend. Nothing.' I wiped away another tear.

'And you mind him having a girlfriend?' A hint of a smile played around Mum's lips.

'No! I don't know. But she's prettier than me and she's skinny and she's good at running and I—'

'Oh, love.' Mum pulled me into her and held me tight. I could smell her perfume and shampoo. Maybe a hint of a cheeky cigarette in the garden while Dad was out. We stayed there for ages, rocking a little bit while I sobbed into her shoulder.

'You don't need him, OK?'

'But I—'

'I mean, you're friends, and that's great, and he's a lovely boy. Maybe something will happen with him one day. I guarantee he won't be with this girl forever.'

I sniffed, wiping my eyes with the cuffs of my jumper.

'But you can't compare yourself to other people like that, alright? You'll drive yourself mad. You are absolutely enough, all on your own. You're lovely, and clever, and beautiful.'

'Nobody's going to go out with me, though.'

'OK, well, firstly, you're way too young to be thinking about that, and you're not allowed to go out with anybody until you're at least twenty-seven.'

I looked up, aghast, and she tried to stifle a smile.

'I'm joking. But you are a bit young. And I don't want you putting all this pressure on it, you know? If and when you go out with somebody, you have to remember it's a nice thing, but it's not the most important thing. You have to be happy with yourself before you can be happy with anybody else.'

'Were you happy with yourself before you met Dad?'

The atmosphere in the room shifted ever so slightly, like a cloud had gone over the sun. Mum cleared her throat, and then she loosened her grip on me and stood up.

'I know Dad loves me. Even if I make it hard sometimes.'

Now that I'm ring-free and can focus, I return to the kitchen and the business card Reg gave me. I find Dad's old landline phone on the windowsill, wedged in amongst some packets of completely inedible food, if the photos on the front are anything to go by. God, I hope Dad wasn't eating this stuff as well as hanging on to it for dear life. Not that I could have done much better. I can't cook for shit.

Anyway, I have the phone in one hand and the business card in another, and all that remains is for me to practise what I want to say before I feel ready to make the call. I have never gone into a phone call unrehearsed, nor will I ever. If I don't practise what I'm going to say I worry that my mind will go blank when somebody answers. And then my mind *will* go blank because I'm worried it'll go blank, and it's all a vicious circle. Better just to rehearse. I hold the phone to my ear to make it even more realistic.

'Oh, hello,' I say out loud to the kitchen at large. I put on my best phone voice, really try to sound authoritative. 'One funeral, please.'

No, that can't be right. Try again.

'Yes, hi. Reg Angove gave me this number and said I should talk to Mr Trelawney. My name's Charlie Trewin. My dad . . .'

And then my words run out, which is fine, because that is exactly why I'm practising at all. I puff out my cheeks and put the phone down on the side so that I can shake out my hands. I blink extra-hard a few times because my vision is getting foggy out of nowhere. Come on, Charlie. You can do it.

I pick up the phone again. This time I actually dial.

'Hello, Trelawney and Associates, Jade speaking.'

'I—' I stammer.

'Hello?'

'Yes, I—'

'Hello, can you hear me?'

And then I hang up the phone. Everything in the kitchen is starting to spin, the piles of junk are blurring into one. I can't get enough air in. I sink sideways into one of the chairs at the table. It's far too hard to be sinking into, but it's that or I end up on the floor. I rest my forehead on the tabletop. A pile of empty crisp packets rustles under my face, and I get a faint whiff of cheese and onion. I close my eyes and try to breathe. All I can hear is the clock ticking, and if I keep my breath exactly in time with that, it actually does help.

◆　◆　◆

I nearly jump out of my skin when I hear the front door open.

'Ooh, you bastard,' someone says as they trip over the collapsed heap of papers still cluttering up the hallway. It's—

'Lowenna?'

She materialises at the kitchen door and I can see her properly for the first time. Her hair's been cropped short, in place of the 'old lady' perm I remember her having when I was a child. She walks with a stick, and her shoulders have curved forward as if they're trying to reach her stomach. But her smile hasn't changed. It's still as conspiratorial as it used to be when she'd hand me packets of Rolos over the fence and instruct me not to tell my parents.

'I hadn't seen much movement over here so I thought I'd come and check you hadn't offed yourself.'

It's so wildly inappropriate that I laugh in spite of myself. When I do, the weight that had been pressing me to the chair gets a tiny bit lighter. I find I can sit up straighter.

'Of course not,' I tell her.

'Well, you can't be too careful, can you? We all learned that the hard way. And you don't look well, Charlie.'

'I . . .'

How are you ever supposed to respond to that? I wish it were the first time I'd heard it but the man who owns the newsagent's near my flat in London seems determined to destroy my self-esteem with very similar observations, so I'm used to it. Eventually I settle for: 'I didn't sleep very well.'

'Come on, Charlie. You look like hell. It's more than one bad night's sleep.'

Lowenna regards me with a cool, steady gaze. I can feel myself turning red under her scrutiny, but I don't know what she means. I am very happy, and if I don't look it, then that's just an unfortunate quirk of my face.

OK fine, I *might* know what she means, but it's difficult to pin down to any one thing.

OK, fine, I know exactly what she means but I came here to get away from it and I am not about to bring it up.

'Fine, don't tell me,' she eventually relents, lowering herself onto the chair next to me. 'Make me a cup of tea, though.'

I suddenly feel panicky. She looked into my soul before she'd even sat down – what's she going to figure out over the course of a twenty-minute cuppa? I absentmindedly brush my now-naked ring finger with my thumb and I'm sure *she sees me*. She's a witch.

'Actually, Lowenna,' I say, mustering all the confidence I can to keep the tremble out of my voice. 'I was just about to go for a walk.'

She narrows her eyes.

'Well, you could have said something before you let me sit down. It takes me weeks to stand up again. It's alright when you're young.'

'Sorry.'

'No, it's fine. 'Course it is. You need some air. Come here.'

She holds out both of her hands to me and I take them in mine. She uses them to hoist herself up to a standing position and I'm shocked by how light she feels. There's nothing of her. I think I've . . . *missed* her? And now there's hardly any of her left. I blink away the tears that come out of nowhere. Stop it, stop it, stop it.

I try to smile as I wave her off at the front door. She used to just hop over the straggly excuse for a hedge between our gardens but I guess it's too high for her now. The amount of time I've missed knocks the breath out of me, but I smile and keep waving until Lowenna gets back inside.

CHAPTER THREE

I know Lowenna's going to watch out of her window to make sure I'm telling the truth about my walk, so I pull on some old trainers I didn't think were cool enough to take away to uni. They'd probably go down a storm with today's teenagers, though. It's so unfair.

I'm nervous to go outside, to be seen back in the village, but I imagine it won't be a surprise to anyone. Good news travels fast, but dramatic news travels quicker. I suppose there's always the chance they won't recognise me – Lowenna certainly seemed to think I'd been ravaged by time.

I make sure to get out of the door before the crushing weight circling over my head can pin me down. The sky is such a bright blue that it looks as if somebody's turned the saturation up too high on Instagram. The sun is hidden behind the trees so it isn't warm, and I shiver. But I can't go back inside now. I can't even look at the phone, or the mess, or . . . I just can't deal with it. The whole place.

When I reach the end of the garden path I turn to look back towards the house and, sure enough, I catch sight of Lowenna standing in her window, staring out with narrowed eyes. I pause. She shoos me and lowers the net curtain.

The house itself looks the same as it ever did. I mean, it's hundreds of years old so you would really hope so. Around the time that Mum did what she did I used to find it comforting to think that so many hundreds of families had lived here before us, and hundreds would probably live here after us, and everything that felt so huge, and sad, and overwhelming, was really just a tiny blip in the history of this place.

The thatch on the roof could be in better nick, and the whitewash on the walls is a bit grubby, but it's not terrible. Nothing stays pristine here because a seagull *will* eventually pull it to pieces or shit on it. It's the circle of life. The yellow paint on the window frames has peeled to reveal red underneath, and a hint of blue beneath that. Mum did always love a bright colour. Sanding before starting an impulse DIY project, not so much.

The windows themselves are tiny. It's probably a good thing, since it means people can't see the chaos inside from the street. The flower beds under the windows are unkempt, but pretty. Hydrangeas and dahlias share space with weeds, and everything – whether invited or not – is putting out its last flowers of the year. One final display before the storms start rolling through.

The oak tree by the garden gate has dropped a couple of leaves, and it's also put out a root that's sent a crack right across the path. Mum and I planted an acorn for fun one autumn when I was very small and, well, it's all got a bit out of hand. I close the gate behind me and look both ways before I cross the road, even though it's only really busy during the summer holidays, and I don't even know if that's still the case.

We sometimes used to notice holidaymakers taking photos of the house during the summer. I imagine that's probably worse now. It'd go down a storm on Instagram. Sometimes Dad would stand in the window and pull faces, which people were too busy focusing on the thatch to notice. I wonder if anybody ever got their photos developed and noticed. I'd love one of those now.

I walk past the houses of old school friends and remember the times I spent laughing in all of them over *Smash Hits* magazine, or

Pokémon cards, or whichever radio show we were listening to (and taping the songs from) religiously at the time. Up until The Day Everything Fell Apart™, anyway. I pass the community gardens my class used to help plant every spring. Everybody else thought it was lame, so I pretended I did too.

I spot a couple of familiar faces as I walk, and they call out friendly 'hello's. I don't stop to chat, but I smile and nod by way of greeting. Maybe they start discussing me and my latest tragedy as soon as I'm out of earshot. Maybe they don't know yet. I dig my fingernails into my hands and try not to think about it.

It doesn't take long to get to the beach. Although 'beach' might actually be too strong a word. It's only a little cove nestled in a dip where the cliffs drop away before rising suddenly again a hundred metres later. They feel a lot like walls which, depending on the day, can make you feel secure or trapped. I've had it both ways. I'm not sure which it is today.

I kick off my shoes and the feeling of the sand under my feet is like I've never been away. It's chilly, damp, and a little bit stony, not like the warm sands you imagine when you look at holiday pictures from around the world. But it's nice in its way. It's familiar.

I plonk myself onto the damp ground and watch the waves languidly advancing and retreating. The sea is the kind of turquoise you wouldn't believe was possible in England unless you saw it frequently when you were growing up. It's crystal clear and I can see the dark shadows of the rocks below the surface as if through a window. A little group of boats bob together further out. A cloud of seabirds hovers around them, sometimes darting closer, sometimes moving away, presumably having been shooed by a fisherman.

I can't remember the last time I was on a beach, and the lost years hit me straight in the heart again. I can picture Dad chasing me around with a bucket of water. I can see him picking me up and chucking me in the sea. I can even see when he tried to take me fishing off the rocks, accidentally caught an eel, and threw the entire rod into the water while Mum laughed and I screamed my head off. It's disorientating to think that this is the same place but it doesn't exist in the same world any more. The one with Dad in it. The one with both of them in it.

I take a couple of breaths, tangy with salt, then close my eyes and listen to the waves rearranging the shingle at the shoreline. Then, before I really have a chance to overthink it, I'm on my feet and I've whipped off my T-shirt. If you'd told me twenty-four hours ago that I'd find myself at the beach in only my bra, I'd never have believed you. But I don't want to waste even more time with second-guessing. I strip down to my knickers and leave my clothes in a pile on the sand. I know I'll regret it in about ten minutes' time when they're all a bit gritty. But to be fair, swimming in my bra and pants probably isn't my smartest idea either. And yet that's what's happening. I just want to switch my brain off for once in my life. Common sense is no longer at the wheel.

The tide is in so it takes no time at all to get to the water's edge. I glance around, but there's nobody nearby. It's off-season, after all. There are a couple of old ladies towelling themselves off at the other end of the beach but they're too deep in conversation to even think about stealing my clothes. I'm pretty sure I could take them if they did, anyway. And, crucially, that's just not the way the world works here.

I pause at the edge of the water, the anticipation of the cold briefly making me rethink my choices up to this moment. Then I pluck up the courage and take my first step into the shallows. I take another, then another, before my body has time to register what I'm about to make it do. I stop to scoop up some of the icy water, and I splash it on my face like I was always told to. It apparently helps your body acclimatise, although I always wondered how a tiny splash of water on the face could prepare acres of skin on one's torso or limbs. Goosebumps spring up on my arms. They feel no more prepared.

The shore drops away quickly and it only takes a few steps before I'm up to my waist and faced with the choice of diving in gracefully, or losing my footing and tumbling in sideways with a squawk. I choose the latter. Or rather, it chooses me.

The cold takes my breath away. I tread water until I have it under control. Next comes the cold that somehow seems to move under my skin. I wait for my internal temperature to meet that of the water so it will stop. Underneath the surface my bright-red nails look extra-intense, and I stretch my arms out, watching the light making patterns on my skin through the surface.

I stick my head under and try to count to ten. I make it to five before I'm forced to the surface by a sudden, splitting headache. Once it subsides, I do it again. Eventually I can stay under there until I get to twenty. I dive completely under and all sound disappears. My hair floats around my face, framing my view of the reef. I swim closer, looking for signs of life.

While I'm still under the water I flip onto my back and watch the rays of the sun dance through the ripples of the surface. It's stunning. I'd forgotten. I used to swim on my back under the water every time we came to the beach. I wish I could stay down here forever.

It takes absolutely no time for me to run out of air, though, so I'm back at the surface before I know it. As I breach (can I say that about myself if I'm a human being and not a porpoise?) a gull screeches and jolts me back to earth.

Who the hell do I think I am, enjoying myself? I have actual things to be doing. Even if I weren't here, and everything weren't upside down, I would still have actual life to be getting on with. I don't have time to mess around. And I should be making a phone call. I have *one* job, and it isn't this.

The spell of the water well and truly broken by a surge of disgust at myself, I clamber unsteadily back to the beach. I try to put my feet on the ground while I'm still out of my depth at least three times, and style it out as if it's some cool new technique. I'm sure I'm not fooling the few bemused customers having drinks at the beach cafe.

I stagger onto the sand, shivering. My skin is now an angry pink colour, dotted with goosebumps. Every scar I've ever picked up in my life has suddenly reappeared. And this time they're purple. The elastic around my bikini line has shifted and I look a bit like the 'before' in a Veet advert that would never make it to air. I shiver and wonder why Bond girls never look like this when they saunter out of the ocean after enjoying a dip. Probably because they're in some glamorous Caribbean destination, I decide. And that is the only thing that separates us.

It's only now that I realise the error I've made. I'm dripping wet, in my underwear, and I can't get dry to put my clothes back on. Wonderful. I suddenly feel convinced that the people eating burgers and chips on the cafe terrace are all actively watching and judging me, as if they don't have their own family and friends to be focusing on. It's ridiculous, and patently untrue, but that's how my brain works. I shiver again. I'm so fucking stupid.

I scoop up my clothes and hobble over to some rocks. The shingle is no joke under freezing feet. I lean against a rock and hold out my arms and legs as if I'm trying to dry the fake tan I bought once in a fit of especially low self-esteem and never actually used. Every single hair on my arms stands on end.

◆　◆　◆

When I've eventually dried enough to fight my way back into my leggings (no mean feat with damp skin, thank you very much),

I climb the steps up to the road. I should move fast, because I'm definitely going to end up with the wet shadows of my underwear soaking through my outerwear, but I have to pause to take it all in.

The view across the bay is beautiful. I never appreciated it when I was growing up here. All I saw in the crags and the calling seabirds was the lack of things I thought all other kids must have: places to hang out until way past bedtime, and streets full of people my own age to hang out with. I fantasised about a Carncarrow where the cliff sides, studded with bright-yellow gorse and frothy pink thrift flowers, were replaced with brightly lit cinemas and fast-food joints you didn't need a car to get to. If I'd had my way I'd have paved over the entire bay and built a shopping centre in its stead, so I could live like all the girls my dad didn't like me watching on TV.

Now I look out at the same bay and feel my heart lift. I can't remember the last time I felt that happen. It's the lack of people that really gets me. The same lack I felt so hard years ago. I can't imagine one part of London where I could see for miles without a single other human entering my field of vision, and I didn't realise how much I actually wanted it. Which is not to say that I *hate* other humans. I just never know how to act around them, I guess.

There's no such thing as hellishly packed streets here. I mean, there kind of is for a few weeks in high summer, but no local in their right mind would be out and about then anyway. And if you desperately wanted to have your face forced into the armpit of a sweaty man in a suit on public transport, you'd have to travel hundreds of miles for the privilege. There are no sirens, or car alarms, or—

I am roused by the joyful and insistent beep of a horn and somebody yelling at me from the road. I jump and see Jason Cardew, who used to run the chip shop. And, I can only assume, still does because he's leaning halfway out of the driver's-side window of a shiny new van emblazoned with giant letters that say 'Chip Happens'.

'Charlie! Like the new wheels? I just picked her up.' He grins at me triumphantly. I wonder if he's even noticed that I left for thirteen years.

'It looks great.'

'I didn't know you was back in town.'

'No, well, I had some things to take care of,' I tell him vaguely. I know I should tell him about Dad. I should tell everyone. I can't just rely on the rumour mill to do my dirty work for me.

And yet I can't bring myself to form the words. When I can't avoid them altogether, it's nice to have the people here greeting me like they're happy to see me. I can't go back to tilted heads and comforting hands on my arm. I don't want sudden silences when I enter a room again.

I still have nightmares about going back to school after Mum died. I was escorted to The Office on my first morning. It was a scary-sounding place back then because I think we all assumed that the people who worked in offices knew everything. Of course, now I'm an adult who works in one I know we were very wrong indeed, but that's by the by. When I got there, Mrs Trenton, the headmistress, made me a cup of tea even though I didn't drink tea. She tilted her head in the way people always did and placed a hand lightly on my shoulder. She told me all the right stuff – I could let her know if I needed anything, I could talk to anybody any time, everybody was here for me. I nodded constantly, thinking that might move things along faster.

When it was finally time for me to rejoin the world, Mrs Trenton squeezed my shoulder again and steered me along the corridor to my classroom.

'I know where it is, thank you.'

I didn't want to sound rude, but I also didn't want Mrs Trenton to think that I'd forgotten the way. I'd only been gone a couple of weeks, after all, and most of that time had been spent watching Dad stare into space and wishing I had anything else to do.

'I know you know, I'm just here for moral support.' Mrs Trenton gave my shoulder an extra 'little' squeeze. If I had to pick one overriding memory from that time it would be the bruising. People don't half love to prod and pinch bits of you when they know you're sad.

Mrs Trenton pushed open the door to reveal Miss Lake, my form tutor, mid-lecture. You could tell roughly how long she'd usually been speaking based on how many students had wilted over their desks. I think the split that day was about seventy–thirty in favour of drooping. She didn't spot us immediately.

'. . . So please just be gentle with her and try not to say anything stupid, OK? Suicide is very sad, and you might have questions, but—'

'Morning, Miss Lake!' Mrs Trenton interrupted, far too loudly. 'Look who I bumped into in the hall.'

She pushed me over the threshold.

'Oh, hello, Charlie, love. Nice to have you back.' Miss Lake smiled, overcompensating for being caught talking about me. 'Isn't it?'

The class jumped to attention when they caught her threatening tone, and voiced their agreement, albeit lukewarm.

My face burned. It was part embarrassment, of course. Nobody likes to be talked about without their knowledge at the best of times, least of all self-conscious girls. But it was also, I don't know . . . disappointment, maybe? I was sad about Mum. In fact, 'sad' doesn't even come close. My life had come crashing down around my ears and I no longer knew which way was up. Dad was being weird, and Lowenna kept turning up at funny times to cook for us. But school was the one place I thought I'd be able to get back to normal, and that was the moment I realised it wasn't going to happen.

I could feel eyes on me as I glared at my desk until my cheeks stopped burning, but when I looked up I mainly saw butterfly clips and spiky hair gel flicking back to face the board. Mae Fletcher gave me a sad little smile, and that was when I knew I was forever going to be The Girl Whose Mum Killed Herself.

'You fancy a lift back home in the Batter Wagon?'

Jason's question brings me back to myself, here, standing on top of a cliff, with nobody staring at me, and the underwear I swam in very much starting to soak through my clothes. I should have taken it off, I now realise. Hindsight's a wonderful thing. The bra-shaped wet patch currently blooming on my T-shirt is not. I shake my head.

'No. Thanks, Jay.'

'Suit yourself. Catch you later, eh?'

He pulls away and I begin to walk.

◆ ◆ ◆

The sun is shining from behind the thatch when I get back to the house. It makes the place look like it has a halo. But I can't stop to stare at it for long. I. Am. *Freezing*. My hands are a fetching shade of purple and I'm glad I didn't lock up when I left because they're shaking so hard I don't think I could aim a key in the right direction if I tried.

I pick my way upstairs, partly because of all the piles of crap, and partly because it's quite difficult to walk on numb feet. I discard my wet clothes on the bathroom floor and jump into the shower until my skin begins to turn a normal colour again. I don't even have the temperature turned up that high but the water feels boiling. The heat is giving me goosebumps now.

Dad still has (had?) (has) (no, *had*, I suppose) the same shower as he did years ago so I know exactly where I need to point all of the dials, which makes a nice change. The shower is temperamental but at least I know its quirks, unlike the overly high-tech rain-head one I've never got the hang of back in London. This one sputters and is prone to sudden drops in temperature followed by burning overcorrections. Even so, I feel safe here. Nobody can get me. You can't be expected to make phone calls when you're locked in the bathroom and, unfortunately, a hot shower is medically necessary right now. Whether that shower *has* to be an hour long is probably up for debate. But I can't be part of that debate because I'm in the shower.

I stay there until it starts to get dark outside. I pray I won't trip as I climb out, and feel around for a towel. Back in my room, I put on my pyjamas and dressing gown, and sit down on the edge of my bed.

I can feel that weight starting to gather just above my shoulders again. It's starting to press them down. Something begins jumping in my chest, slowly at first, and then faster and faster, demanding attention I don't want to give it. Now that I'm alone, in the gloom, in my childhood bedroom, starting to shiver again because I think the cold from the sea has entered the very core of my being and a shower isn't going to cut it, I . . . I don't even know. I suddenly feel stupid. Callous, even. Small. I've wasted an entire day. Before I become completely paralysed I pull the duvet over me and curl up.

Maybe I'll wake up a better person tomorrow.

CHAPTER FOUR

In the morning I jump out of bed before whatever sat on my chest for half the night can get me again. I pour myself some only-just-not-stale Rice Krispies and pick up the business card Reg gave me. Nothing is stopping me today. Nothing, nothing, nothing. A million people have dealt with this kind of situation before me, and they've taken it in their stride, and I am *not* special. I am not beholden to the tightness in my chest. The tightness in my chest does not control me.

I psych myself up and spend maybe five minutes speaking to the same bored-sounding receptionist I spoke to yesterday, and then I have an appointment. It is worryingly soon and I need to go. I don't even have time to dwell on how easy that was, and how much of a meal I made of it yesterday.

Once I've left my unwashed bowl in the sink (I'd like to pretend that's because I'm in a rush, but it's really just my preferred method of dealing with washing-up) I grab my bag and head for the door.

It's then that I notice the corner of a piece of paper sticking through the letterbox. It brings me to a halt. I cast my mind back but I can't remember if I've seen it before or not. I pull it out, expecting a leaflet, but it's actually a handwritten note, which has been concertinaed against the flap because the thing is so rusty it never opens properly.

Charlie,

Just tried to speak to you but you were out. Your phone is also off. Please call me ASAP.

Pauline x

It pulls me up short. I stare at the phone number she's scribbled at the bottom of the note and underlined twice. I look up at the clock. There's a very good chance that I'm not going to make it on time as it is.

I look back at the note, then back at the clock. And then I take one of those deep mindfulness breaths that don't really work, put the note on top of a pile on top of a pile on top of a chest of drawers, and leave the house.

I really don't have the time to dilly-dally, but I do still find myself slowing down as I head into town. I can't help it. It's another lovely day and if I didn't know better I'd say we were somewhere actually good, what with the palm trees and the sunshine, rather than somewhere lives fall apart.

Signs on the B&Bs all the way down the hill to the high street proclaim that there are no vacancies. I catch the eye of the occasional guest at breakfast as I walk past the big bay windows. I glance away quickly so they don't think I'm a creep. When I round the last corner I finally see glimpses of the harbour between buildings. I can smell the sea beyond that.

There are a few figures moving between the crooked buildings of the high street. The sun glances off the cobbles and makes the road practically shine. I wish I could follow that glimmering path instead of doing what I actually have to do. The high street is dotted with figures who pause and gaze into shop windows, and I'm kind of jealous.

I'm also about to be late, I realise as I glance at my phone. I check the address on the business card, squint up at the numbers on the buildings nearest me, and hurry past a few brightly coloured shopfronts until I find the right place.

◆ ◆ ◆

I can't stop tapping my foot on the floorboards, which must be driving the receptionist insane. Luckily she's nice about it. I suppose she must be used to all sorts, working here. At least I'm not crying. I wonder if she remembers me from school. We weren't in the same year, but it wasn't exactly a big place. I wonder if she's texting someone right now, telling them I'm back. Crazy Mum Girl. Dead Dad Girl too, now.

I wonder what this Pauline woman wants. I met her very briefly at the hospital as she left and I arrived, but we didn't speak beyond a very small, scared hello and goodbye. Probably something about condolences, I imagine. Isn't it always, in the days just after? I knew it would start sooner or later. Maybe she wants to be the first to bring round a pasta bake. Lots of pasta bakes last time, I seem to remember. My stomach rumbles. No. Focus on the job in hand.

The funeral director's waiting room contains a faded corduroy sofa in a horrible dusty pink. There's a gigantic pot plant taking up one corner and basically swallowing a little table of old magazines. There's a water cooler next to the door and a long, low pine coffee table in front of me, with a box of tissues sitting in the centre, the only nod to this being worse than any other run-down waiting room.

I was worried I'd be trapped in a room with a bunch of other people who were all weeping and wailing, a parade of misery. Instead, it's just me. And obviously the receptionist, who I now seem to remember was surf lifesaving county champion once upon a time. I was always mystified by the sporty kids. Whatever, we're both here now. How the mighty have fallen, whichever one of us that was.

'You can go through.' She smiles benignly, and I cannot figure out if she recognises me or not.

And that literally does not matter at all, I have to *keep* scolding myself. This is not about me, or who recognises me, or who's talking about me. I am here for Dad. I am here for Dad, and I know what I'm doing, and I have my shit together.

I give the receptionist – Jade, I've just remembered – a nod and a smile, and walk out of the waiting room and across the hallway. I briefly consider making a break for it out of the front door, but that doesn't seem like something an adult would do, and I am an adult. I'm an adult, I'm an adult, I'm an adult.

The door to the office opens as I'm contemplating my escape. It makes me jump.

'There you are,' says a man in a respectable suit, which wouldn't look out of place in my office in London, but definitely seems out of place when I can hear seagulls outside. 'I thought you'd got lost!'

I crack a weak smile and follow him into the room. He indicates a chair and I sit down.

'Tea?' he asks.

I nod, even though I know I'll probably feel too awkward to drink it so it'll end up going cold on his desk. There's just a lot of tea in these situations. You kind of have to go with it. It's all coming back to me now.

'My name's Trelawney. Fred Trelawney.'

'Hi. Charlie.'

'Well, I know who you are, of course.' He nods. 'Terrible business with your mother.'

My face burns and I swallow.

When he's made me a drink, Mr Trelawney presents me with a stack of brochures and sits on the other side of the table. It's amazing to think that he's friends with Reg. He's very polished. His hair is grey but styled, but also not *so* styled that it looks too styled, you know? Plus, the suit. He seems quite suave. I go a bit shy. Jesus Christ. Rein it in, Charlie.

He puts on a pair of glasses, and then adopts the same posture we were taught to use at work when having serious meetings – looking straight at me, not hunching, with his wrists facing upwards and arms uncrossed to signal his openness.

'Now,' he begins. 'Have you given any thought to the kind of casket you'd like for your father?'

And just like that, I remember why I'm here and the spell of his smooth suit and subtle aftershave is broken.

We talk about things I've never, ever considered before – we move from caskets, to urns, to the outfit I want to be the last outfit Dad ever wears, and at some point I step out of my body and watch myself nodding along to questions I can't even hear because there's too much white noise.

If I were to put comfort above all else, Dad would wear the ratty old tracksuit bottoms I assume he must still have in the house somewhere because, well, we all know why. I suppose they might have fallen apart by now. Or he could wear the smart suit he only ever got out for weddings. In all honesty it was not *that* smart – he'd had the thing for my entire lifetime and then some. But he always held himself differently when he got to wear it – he'd throw his shoulders back and hold his head a little higher. But people, me included (and assuming he didn't discover high fashion in his later years), would most likely remember him in jeans, a T-shirt, and a beanie hat worn slightly too high. A hoodie if it was cold. But that doesn't feel like the right choice either.

I don't know what I'm doing. I don't know why I'm here. I mean, I obviously *do* know why I'm here, but I strongly don't think I'm the one who should be here. But that thought hurts in itself and then I just—

'Charlie?' Mr Trelawney says. He lays a gentle hand on my arm and I jump. 'This is all a bit much, right?'

I consider denying it. But all of my determination to be an adult with my shit together seems to have stayed out in the waiting room, so I nod, and my chin wobbles, which makes my heart start to pound because I really don't want to cry in a stranger's office with the former county surf lifesaving champion across the hall. Even if they *do* put out tissues for that exact reason.

'Why don't we talk about personalising things?' he asks, after giving me a tactful moment to get myself together. 'People tend to feel more comfortable with that side of it.'

'OK.'

'Did your father have a favourite piece of music?'

I remember us dancing around the room when I was a child. He'd put on The Beatles or Bay City Rollers, and I'd roll my eyes and pretend to hate it as he twirled me around the kitchen. Mum would laugh along. Eventually she would cut in and spin me around, and then Mum and Dad would dance together and I'd roll my eyes again, this time because the attention was no longer on me and only children are the worst. I don't remember there being much music in the house since Mum.

I open my mouth and close it again.

'I might need to check. See if he had any CDs, or . . .' I tail off.

'Of course. Were there any readings you'd like to include?'

'Like what?'

'Well, some people like to have a poem, or a story they would read as children. Maybe a Bible passage. Anything like that?'

I open my mouth. And then I close it again. God, I must look gormless. But, honestly, I can't remember the last time I read *anything*, let alone something that would be meaningful enough to include in an honest-to-God funeral. I don't think the tweets I scroll through in the work toilets to fend off panic attacks count as 'reading'. I'm fucking this up.

I do remember Dad scooping me onto his lap when I was little and reading me story after story, anything I wanted. He gave perfect voices to witches, adventurers, even Twits. I would laugh my head off. Sometimes I would make him read the same story over and over again, scolding him if he didn't get the voices exactly right every time. But I don't think I've inherited his talents, and I doubt that's what Mr Trelawney quite had in mind.

'Can I think—'

'Of course you can.'

'OK, thank you.'

'Right. Well. We've got a *bit* of a plan, at least.' He sounds surprisingly cheerful since it feels like we've achieved very little indeed. 'We know when we want it, and I can get to work on urns and caskets and suchlike. And in the meantime, you can have a dig around and figure out the personal touches. How does that sound?'

I nod because I don't think I can reasonably say 'terrible' after he's been so patient with me, but I'm starting to hear the roaring in my ears again and I need to get out before the walls start closing in. I stand up, banging my knee on the desk in the process.

'Oh, Charlie . . .'

I turn around, one hand on the doorknob. He's starting to collect the brochures I left scattered everywhere.

'You might like to have a chat with Pauline about all of this. I'm sure she'd be able to give you a hand.'

I swallow and nod, then wrench open the door.

I stumble out of the office – literally stumble – and try to catch my breath. I put my hands on my knees like Olympic athletes do after they've run a big race, but all I've done is walk two steps out of a building and on to the high street. It's so sunny out here it's frankly quite disrespectful, given the circumstances. I still shiver, though, because somewhere along the line I started sweating while we were chatting about coffins, and the usually pleasant breeze suddenly feels chilly. I can smell the mud and seaweed from the harbour as I try to take deep, steady breaths. A couple of shoppers stroll past. All I see is their shoes.

'Are you OK?' someone asks. I quickly rearrange my face and straighten up.

I start to answer but the words disappear as I take in the man standing in front of me. He's also wearing a suit, which looks even more out of place now that I'm outside in the sunshine, standing next to a palm tree. He's grown stubble that never used to be there, and there's the very faintest crinkle in the corners of his eyes that proves it really has been thirteen years since I last saw him. He gives me a massive grin, so I guess I can't have changed much either. Maybe Lowenna was exaggerating.

'Adam!' I laugh and he pulls me into a hug. He still smells the same and my chin still exactly fits against his shoulder. After a moment we break apart, suddenly embarrassed by the enthusiasm of our greeting. I assume. I know I am. And here, of all places. And now, of all times.

The office door is slightly set back from the main thoroughfare of the high street, and people glance at us curiously as they walk past.

'What do you mean, you're leaving?'

'I just . . . I can't stay here, can I?'

We ducked into the doorway of a boarded-up shop to get out of the rain. People barely glanced up as they passed, they were too busy holding their hoods up and fighting to keep umbrellas the right way round. Of course I did not have a coat.

'Of course you can.'

'And what? Be reminded of her everywhere I go forever? I can't take it.'

'And you think you'll feel better if you run away?'

I scuffed at the doorframe with my toe.

'I'm not running away. I'm going to university. People do. And I have to try, don't I?'

His shoulders slumped and he pulled me into a very damp hug.

'I'll miss you.'

It wasn't the last time we saw each other, but I guess it was the last time we knew what we were to each other. After that we were pen pals, I guess, until he found somebody else, and I pretended I had too so he wouldn't feel bad, and eventually the messages got shorter and shorter until they dried up all together.

'Hi,' I eventually say to break the silence.

He smiles. 'Hi.'

There's another awkward pause. Where do you start after a thirteen-year gap?

'I work here now,' he tells me. Then his face drops. 'I'm so sorry about your dad.'

'Thanks.' I smile weakly and I mean it. 'I don't really know if I'm coming or going at the moment.'

'Well, right now you're coming with me and we're going to get coffee,' he tells me confidently.

'Don't you have, I dunno, people to . . .' I gesture vaguely, not entirely sure what he does, and not *really* wanting to know in any great detail.

'No.' He shrugs. 'We've got one village's-worth of customers, and at the moment everybody's pretty healthy, so it's all good.' His face falls. 'Sorry, was that insensitive?'

'Yes, but it's fine.'

His embarrassment makes me laugh. I feel bad. But it's so nice to see him that I allow that to be the only thing in my head for one lovely moment.

He ushers me a couple of doors down and into a painfully trendy coffee shop which acts like it never used to be a gift shop that gouged tourists looking to buy tacky fridge magnets and crabbing lines. We buy flat whites and sit at a table in the lane outside, where it's really far too narrow to have outdoor seating. We have to breathe in massively to allow an elderly couple carrying shopping bags to get past. I fiddle with a couple of sugar packets, not sure what to say next.

'God, I just can't believe you're back, Charlie,' Adam begins. 'I thought I'd never see you again.'

'I would have thought you'd think that was a good thing.'

'Are you kidding? Why shouldn't we catch up?'

'I just thought, with how everything ended, with me leaving, I dunno.'

45

'We were basically children. People drift apart. It happens. I don't hold a grudge. Do *you* hold a grudge? Do you hate me?'

'No.'

'There you go, then. Your dad said you'd been doing really well upcountry.'

It stings, just for a second. I shouldn't be here. I don't get to enjoy coffee in the sun. Not right now. Not when I lied for so long. 'Doing really well', indeed. I feel a flutter of panic and I puff out my cheeks as I breathe it away.

'You OK?' Adam lays a hand on mine, and I try to cover a – I don't want to say 'gasp', but not *not* a gasp.

'Yeah.' It sounds strangled. 'Just . . . I don't know.'

'What?'

And I guess I can tell him anything. I always *used* to be able to tell him anything. And he still seems up for it.

'I sometimes wonder if I made a mistake. Leaving, I mean.'

He raises his eyebrows, which I get, because who knows? We might still be together if I hadn't gone to London. Would that have been healthy? Almost certainly not. But it makes you think.

'I mean, I dunno, I think I was right to leave here, with the memories and all, I just . . . *London* is . . . a lot.'

'And you're on your own up there?'

'Well, I . . . There's . . . I don't . . .' I should obviously tell him about James. I do know that. He won't care. Our last contact before today was an email a decade ago. But I'm not comfortable with my old life leaking into my new life. Or my new life leaking into my old life. Everything just needs to stay exactly where I left it. In the end, I dodge the question because I am who I am. 'Can we talk about something else?'

'What did you have in mind?'

'How about, you work for a funeral director?'

He laughs.

'I do work for a funeral director. But you know what it's like here. There's not a ton of options and I didn't get to just up and leave like you' – ouch. Harsh, but fair – 'plus I had to look after Grandma. Which reminds me, have you seen my grandma yet?'

'Yeah. She thought I was a burglar the other night. I think she was ready to come over in her nightie and beat me up. And then she broke in yesterday.'

He laughs, and then looks serious. 'She'll be really torn up about . . . y'know.'

'Yep.' There's that strangled sound again. 'Carry on.'

'Sure. So I knew I didn't want to work at the chippy for the rest of my life but I didn't have a whole lot else going on. And then Mr Trelawney was looking for help and I jumped at it. After all, fishing's going down the pan, farming's a nightmare, tourism's risky – but there's always business in, well, *that* business,' he tells me, then indicates his suit. 'And the rest is history.'

I grin. 'Very stylish history it is too.'

'Still not up for talking about you?'

'No, thanks.'

'Cool.'

◆ ◆ ◆

I stop in to the florist after my coffee with Adam. It's not exactly on my way home, but I just can't face that yet. So, I walk along the high street, past boutiques selling overpriced stripy tops and fancy-looking bakeries with focaccia in the window (I mean, focaccia? In *Carncarrow*?), until I reach the square.

The church is the first thing I see. It's a neat little building, not much bigger than a house. The clock isn't quite keeping the correct time, but it's close enough. The yard around it is overgrown and dotted with wonky gravestones, worn smooth over a century. Dad used to take me in there and tell me stories, which I now realise he probably made up, about the adventures of all the people who were buried there. He made the village sound like the centre of history. The grey stones of the church walls are dotted with bright-yellow lichen, and a pinboard by the gate is covered with notices. Strings of bunting have been tied to the tiny spire. They fan out across the square, each string attached to buildings on the other side, and a canopy of fluttering triangles draws my eye everywhere.

There are a few new restaurants with nice outdoor seating areas. We would possibly call them bistros, I suppose. They certainly seem to call themselves that. They're a step up from the pasty shops and amusement arcades I remember from years ago. There's also an estate agent whose window I'm suddenly too scared to look in. The florist is tucked between a surf shop and the key cutter's. And, yes. Flowers are why I'm here. Focus, Charlie.

I feel like flowers are a thing you're supposed to do. Mae Fletcher, my former classmate, shows me brochures. If there's one thing I'm taking away from this experience so far it's that there are So. Many. Brochures. These ones show the arrangements I might like to choose from – from bouquets of tasteful lilies all the way through to names rendered in, well, tasteful lilies. There's a lot of tasteful lilies.

There's a hollowness in my stomach which actually feels quite familiar – it happened when James and I went to a florist to talk about wedding flowers too. Maybe I just hate flowers. That'll be it.

It's just that every single suggestion the very nice florist lady gave us at that appointment made me more and more sweaty. James kept rubbing the small of my back in a way that I'm sure he thought was loving, but it was making me want to strangle him. I dismissed idea after idea, and then I was so nervous that somebody might read too much into my lack of enthusiasm that I gave a short monologue about how I thought flowers were over and I wanted to have an arrangement of artistic twigs as my bouquet. Luckily, I've swerved setting a date so far. But when we do, I guess I'm carrying fancy sticks down the aisle.

All of which to say, I think florists generally set off panic in me. I know absolutely fuck all about flowers and now I have to choose somebody's Last Ever Bouquet. When Dad brought me in to choose some flowers for Mum he said I could get whatever I liked. I picked sunflowers without a second thought because they were fun so they reminded me of her, and I thought they might cheer us all up when we saw them at her service. But now:

A) I'm painfully aware that people are going to be looking at my choices, because I'm no longer a youngster who gets a free pass. They're going to judge me. I can't pick something uplifting because you can't just waltz back after a thirteen-year absence and be all 'LOL sunflowers'.

B) I'm overwhelmed by the idea that this is my final gesture. I have to say everything I want to say in a language I do not speak, and I will never get another chance.

One of the brochures slips out of my hands and I have to stop and take some of those useless mindfulness breaths again. As ever, they do not help. Mae fetches me a glass of water and pats my arm until the dizziness subsides.

'It's OK,' she keeps telling me. 'God, Pauline must be beside herself too.'

And there's that name again. When I hear it it makes my stomach squirm in a funny way and I really don't know what to call it. It's kind of . . . FOMO? Like, everybody knows it and I don't, and nor do I have any right to, but . . . I don't know. It's just making me feel worse, if that's possible.

Twenty head-spinning minutes later, I'm back outside, staring at the war memorial, and I'm not quite sure what happened. I *am* certain that I achieved nothing. I clutch Mae's card in my clammy hand. I promised to call when I felt more up to it. I wonder what 'more up to it' even feels like. I hope I figure it out soon because there's starting to be a lot riding on it. On the plus side, my collection of death-related business cards is really taking off. Maybe I'll be a hoarder too by the end of this. I seem to be a prodigy. And we all know I have the genes.

I pop into the corner shop on the way home. It's the closest thing we ever had to a supermarket. For actual choice when you want to buy food you have to drive twenty minutes to Big Tesco, which is also the only Tesco, and which – I realised as soon as I moved upcountry – isn't even that big. But for everyday essentials you go to Karnkarrow Konveniences. The owners know everything from who currently needs to add a few prunes to their diet to which unfortunate teenager with a recently deceased mother has secretly started her periods.

I've never quite forgiven Mrs Rowe for telling on me to Dad. As far as I was concerned we never needed that particular chat to happen. I had, after all, read many informative agony-aunt columns in teen magazines. I was an independent lady, I had listened to Destiny's Child, and I did think I could handle this.

The tiny shop has everything you could ever really need, just not all at the same time, and almost certainly not when you might need it. Right now, in very early September, tins of soup in a thousand flavours already fill one shelf while another is full of gravy granules. But in three months' time this place might be filled with salad dressings and ice cream wafers, even though everybody will be thinking about Christmas dinner. It's a 'take what you think you might need one day when you see it' kind of situation. Throughout every day Mrs Rowe plays a delicate game of Tetris to fill the gaps as they appear. The woman's spatial awareness is flawless – she could have tutored Dad in the art of stacking stuff. He actually made her jump once, right at a crucial moment when she was trying to squeeze a bag of pasta into a gap half its size. An entire shelf came crashing down and couldn't be put up again. She was frosty with both of us for weeks afterwards.

I enter the little shop with an electronic 'ding dong'. I keep my head down and make a beeline for where I hope I might find some cleaning products. It just so happens to be in the same place as the tampons.

'Time of the month again, love, is it?' Mrs Rowe trills as I rush past, avoiding eye contact.

'Not yet, Mrs Rowe, thank you!'

I peruse spray bottle after spray bottle of violently coloured liquids, all promising to kill very specific kinds of bacteria, each in very specific sets of circumstances. It is, without question, a con, but I load up with one of everything just to be on the safe side. That ache in my stomach is back but I ignore it and reach for a packet of J-cloths.

I pause as I near the counter with my heap of stuff. Goosebumps prickle on my arms and I feel a little bit like somebody's sucked the air out of my lungs.

'You alright, Charlie?' Mrs Rowe smiled down at me over the counter. I hid behind Mum's leg and chewed the sleeve of my school jumper. I wasn't always quite that clingy, but Mum had been away and I was happy to have her back. And, fine, I may or may not have thought Mrs Rowe looked a little bit like a witch from certain angles.

'She's alright, aren't you?' Mum smiled at me too. 'Doing so well at school! You're really getting into it. She loves reading. Don't you love reading?'

I nodded, and Mum chucked me under the chin and laid her hand on my head. Mrs Rowe made approving noises before pressing a few buttons on the till. The drawer crashed open.

'And what about you, love?' She took Mum's hand over her few bits of shopping. 'How are you?'

'I'm great, thank you.'

'But how are you really*? In yourself, I mean? They were able to help you at' – she glanced at me – 'on your break?'*

'It was really good, Mrs Rowe, thank you. I'm getting there. And thank you for keeping Martin and this one stocked up. You're a life-saver. But we'd better go, madam, hadn't we?'

She placed a hand over Mrs Rowe's for a moment, then gathered up the bits on the counter. Then she handed me the cornflakes, because I was always Official Cornflakes Carrier, put a hand on my back, and gently steered me towards the door.

I deposit my haul on the counter along with some bin bags and a bottle of gin.

'Bit of cleaning, love, is it?' Mrs Rowe asks lightly as she rings up a full armload of cleaning products.

'Just a bit, Mrs Rowe.'

'I've not seen you around here in a while.'

'No, Mrs Rowe. I've been away.'

'Well, you want to take better care of yourself. You could carry this lot home in the bags under your eyes.'

She regards me neutrally, and I try not to give her anything in my facial expression either. The truth is I haven't slept *that* badly since I got here. If there are bags under my eyes I carried them from London. I gather the handles of my bags (carrier) and turn to leave.

'Sorry to hear about your father, Charlie.'

I turn back. 'Thank you, Mrs Rowe.'

She squeezes my wrist across the counter and looks deep into my eyes. I can't look away. This is way more intense than Tampon-gate.

'You know you can just let it settle, don't you? Don't rush to bury him before we've even had the funeral.'

I pause. I know what my huge haul of disinfectant must look like. But I have things I have to get back to. Life goes on, even when we don't really want it to. Mrs Rowe releases me.

'Thank you,' I say as I leave.

I get home – I mean, back to Dad's, obviously – and finally switch on my phone out of curiosity. It jumps into life as message after message comes through – voicemails, texts, actual honest-to-goodness emails. I immediately wish I hadn't looked and switch it back off without reading anything. My hands feel clammy. It's not like I planned to run away, and that is categorically *not* what I've done, even though it might look a lot like what I've done. But I feel guilty anyway. I stare into space and wait for my heart to stop pounding.

CHAPTER FIVE

It feels like the house has got smaller since I've been outside. I guess it's something to do with the contrast between the airiness and sunshine, and then sitting in a kitchen with a tiny window that's partially blocked out by the old wine bottles stacked on the sill. Or it's just the sheer amount of shit in here.

Each time I've left I've kind of forgotten what it's like and assumed I must be exaggerating it in my head. And then I come back and have to move a stack of neatly folded tea towels I remember from, like, thirteen years ago to make space to put my cup down. So I guess it really is that bad after all.

It's the quiet I hate. I'm not used to the house being empty. It's not natural. I at least expect the TV to be on when I come in, maybe a couple of lights, or the clatter of something in the kitchen. It was never *just* me here. I pull my phone from my back pocket without even making the conscious decision to look at it. I don't even know why. There's nothing to see. I mean, there's a couple of texts from James when I switch my phone back on, but it's not like there's going to be anything new from the one person I actually want a message from.

I take a couple of steadying sips of tea before deciding that won't do the trick and fishing my bottle of gin from the stripy plastic bag. I pour the tea into the sink and refill my mug. But only halfway because it's only lunchtime and I'm not an animal.

I lean against the sink and contemplate the scene before me. It kind of feels like I'm in a helicopter over the Grand Canyon. There's one steep valley before me, which provides a route from the kitchen sink and all the way to the front door. There's a tributary in the direction of the table, and a route off to the living room. Maybe geography wasn't such a waste of time after all. The sides of the valley are just unbelievable amounts of crap. Heaps of recipe books, packaging, and food give way to piles of shoes, suitcases, and a load of black bags which could contain anything. I don't even know where to start.

I drain my gin mug and wipe my mouth with my arm like a lady. I have one job to do, and it won't get done if I just stand like a lemon by the sink letting everything overwhelm me. Even if there *is* a voice in my head getting louder and louder, suggesting that I should just leave now because nobody really wants me here anyway. I refuse to listen to that. Although I will admit that I take another swig of gin, straight from the bottle this time, just to drown it once and for all.

I decide to find the record player. It feels logical, because where there's a record player there's records, and then I'll know the kind of music he was into, and then Mr Trelawney will stop thinking I'm totally useless, and maybe so will I. I know there's a record player here somewhere because it was here when I was a teenager and if there's one thing I'm certain of it's that nothing which has ever entered this house has left it. Apart from me. Nope. Unhelpful thought. Stop it, stop it, stop it.

I creep through the Grand Canyon of Junk in the direction of the living room. I'm afraid to touch the sides just in case I knock something over, cause a domino effect, and trap myself here forever.

I mean, I suppose it *would* serve me right for running away like I did. But still. Let's not.

The living room is a shithole, which should surprise nobody. I haven't seen an actual, old-school, 3D television set like the one that still has pride of place here in years. It has buttons you literally have to press inwards until they click, and a wire aerial that Dad would sometimes pay me 50p to hold up for ten minutes if something big had happened in the news and the weather was bad. I hear roaring my ears. It sounds like the static from that ancient TV, except the TV isn't on. I shake my head.

One wall of the living room is entirely lined with bookcases. Books lie on top of the books stacked on the shelves. They're also piled on top of the bookcases themselves, and as I look up they seem to stretch upwards forever and it feels like they're going to tumble down and bury me. I drop onto the sofa and put my head between my knees. This is not a good start. Stay focused. Stay focused, stay focused, stay focused.

My eyes alight on a huge cardboard box in one corner, which seems the right kind of size. It looks like it mainly contains bills. Except that when I get beyond the top layer I start to turn up photographs and drawings. Goals immediately abandoned, I stick my hands in up to my elbows and grab handfuls of paper. Here's a picture of Mum giving me a piggyback. Her eyes are closed against the sun and I'm laughing my head off. Here's one of Dad with Mum on the beach. It's a proper golden-hour #selfie, except it was definitely taken in the eighties because Mum's perm is absurd, as are her glasses. Probably quite stylish now, though. Mum's arm is extended as she holds the camera, and Dad is staring at her so adoringly I almost feel like I should look away.

None of the photos are from anywhere further flung than the next bay from Carncarrow. Dad never saw the point of going on holidays, and so we never did.

'Why would you bother when you live on holiday already?' he'd ask. Except my friends always seemed to be jetting off to glamorous places (Benidorm! Disneyland Paris! The Lake District!) and I felt self-conscious telling them I'd spent another summer holiday on the beach two minutes from my house.

I find a bundle of school reports and leaf through. To sum up: I was a good student. There are a lot of references within the later reports to my 'tragic circumstances' and how I was 'overcoming adversity', and after I read that a few times I start to feel like my teenage self again. Nobody could ever see anything I did, anything I achieved, without seeing it through the lens of what Mum did. I knew they had my best interests at heart, but that was also when I started to feel like I'd never be anything on my own. I worried that that one horrible day would follow me around forever, marring even the positive events in my life.

There's drawing after drawing of three stick figures and a house in the box as well. Sometimes the smaller female stick figure is off on her own with the bigger ones in the background, sometimes all three are holding hands and smiling. The house is always the same – red front door and thatched roof, just like ours. You can tell they're dated because the knockers hadn't built up yet. And because they were all done by a five-year-old and there hasn't been one of those in the family for decades.

As I pick up a handful of paper something smaller than the rest flutters to the floor. I pick it up and turn it over. It's a ticket to *Snow White and the Seven Dwarfs*, the local am-dram panto one year. For some reason it happened in January rather than over Christmas and it was absolute chaos. Reg played the wicked stepmother with a level of enthusiasm that was, frankly, alarming. Mum got roped into playing one of the dwarfs, with shoes tied around her knees and bright-red cheeks. I conducted myself with an 'I'm with the band'-type energy because I hadn't yet learned that being on stage doesn't make somebody famous. I remember being convinced I was some kind of VIP because my mum was up there. I ate an unholy amount of cola-bottle sweets and bounced along to all the songs, while Dad sat next to me, cheering and booing louder than anybody else. And then, afterwards, I threw up an unholy amount of cola-bottle sweets.

I finally stop and look at the chaos I've created within the chaos that was already here. Looking at the paper remnants of the past has made me feel weird. There's so much here that could directly contradict my belief that nothing good happens in Carncarrow, but the very fact that I'm here now means I was correct. My stomach's doing very unpleasant somersaults and sweat is starting to prickle at my hairline. There's not enough air in here, that's all it is. Looking through memories is a nice way to spend an afternoon. It's nice. Nice, nice, nice.

I tip everything back into the box in no particular order, stand up, and stretch. I was barking up the wrong tree in here, which is fine. I just have to move on. Which I'm great at, famously. My stomach does another backflip. Stop it.

The hallway mostly seems to be shoes, and coats, and bags. So far, so reasonable, except there are too many for one person. Or even the original three people. It's like the whole of Carncarrow came to visit one day and forgot all of their stuff when they left.

I give a couple of the black bin bags an exploratory poke, just in case, but there's nothing that feels like a record player. One hasn't been tied and flops open to reveal a gaggle of forlorn-looking teddy bears. I've never seen them before. It looks like the opening of a very haunting children's film.

After negotiating my way around the books piled up the stairs (this from the man who once told me that if I left things lying around I might trip over and die) I stick my head around the door of the office. Nobody ever really worked there, but the box room became 'the office' when we got a computer so gigantic it needed an entire room to itself. This room was ninety-eight per cent junk even before everything fell apart and the hoarding began.

But the office is where I hit the mother lode. Not one record player, but three. There are records piled against every wall as well as being stacked on the desk.

Almost as soon as relief arrives, it disappears. Because, I mean, now what? There are thousands of records here. I don't know if Dad ever played *any* of them. I still don't know what kind of music he would want to be the last thing he ever hears. If he'd even hear it. Let's never go *there*. I suppose what I had really hoped to find was one album called *Hi, Charlie, play this if I die and you can't go wrong*.

The room spins and I have to sit down. There's a chair but it's buried, so I just drop onto the carpet. Piles of records tower over me, suddenly menacing as they block out the light. My chest hurts and I try to massage it. I don't know what I'm doing.

I've just let out a strained little noise when I hear the door handle turn downstairs. I freeze. The door opens and I can hear somebody wiping their feet on the mat. I wonder if it's just another nosy neighbour, or a serial killer this time. People have *got* to stop just letting themselves in. I wonder if I'd seem like a bitch if I put a safety chain on.

'Charlie?' a woman calls. 'Charlie, are you here?'

I hold my breath. I'm not sure why.

'Charlie!' She has more of a singsong tone now, as if she's playing hide-and-seek with a child.

I struggle to my feet, terrified that if I make one wrong move I'll end up buried under vintage vinyl, and tiptoe downstairs. I don't know why I'm creeping around. We're both in the same house. I can't hide.

There's a woman sitting on the chair in the hallway, surrounded by a sea of shoes. I recognise her, but I can't place her. She must be in her sixties, I suppose. She's very well dressed. Her blonde hair is lacquered into a bun and she has rings on every finger. She's wearing a floaty blouse and a bright-pink skirt. Her very presence makes me feel self-conscious about my own appearance, and I tug the faded old T-shirt I dug out from my old wardrobe. Mrs Rowe certainly wouldn't be commenting on *her* eye bags because she doesn't have any. She is quietly crying, though.

I stare at her, mouth open, not at all concerned that I might look rude. It's OK when Lowenna and Reg let themselves in here because they've been doing it my entire life, and allowing them to continue is the path of least resistance. But this woman is a stranger whose face I can't quite place.

'Who are you?' I finally ask.

The woman laughs through tears, but then she catches my eye and realises I'm serious.

'I'm Pauline,' she tells me. 'We met at the hospital.'

'Oh yeah. Dad's friend, right?'

'Well, actually, I'm your father's partner. Or I was.' She dabs her eyes again, finishes removing her shoes, and then heads to the kitchen and flicks the kettle on. 'I'll make us some tea, shall I? We should have a catch-up.'

I don't move from my position in the hallway. It's like I'm back in the sea again because suddenly I can't hear anything over the roaring in my ears. She's Dad's *what*? I look around the hallway, bewildered. I haven't seen any sign of her. She hasn't made a single mark on this house. Or, at least, I don't think she has. It's admittedly quite difficult to tell amongst the chaos.

How could she put up with Dad when everything he touched turned to a jumble sale? Surely that's not conducive to a good relationship. And what about Mum? I don't really think I believe in the afterlife but I am absolutely certain that if she has been forced to sit in heaven watching her husband move on with another woman I will throw up. In fact, I think I'm going to throw up anyway.

◆　◆　◆

It's just, I remember Dad after Mum died. He just sat on the sofa. He just sat on the sofa straight after breaking down the bathroom door and finding her on the floor, surrounded by way too many pill bottles. And then I either sat with him or hid from him for a couple of weeks until Lowenna took me in hand and said I should get back to school. And then he just carried on sitting there, as far as I know, for weeks on top of that. I would leave the TV on when I went out, like you might do for a cat in need of company, and then I'd come back hours later and it would still be on the same channel. Lowenna would bring him a sandwich sometimes in the middle of the day, and it would still be there when I came back.

It had become full-on summer by the time Dad was up and out of the house again. He started slowly, going for walks to the beach and back, or popping for a pint of milk when we needed one. A few people came round to see him and he made eye contact, acknowledged what they were saying instead of staring through them.

I thought we were in it together, even if we weren't literally 'together'. Or, y'know, very good at talking. But apparently he just decided not to be sad any more. And I know people should be allowed to move on, of course they should. I have nothing but admiration for people who find love again. I fully support the people who write their romantic stories in magazines or who go on *This Morning* to talk about how they got married at eighty, or whatever. I retweet inspirational love stories just as much as the next millennial woman with too much time on her hands. Good for them. Good for everybody, honestly.

But this is my dad getting over my mum, and as far as I'm concerned that should be impossible. If I really dug down into why I wake up every day in London feeling like somebody's sitting on my chest, I'd be big enough to admit that I never got over it. Not really. But that's fine because I'm thinking about Dad, not me. I'm not the one who's no longer here to explain their decisions.

My throat constricts and I race past Pauline, who's stirring a couple of mugs in the kitchen – she certainly found those quickly enough – and into the downstairs toilet. Six packs of twelve rolls of toilet paper tower over me as I heave over the avocado suite he never changed. When it's over I collapse, teary and sweaty, onto the beige carpet. How did a man who had beige carpet around his toilet until the day he died ever manage to get a girlfriend?

'Are you OK, sweetheart?' Pauline appears at the door. She looks down at me and smiles sweetly. I avoid her eyes. 'You've been through such a lot. It's a lot to take in. There's some ginger biscuits on the side. Good for the stomach.'

She pulls me to my feet and helps me into the kitchen, and all I can think is that she knows where to find ginger biscuits. Like somebody who's spent a lot of time here might be able to find ginger biscuits. I basically haven't been able to find anything except cereal and my own unmoved possessions since I arrived.

'Now. Why don't we have a chat?' she asks, offering me the biscuits which she's laid out on a plate I've never even seen before.

'What do you want to chat about?' I ask sullenly. I'm fully aware that I'm behaving like a child, but what I'm not aware of is how to stop.

'Well, how are you, first of all? I've been so worried about you.'

'You've been worried about me?'

'Of course I have.'

I'm finally starting to work out what the weird stomach ache and the ringing in my ears are about. Because, I mean, I thought we could tell each other things. I would have thought that Pauline might be something he'd tell me about. I suppose it's probably kind of a double standard. Because while I think it's fine for me to have omitted some of the boring minutiae of my life, I can't help but feel that he should have been sharing everything. And this wasn't boring anyway. This was big. This was him finding something – no, some*body* – that made him happy after so much shit. So, did he not say anything because he thought I'd be upset? Or, and there's a stabbing feeling in my chest at the very idea, because he thought I might not care?

'Thanks, that's nice,' I say.

Pauline gives me a funny look.

'You OK?' She frowns. 'Aside from the obvious, I mean.'

I clear my throat. Don't be a dick. Keep it together.

'I just . . . I don't know why he didn't tell me.'

'Oh, look, he didn't know, love. The doctor said you don't sometimes with aneurysms and then if it ruptures . . .' She shakes her head. 'But you got here, and that's good.'

'Oh, no, sorry, I mean . . .' Oh God, I hope I'm not about to say something really hurtful but, let's be honest, it's coming out anyway. 'He never mentioned you.'

Pauline purses her lips. After a moment, she nods. After another moment, she gives me a rueful smile.

'I did wonder if he would have.'

I shake my head, shrugging.

'Oh, Martin, what were we ever going to do with you?' she sighs, looking somewhere into the middle distance.

'You're not . . . upset?'

She takes a deep breath, which she blows out slowly, deliberately. What must it be like to be so in control of one's emotions?

'Well, it's not my favourite feeling, but I guess I can't say I'm surprised.'

'But—'

'Look, Charlie, you know your dad. Knew your dad. He wasn't very good with . . . Well, a lot of things. Emotional things. Maybe he was waiting 'til we'd been together longer. And with everything that happened with your mum, he probably just thought you'd be upset. Absolute bloody wuss, if you ask me.'

I smile weakly and try to swallow the lump in my throat.

'Oh, Charlie' – Pauline looks at me with concern as she catches my lip trembling – 'you mustn't take it personally. Whatever his reasons, they were to do with him, not you.'

I nod, then let out a sob. I desperately wish that I hadn't, because once one's escaped it's all over. Pauline has the good grace to look concerned and sympathetic even though after ten minutes with no let-up I can feel snot running down to my lip so she must be using everything in her power not to shudder. She brings me a tissue. Then she brings me a roll of paper towels. Then she moves her chair next to mine and pulls me into her, her rings digging into my neck as she holds me tight. I sob into her shoulder. She smells nice – like perfume mixed with just the faintest hint of cigarettes.

Eventually the rush of emotion ebbs away and Pauline releases her hold on me. I'm left hiccupping at the kitchen table as she busies herself in another cupboard. The only sounds for a minute or so are the clock on the kitchen wall blithely ticking away completely the wrong time, and the clinking of glass somewhere in the region of where Pauline's bottom is sticking out of a cupboard.

'Aha!' she declares triumphantly, as she backs out. She's holding two glasses and a bottle of something purple and viscous. 'I knew he wouldn't even have opened it, the lying sod.'

She wipes dust from the bottle with her sleeve and pours the contents into the two glasses.

'Sloe gin,' she tells me as she slides me a very generous glass of it over the table. 'I made it last year but your dad hated it. "It's not a Doom Bar, though, love, is it?"'

Her impression of him is so spot on that my eyes fill with tears again.

'Oh now, come on, Charlie. Drink up. You'll feel better.'

I take a big gulp and momentarily feel like some of the skin has been burned from the back of my throat. This is like no sloe gin I've ever tasted. I choke.

'See?' She smiles warmly.

I give her a thumbs-up as I cough up fruit-flavoured lighter fluid.

◆ ◆ ◆

'So, how long were you and Dad together?'

We've been making small talk, gossiping about people in the village, but this is the elephant in the room and now that I have a few drinks in me I finally feel ready to hear it. Pauline glazes over, smiling.

'About eighteen months.'

I nod and exhale. Eighteen months I can cope with. Eighteen months isn't too dramatic. If it had turned out that they'd got together a decade ago I was likely to lose it again.

'He gave me hell when I took over the pub. Total arsehole, honestly. They don't like their out-of-towners, do they?'

'Not at first.' I smile in spite of myself.

'Anyway, he took me out to say sorry and we went from there. Nothing mad. He wasn't about to get married again or anything, obviously. He told me about your mum and how that was for him, you know, with her—'

'Can we not—' I take a shaky breath. 'Can we not talk about that?'

'Of course.' She reaches a hand over the table and squeezes mine. 'Sorry.'

'No, it's fine, it's just . . . y'know.'

'I probably don't even know the half of it anyway.'

We both sip our drinks.

'So, you and Dad . . .'

'So, we'd go out for dinner, go to the cinema, get coffee, I don't know. It wasn't exactly raunchy' – I try not to shudder – 'but we had a lovely time together, and it's just nice to have someone you look forward to seeing, isn't it? Someone who cares what you're doing, who wants to look after you. Eighteen months is no time, really. I do wonder where it could have gone—' Her voice cracks, and she looks at me with shining eyes. 'You probably think it sounds really boring.'

'I think it sounds amazing.'

'He told me all about you, of course.'

'Yeah?' I'm not totally sure I'm ready to hear it but I've been a big, brave girl so far.

'He said you were amazing. That you'd obviously been through . . . everything. But you'd come out the other end and you were making something of yourself. He said he wished he got to see you more but when the two of you were together it just reminded him that your mum wasn't any more. He could see the hole she'd left when he saw you, is what he said.'

I blink too hard and nod.

'I get that.'

We sip our drinks in companionable silence for a while as the last of the daylight tries to stream in past the insane number of wine bottles on the windowsill. It might not be that insane any more, I suppose, if Pauline was in the equation. I wonder what my life would have been like if she'd come into it earlier. It's a moot point, though. If she'd been in my life earlier it would already mean that I hadn't dropped off the map and everything would have been completely different anyway.

'Oh my God, we're so off-topic,' Pauline eventually says (or, if we're very honest, slurs), putting down her glass and leaning across the table to me. Her skin is pink from the gin. 'I actually came to ask how you'd feel about being involved in the funeral. Like I said, I know you two didn't—'

'Oh, I already went to Trelawney's.'

It comes out too abruptly. The booze has taken away my ability to moderate my tone. Pauline sits back in her chair.

'Oh. I see.'

I can see her mulling this over and my hairline prickles. I've been an idiot. I should have thought . . . but should . . . have thought what? That someone else might want to be involved? But how would I know that? Objectively I can see that there's been a simple miscommunication. But I can feel the flush rising up my face, and I can see a similar one rising up hers, and I have a horrible feeling that objectivity is about to fly out the window.

'No, I'm sorry – what?' she demands.

'I went to Trelawney. It was just to find some stuff out, really, I . . . I didn't know. About—'

'I tried to get in touch, Charlie. You didn't call me back. I wanted to do the decent thing and include you before I just ploughed on.'

'I'm sorry, I just thought I'd better make a start. I got your note, and I was going to call, but—'

Pauline holds up a hand. She's laughing, but her eyes are brimming and angry.

'Do you know what? I should have known. With everything I've heard about you, I should've known.'

'What—'

'That you'd be selfish. Just because you're in a rush to bury the past doesn't mean we all are.'

'But, I—'

'And I'm sure you "didn't know" and you "didn't mean it", but your actions have *consequences*. You're not some naive teenager any more, you should know this by now.'

'I just—'

'You "just" need to try thinking about other people for once in your life. You're just like your mother.'

She sits back, and I clench my jaw as hard as I ever have in my life. I'm obviously angry about what she's just said to me. It's all very unfair. And to bring *Mum* into it? She didn't even know her. But more than that, I can feel the brief glow of mindless (and yes, drunken, so sue me) happiness fading back to the same old, same old. I wasn't ready. But here we are.

She regards me coldly. She's waiting to see what I have to say, and I try to look anywhere except into her eyes. Because despite all of my self-righteous anger I'm worried she's right. I mean, I *know* she's right. I always wonder if people look at me and think that Mum and I are the same. Because I do worry we are. I know it's a slippery slope to end up where Mum did, and sometimes I wonder if I'm still at the top or if I'm already halfway down. Maybe she didn't even mean *that*, but . . . I don't know. The sudden rush of embarrassment makes me defensive. And that, along with the disappointment of losing that tipsy, giggly glow, brings me to the end of my tether.

I take a deep breath to steady my voice and finally look up, my eyes meeting Pauline's cold ones. I draw myself to my feet.

'Shove it up your arse, Pauline.'

She stares at me. I don't think either of us can quite register the turn this has all taken. Her mouth sets in a hard line, because what can she say? She can't exactly discipline me. She can't yell at me and send me to my room. So, for a moment she just looks wounded and I feel more like shit. And then I feel even *more* like shit for only thinking about how *I* feel like shit when I've just been very rude to somebody I was growing to like.

When the silence becomes unbearable I open my mouth to speak. I want to change my mind, to take it back, to tell her how sorry I am for leaving her out. I want her to know I was just lashing out because . . . well, just because. But before I can articulate any of that she stands up, turns on her heel and leaves, slamming the kitchen door behind her.

CHAPTER SIX

After Pauline's gone, I stare blankly across the table at where she was *just* sitting. Dregs of purple alcohol remain in the bottle, so I pick it up and drain it. The room spins when I stand up. I stagger out of the kitchen. I reach the front door before I realise I have nowhere to storm off to. I don't think Adam would thank me for showing up, unannounced and tear-stained, on his doorstep any more. So I turn around and climb the stairs to bed. The sun's *nearly* down, so it's almost acceptable. There are a couple of crashes behind me as I struggle to keep my course straight.

Up in my room I lie down, fully clothed. I want nothing more than to blank out everything that's happened today. For the last three days, in fact. I never dreamed I'd be wishing to be back in London on the seemingly unstoppable hamster wheel of work, tubes, and wedding appointments, but we are where we are.

I close my eyes and pretend I don't exist until I finally pass out.

◆ ◆ ◆

I have such weird dreams over the next I-don't-even-know-how-long. In one of them I'm visited by Lowenna, who knocks on the door and, when I open it, just continues to knock on thin air. When

I touch her on the shoulder to let her know I'm there she continues to knock, but this time she does it directly on my forehead.

I see Mae Fletcher walking down the street towards me and dive into a hedge to avoid her, only to find out that she's somehow also in the hedge, trying to see who I'm hiding from.

In one dream, we have the funeral, attended by everybody in the village, and it's beautiful. I can't stop crying. But then the coffin falls off the stage and it's empty. Nobody around me seems to be surprised. Instead, they simply plough on with a beautiful rendition of 'The Lord is My Shepherd'.

I open my eyes slowly, blinking away the tiredness, and I see Dad sitting on the end of my bed. He looks at me sadly and gives me a little smile and a nod, before beginning to fizzle out at the edges like the picture on his ancient TV.

'No!'

But he raises a hand in farewell and disappears entirely.

I wake up with a start and a stifled yell and immediately sit up to check the end of my bed. I don't know what I expect to find, apart from the end of the duvet, twisted around my feet where I've been tossing and turning. My heart sinks a little, then I laugh at myself. As if he was ever going to be there.

That's when the pounding in my head hits. At first it could be mistaken for a side effect of my sitting up too fast, but soon it's crept over my skull and somehow infiltrated the deepest recesses of my brain. My mouth feels like cotton wool and my stomach churns – not enough to make me sick, but just enough to mean that I can never feel totally safe. A classic Trewin hangover. I feel bad about how things ended with Pauline, but at least she got some delayed revenge by plying me with unseemly amounts of gin.

The light through the curtains isn't that bright yet so it can't be too late. Not that I know what I'm supposed to do with myself today anyway. I pull the duvet up to my face with a groan and try to ignore the pain in my head until I drop off again.

The next time I wake up it is unquestionably late in the day. It must be sunny outside because it's dazzling in here even with the curtains drawn. I can't imagine wanting to be outside – or, indeed, upright – ever again.

I can hear whirring and slowly (so slowly) get to my feet. I honestly moved faster that time I put my back out during session one of week one of the Couch to 5K programme. When I open the curtains a crack, a shaft of light hits me directly in the eye and I hiss like a vampire confronted with a crucifix. I take a moment for my eyes to adjust to the horror of actual sunlight, and then I peer out of the window.

Beyond the peeling paint of the window frame and the seagull-splattered glass, Lowenna is working away in her garden, which makes me feel very inferior. She has more energy than me this morning and she's been around for nine decades. And, I mean, she wasn't up to her eyeballs in very strong homemade booze last night, but still.

I watch her push a lawnmower which is probably older than I am up and down her neat front lawn. In contrast, Dad's grass is tall enough to hide small children, and sways defiantly in the breeze. Another thing that needs to be sorted. All of the jobs starting to pile up are enough to make me want to lock myself in my childhood bedroom, never to be seen again. Like Miss Havisham in a tatty old nightie.

As I watch, Reg strolls into view. He has a copy of the *Daily Mail* tucked under one arm, and a loaf of bread in a plastic bag swings by his side. Lowenna accosts him and he pauses. They stand together by her garden gate and chat. I can't hear what's being said, but I figure out that it must be about me, or Dad, or a combination thereof, when they both look up at the house. I throw myself onto the floor with my hands over my head, my heart thumping.

I think I just need a day away from human interaction. I get that sometimes. I'm still smarting from my exchange with Pauline last night. I feel hurt by what she said, but also disloyal for feeling hurt. I feel bad for not thinking about anyone else when I started making arrangements. I feel overwhelmed by the amount of house-work I have in front of me. I feel pathetic because even when all this is over it's not like I have anything to look forward to. It's all just a bit shit.

As I mentally list everything that feels bad right now (do not recommend, incidentally), a tear spills down my cheek. This time I'm not angry. This is pure overwhelm, and it's all I can do to keep from wailing as a surge of in-over-my-head-ness washes over me. I don't know where to start, and I certainly don't know how to fix all of the things that need fixing. And to top it all off there's that Dad-shaped hole that I can't even bring myself to think about.

I crawl over to the bedside table and pick up my phone. It's more a reflex than anything because, I mean, who would I call? And it's not like I'm in the mood to scroll through all of the strangers being happy on Instagram. The glow from the screen is burning my eyes. I don't even make a conscious decision to do it, but I open my texts and scroll to find Dad's. It has been a few weeks, but it still takes a depressingly short time to reach them. The only people who really text me are James and delivery companies.

Hi Charlie hope your ok

Great, thanks! How are you?

No answer. And then, a few weeks later:

Just checking in you ok

Good thanks, hope you are too :)

Happy birthday! Doing anything good today?

Thanks love just dinner with a friend

I now realise the friend was probably Pauline but thinking about Pauline makes my stomach twist so maybe I just won't.

Hi all going well

Yep, all good thanks :) how are you?

Good ta

Hows things

Great, thank you x

And it just goes on and on, lie after lie, right up until that time I dropped my old phone in the sink and got this one. I can't even fathom that I won't be getting a punctuation-free check-in message ever again. I refuse to believe it. I wonder if I could have changed anything if I'd – just once – told him the truth. Maybe he'd have suggested I come down for a visit, I might have noticed something different about him, I could have . . .

I spend a long time on the floor under the window, knees pulled in tight to my chest, weeping. I hate that word, but I really can only describe it as weeping. It's soft and hopeless. Pathetic, really. At one point the doorbell rings. I assume it's either Lowenna or Reg since they were in the area. I don't answer it. They don't let themselves in. Maybe they know it's not the time.

When I finally stop crying – not because I start feeling better, but just because I've run out of steam – my hangover has given way to another headache. Or at least, it's changed shape. Rather than a crashing pain which overrides everything, this one is dull but comes in waves. Just when I think it's better another wave hits and I can't think about anything for five minutes until it subsides.

I crawl back to bed feeling more exhausted than I did when I first woke up. I haven't even shut the curtains. But by the time I realise that, I've already cocooned myself under the covers and there's nothing in the world that could entice me back out. I am one with the duvet. The duvet is me. So I just fall asleep in the full daylight.

It's hunger that eventually forces me into an upright position again. When I was a child and having a tantrum I would shut myself in my room and Mum would tell me with absolute confidence that she'd see me when I was hungry. As it turns out, hunger is still my biggest motivator in my thirties.

I catch a glimpse of myself in the bathroom mirror as I do my first pee in God knows how many hours. I'm there forever. You know the ones. My hair is sticking up in directions I didn't think were possible. My skin is sallow. I was never actually sure what 'sallow' meant before this moment but it's the only word that seems to capture the state of my face. There are dark shadows around my eyes, which are also bloodshot *and* puffy: The Misery Trifecta. My clothes, which were never designed to be slept in, feel like they've fused to my body. I look at my bare legs as I sit on the toilet (classy) and there are perfect imprints of the seams from my old jeans down each one, deeper than I've ever seen them before.

I don't do anything to improve my appearance before I go downstairs. I simply raid the fridge. Lowenna wouldn't know what had hit her if she happened to glance into the kitchen now. Mercifully, she's not out in the garden at the moment.

I make myself a meal for which there is no name. It's comprised of crackers, cheese, ham, and pickle. So far, so normal. Then, I add a bowl of cereal on the side just for fun. I find a couple of potato waffles in the freezer so I stick those in the toaster as well. There's a little bit of ice cream in a tub in the freezer so I have that while I wait. And then I round everything off with half a tub of frozen blackberries from what I *hope* is the autumn just gone, although it's undated, and it's Dad's kitchen, so there are no guarantees. It's as if I've just woken up from hibernation.

Once my gnawing hunger pangs have been quelled, I sit amongst the washing-up and empty containers on the kitchen table and begin to make a list of everything I need to get done.

It doesn't take me long to realise that I'm really just making a list of every fixture, fitting, or pile of junk the house contains. *Everything* needs something doing to it. Listing it all is not the way forward, and it's making my palms sweat, so I stop.

I decide to start by cleaning the windows, because it's physically impossible to stack piles of anything on a vertical surface, so it seems a good warm-up. I move through the rooms systematically. In the kitchen, I move all of the old wine bottles off the sill to reach the glass. In the bathroom, old perfume bottles line the window ledge. I sweep them into the recycling. They leave behind a waft of sickly sweetness as they fall. They aren't Mum's, which means they probably came from— No. Sorry, brain. Stop it. Stop it, stop it, stop it. Move on.

In the hallway there's a massive bowl balanced precariously on the windowsill. It's full of more keys than anybody could possibly have used, the majority of which have no discernible purpose. Frankly, it looks a little bit swinger-ish, which is a thought I could live without. Behind everything on each windowsill there's a scattering of dead flies, which makes it all quite harrowing. I sweep them into one hand as if they were toast crumbs and throw them out of each window in turn, trying not to gag.

When it's time for something a little more challenging, I tackle the bathroom first. There are many and varied creams and medications, and I'm not sure Dad would want me knowing more about them than strictly necessary, so I just sweep everything into the bin with one quick arm movement. Some things are better left a mystery.

I give everything a vigorous wipe down with the cleaning products I bought from Mrs Rowe, the fumes from the bleach burning my still-sore eyes. My arms ache from the effort and I start to sweat, but the movement actually feels quite nice. Do I . . . *like* exercise now? No. Let's not go mad.

I can't bring myself to throw away the toothbrush or the plastic comb that sit in a chipped glass on the sink. I move it out of the way and then replace it exactly as it was – at the same angle and everything. I don't know why.

Once I'm done with the bathroom, I stand in the doorway of the living room to get the lie of the land. The more you stare at the junk everywhere, the more it kind of makes . . . sense? Or else I really am going mad. Either is possible. For the most part, things are where you'd expect them to be, just in outrageous quantities. So, where somebody might have the most recent *Radio Times* on the sofa, Dad has a stack of about fifty issues. Had.

I gather up the entire pile, which weighs an absolute ton, thereby increasing my hope that this might count as a workout, and I dump them all in the recycling. There's a tiny voice at the back of my mind that says I should keep hold of them, that they're sentimental, that they're all I have left of him. But that's patently untrue as I'm standing in an entire house full of memories. I also suspect that the same tiny voice telling him to cling on to every little thing for posterity was the reason Dad collected so much junk in the first place. Well, I've seen where that voice can get you. I refuse to give it the satisfaction.

The sideboard is covered in trinkets – there are frames, ornaments, vases, you name it. I fall particularly in love with a massive brass crab and stash it away in my room while also questioning my choices. But this is not me letting the voice in my head win.

'You're just funny,' I tell the crab. 'That's all.'

The crab doesn't have a lot to say in reply. He just brandishes a giant brass claw in my direction.

I go to the garage and retrieve a box, of which there are, unsurprisingly, loads. I might be able to do a bit of recycling at the very least. I bring it back to the living room and gingerly place all of the bits and bobs into it. I'll take them to the charity shop. They'll think all their Christmases have come at once.

I need a change of scene, so I opt to go through my own bedroom next. At least I know I'll happily throw everything away. I bring a raft of bin liners with me and set to work. It only takes two minutes to lay waste to the walls and tear down every poster. Johnny Depp stares forlornly up at me with half a face, the other half lost to the pile of scraps I'm building up in the centre of the carpet. I bundle everything gleefully into a bag, tie it up, and throw it down the stairs, where it comes to rest amongst the bags of indeterminate stuff that have probably been there for years.

I open every drawer and cupboard and scoop their contents into more bin bags. I'm racing through this part and it feels excellent. I feel almost hysterical, buoyed by my sudden progress.

The only thing left to be cleared is the built-in dressing table I turned into a desk. I pull open one of the drawers and stop short. Inside is a gift. The paper is covered with silver stars, which in turn match the perfectly tied bow. I don't remember this at all.

I pick up the gift and there's a card underneath. I recognise Dad's writing, although it's a little bit rougher than the last time I saw it.

It's for me.

I turn the box over and over again in my hands. I'm not sure I want to open it. Dad didn't give it to me and there must be a reason. I give it a little shake and send a sprinkling of glitter into my lap. In the end, curiosity gets the better of me and I untie the ribbon. I'm a little bit afraid of what could be inside.

Once I've gently peeled away the Sellotape and unfolded the paper I'm left with a plain black box in my hands. I pause again, that underwatery rushing sound back in my ears.

Inside, a necklace is arranged over a tiny, overstuffed satin pillow. My mum's name, Joy, is spelled out in gold cursive letters. I feel dizzy.

I gently lay the box on the desk and turn my attention to the card. The front is a watercolour image of a vase of flowers. Inside, my dad has tried to fit a lot of text into quite a small space, but I can just about make it out:

Dear Charlie,

This is just a little something to say congratulations on your graduation. I'm so proud of you, following your heart up to London and working out what you want to do with your life. You always were a go-getter. <u>My</u> go-getter.

You've not had the easiest of times these past few years but I want you to know that whatever happens your mother will <u>always</u> be here. Maybe not in a way we can see, but I do think she's watching over us. That's what this necklace represents. You'll have her with you forever now. I know she'd be so proud of you too, love.

Never forget that you can do anything you set your heart on, and you will, and I will always be here whenever you need me. You just let me know.

I love you.

Dad x

I cling tightly to the card, spellbound. The silence of my bedroom suddenly seems oppressive, but I'm rooted to the spot because my legs won't stop shaking. I open and close my mouth a couple of times as if I'm going to answer Dad from a decade ago. Instead, the tears come.

I hang on tightly to the card in one hand and the edge of the bed in the other as sobs force their way through me. The necklace simply sits on the desk and gleams, and I can't tell if it's a symbol of hope or reproval.

I'm so mad at Dad for not giving me this sooner, and I'm so mad at myself for not being better at staying in touch. I'm even mad at Mum for being the reason we avoided each other like we did. And I'm sad. For all of us. Because I am normally absolutely fine, but I have to admit we're a pretty sad family. Were.

After I don't know how long, the surge of grief becomes a more manageable trickle again. I hiccup and try to steady my breathing. The front of my top is damp from the tears that have dripped there and I wipe my nose on my sleeve because we all know I'm way past dignity at this point.

I pluck the necklace from the box and hold it up in front of my face. The word 'Joy' shines as it swings and then comes to a stop. Then I slip it on and do up the catch. It comes to rest on my sternum, and I reach up to touch it for reassurance. I don't think Dad would be upset that I found it and have chosen to wear it. I just think he'd be upset that it's taken so long.

My eyes threaten to spill over again, but I take a couple of deep breaths, touching the necklace and trying to draw strength from it, and the feeling that I'm about to fall into a pit recedes again.

Which is not to say that I feel OK. I think I'm ready to talk to an actual human. And there are a couple I should probably start with.

CHAPTER SEVEN

I sit on the carpet with my back against the wall, digging my toes into it like I used to when I was complaining about the world to Adam on the landline, so many moons ago. This doesn't feel *quite* the same, but I don't know what else to do. I switch on my mobile, and as I wait for it to power up and the triumphant little tune to ring out, I try to steady my hands. An onslaught of messages and missed calls makes it buzz against the carpet, and makes me jump in the process. Once it's finished, I dial. I can delete everything later.

'What the fuck, Charlie?' James barks when he answers on the first ring. To be fair, I can't blame him.

'I know. I know, I'm sor—'

'You *cannot* just disappear without a trace for days and then phone me and say that you're sorry and expect everything to go away.'

'But I told you—'

'You told me your dad was in hospital and then literally nothing else for days on end. I've been going mad wondering if everything's OK.'

I'm briefly tempted to just hang up.

'I'm fine.'

There are a few seconds of silence.

'My dad died.'

A few tears spill over again. I still haven't really said it out loud that many times, apart from to official Death Industry Professionals. There's another silence on the other end of the phone. Or, not actually silence, but there's nothing apart from James's too-heavy, why-is-he-like-this breathing, which you'd think was just a thing that happened on the phone but which is actually a pretty constant soundtrack to my life. Somehow I'd managed to forget it for a while.

'I'm really sorry, Charlie. I'm sad I never got to meet him.'

Whatever I was expecting him to say it wasn't this. I kind of want to laugh.

'Well, it's a bit late now, isn't it?' I bite back. I can't help it. He makes it too easy sometimes.

'Charlie, come on.'

Be nice. Be nice, be nice, be nice.

'You're right. I'm sorry.'

He lets out a heavy sigh. It's amplified, like, a hundred times by the microphone and I have to hold my phone away from my ear.

'I was really worried about you, you know?'

His voice trembles, and I know he's going to cry. Now, I don't have an issue with men crying. In fact, I'm all for it. I can't get enough of it, honestly. I've seen what not opening up about your feelings can do. The world would be a much better place if we could all just freely express our emotions, regardless of gender. I would probably opt out, personally, but everybody else should let loose if they want. But. *But* . . . I mean, this happens a lot and I never know what to do.

I listen to him sob a couple of times, careful to hold the neutral expression that I've perfected over the years. I know he can't see me, but it's the principle. Once, in our early days, I accidentally lost control of one eyebrow. It escaped up my forehead as I held him and he sobbed about somebody's idea being chosen over his own at work. Apparently that made me 'insensitive'.

'So, have you had the funeral yet?'

'It's in a few days.'

'Should I book a train?'

'What?'

'You know, to be there. To support you?'

'Oh! No. No, thank you.'

'Do you not want me there?'

No. Of course not. But come on, Charlie. Do better. Make something up. I cast my mind around.

'It's not that, it's just . . . Surely you need to be at work? You don't want them to pick one of Hannah's concepts over yours again.'

I'm hitting him where it hurts. Right in the career. It's a low blow, and I hear his shaky inhale as he relives the indignity all over again. I've never felt that strongly about work and I always wondered if that meant there was something wrong with me. But, then again, I'm not the one having tantrums over blueprints.

'No. I suppose you're right.'

We sit in silence for a little while. This was always one of our issues – no small talk. But then, I always reasoned, should you need to make small talk with your future husband anyway? I'm pretty sure we should be able to sit in a comfortable silence. It's just that in our case the silences have become a little too long, and somewhere along the line the comfort disappeared. But it's fine. It's probably just me. I famously have no chat.

'Well, I guess I should go,' James sighs before I get the chance to say anything.

'OK.'

'I miss you. And I'm thinking about you. And I love you.'

'OK. Thanks.'

I jab at the screen as the line goes dead and rest my head against the wall. I rub my eyes. I could happily lie down and have a nap right here on the floor. My head is pounding again and I'm not sure if this sudden fatigue is because I'm exhausted by my frenzy of cleaning, or by our stilted conversation. I'm really, really fighting to think positively about it. We had a good talk. It was good. It was good, good, good.

I stand up and try to physically shake off the awkwardness. I jump up and down a few times. And, while I'm still riding this once-in-a-lifetime phone-bravery high, I dial again. I'm totally prepared for it to go to voicemail, or even to be cut off mid-ring, so it's a surprise when there's an answer straight away.

'Hi, Charlie.'

'Oh, hi, Pauline. Listen, do you think we could, I dunno, meet up? Talk, maybe? I feel really bad about—'

'Yes, that sounds fine. Shall I pop over now?'

'Now?'

I'm not used to things being so immediate. In my world you agonise for weeks before you even manage to ask someone to get lunch, then act breezy when they postpone it for a few weeks. Then you end up having a rushed coffee before going on to better plans elsewhere (them) or telling them it's fine because you have a wedding appointment to get to anyway (me, lying). But I guess it's good to get things over with.

Pauline knocks on the door twenty minutes later, when I've barely had time to practise anything I want to say. I stand on the other side of the stained glass looking at her wavy outline and getting control of my breathing for a second before I open the door.

'I'm sorry,' I say in place of 'hello'.

'Charlie, don't . . .' She shakes her head. 'It's such a nice evening. Shall we go for a walk?'

'Oh.' I had pictured how this conversation might go, and at no point in my imagination were we walking while we had it. But I can be flexible. And she's right, it does look lovely. The sky is doing this ombré thing where it goes from electric blue to bright orange, but you can't quite tell exactly where the colour changes in the middle. The sun has gone down, so the lights in the other houses are on, but nobody's closed their curtains yet. It's totally creepy but I love that. I like to look into people's windows (always pretending I'm not, of course) and imagine what it would be like to live in their houses. To live their lives. To not live mine.

I follow Pauline's lead, and we head in the opposite direction to the beach. We turn right out of the gate and up a hill until little stone cottages give way to bigger houses with gravel driveways and spiky gates. All the while, I wonder whether I should say something, but I don't really know how to start. Pauline doesn't seem in any hurry to speak, so I keep pace with her and take everything in. Even the big houses run out after a while.

We walk down an alleyway next to the allotments and come out in a lane beside a field. The trees are silhouetted against the dusky sky, but the sun has long since disappeared. On the other side of the field I can just make out a couple of farm buildings. Bright-yellow light spills out of one, and a figure moves around in the patch of brightness. An owl hoots somewhere. The lane we're standing in is bordered on both sides with a tangle of wilting late-summer flowers. The scent they give off is . . . well, it's making me feel a bit sick, actually. Or maybe that's nerves. There's the occasional sound of movement in the undergrowth and the canopy of branches above us. It's all very lovely, but the darker it gets the more I feel certain we're going to find out that we're being followed by the Blair Witch, and I still haven't had a chance to apologise.

'Pauline,' I begin, stopping in my tracks and tugging her arm. She turns around to face me. 'Listen, I just need to say it. I'm really sorry. It was selfish not to think other people might want to be involved, and then I was so rude. I'm really, really sorry for what I said to you. I was drunk—'

'Which was my fault.'

'Well, yes, but still.'

'Charlie—'

I plough on, voice starting to catch in my throat and tears threatening to spill over. 'And I know I shouldn't have gone ahead and started arranging things without considering anyone. But I just . . . I haven't been around for Dad, and I should have been, and I can't believe this is my last chance to do something for him. I thought this time I'd take control and get things sorted, y'know? I wanted to make amends, but—'

I dissolve into sobs and Pauline rushes forward to fold me in her arms. Her cardigan tickles my face as she rubs my back until the worst of my outpouring has subsided. Then she holds me by the shoulders at arm's length and looks deep into my eyes.

'Now, then. You listen to me. Oh my God, it's OK. Of *course* it's OK. I overreacted, big time. And I should *never* have said anything about your mother. That was so out of line. I should never have brought it up. Can you forgive me?'

I nod. I don't even want to know what Pauline's heard from Dad.

'Shall we start over?' Pauline asks. 'A bit less gin this time?'

I nod gratefully and breathe a shaky sigh of relief. I try to get us walking again. The logical side of my brain (unfortunately smaller than it should be sometimes) knows we'll be absolutely fine, but it's still getting dark fast and I can hear something rustling in the hedgerow nearby. It's making me nervous even though it probably isn't a serial killer, and we're very unlikely to end up on a podcast. But Pauline keeps her feet resolutely planted and a firm grip on my shoulders. It's as if the woman's never seen the beginning of a horror movie before.

'But, Charlie, listen. I have to tell you that, from where I stand, your dad was just as much to blame for the way things were between you. Too bloody scared of his own feelings to be in touch more often. You're just your father's daughter. Please don't be so hard on yourself.'

At that moment a badger steps out of the undergrowth and into the lane, and I scream. Pauline swings around, sees what made me jump, and begins to laugh. It's contagious, and soon I'm crying with laughter instead of crying with crying. We hold on to each other for support, and it feels like ages before I can think straight.

'Honestly, you're a country girl, born and bred, you ought to be ashamed,' Pauline giggles as she wipes her eyes. 'Come on, townie, let's go back. God forbid we get intercepted by a hedgehog.'

We wander back the way we came. I try to hurry us along, back to the road and the sweet relief of street lights. I'm sure Pauline is actually slowing down. She suppresses a smile, so I know she's doing it deliberately. The stars are coming out now and as we leave the trees behind I crane my neck to look at them. In fact, I pay slightly too much attention and stumble over a tree root it's now too dark to see. Pauline reaches out a hand to steady me.

We make it into the village without further incident and stop off at Karnkarrow Konveniences. Mrs Rowe has locked up for the night, but she's sweeping the floor and unlocks the door to sell us a couple of bottles of cider.

'Nice to see you two together.' She nods approvingly as she hands me a surprising amount of change from a ten-pound note. I am not in London any more. 'I always thought you'd get along if you had the chance.'

We take our ciders to the harbour and sit on the wall, dangling our legs over the side. The tide is in and the water is dead flat, the lights from the fishing boats reflected in its surface. As my eyes adjust to the darkness, I can make out the boardwalk crossing the water, smaller boats moored on either side. I used to stamp down it to see how loud I could make my footsteps. There's nobody on it now. I can hear the sea slapping against the bricks on the other side of the wall.

'I was so useless when I tried to do the funeral on my own,' I say.

'I'm sure you weren't that bad.'

'No, I was. I couldn't think of anything – his favourite song, or what he'd want read or anything.'

'Do you think that matters?'

'Yes. It's my last chance to not be shit to him.'

'Well, I think the fact that you're trying matters more than whether you know what his favourite poem is. Jesus Christ, who the hell seriously has a favourite poem?'

I laugh and take another swig of cider. We sit in silence for a while, listening to the halyards clanking gently against masts all around the harbour and the sea splashing gently against the wall. It's quite nice to be able to sit in silence and not have it feel awkward.

'Your dad nearly pushed me in here once,' Pauline sighs.

'He did what?'

'He was fooling around, *pretending* to push me in, but he was showing off. I don't think he realised how close we were to the edge, and then I lost my footing and I honestly could have smashed my head open. The tide wasn't even in.'

She pauses and I picture the scene. It's so nice to think of Dad having fun, even if it does give me a pang of regret for not having been in contact more. And sure, it would probably be better if he didn't come close to committing manslaughter, but beggars can't be choosers. I wipe my eyes and smile.

CHAPTER EIGHT

The next morning I'm woken up by my phone ringing. I leap out of bed, heart thumping. But then I remember the worst has already happened – twice, in fact – so I've relaxed by the time I find it and pick it up.

'Hello?' I croak. I glance at the clock. It's 8.30. This is unacceptable.

'Good morning!' Pauline is too cheerful considering the hour. I wish I'd known this about her before we made amends. I might not have been in such a rush. No. Stop it. I'm a morning person. Mornings are wonderful. So much potential. Mornings, mornings, mornings.

'Morning.'

I'll work on it.

'I wanted to see if you fancied coming to Trelawney's again today? I thought maybe we could both go and get this thing straightened out once and for all.'

'Um, I don't . . .'

How can I tell her she'd be better off without me? I already told her I made a crap start. I don't know how I could have made it any clearer.

'Come on, Charlie, we should do this together. I think your dad would like it.'

I rush through breakfast and meet Pauline in Trelawney's waiting area. The receptionist glances up as I enter. I cross the room to sit next to Pauline.

I've barely sat down when Adam throws open a door.

'Jade, do you have— Charlie.'

He freezes as he spots me. It still looks weird to see him in a suit.

'Hi,' I say. It doesn't come out the first time, so I have to try again. 'Hi.'

'Hi.'

He holds my gaze for the briefest of moments, and I mean he *really* holds it, and my stomach does something funny, and it feels weird. Then he leaves us with a breezy, 'Sorry, carry on!'

'Wait, didn't you want—' the receptionist begins, but he's already disappeared.

My face suddenly feels hot. I pick up a copy of *OK!* magazine from the early noughties and flick through, admiring the bucket hats and baggy denim and studiously avoiding Pauline's stare, which is *not subtle*.

'Back again, I see,' Mr Trelawney says as Pauline and I take our seats opposite him. 'I understand there was a little miscommunication before. But don't worry, she's left you plenty of gaps.'

He says this to Pauline as he hands her the bundle of brochures I had my chance with last time but am clearly not worthy of. I want to walk out. I tap my foot, but Pauline places a conciliatory hand on my knee and I stay put.

She produces a little stack of CDs from her handbag and passes them to Trelawney. Then she opens one of the glossy brochures, and we both crane our heads over it. We can do this.

◆ ◆ ◆

'So, talk to me about Adam,' Pauline says innocently as she stirs a frothy coffee after our appointment is over. We made excellent progress and managed to only sob a couple of times each, so we earned cake. It would be unhealthy to keep using alcohol as a crutch, after all. Enter: sugar.

Pauline gives me a sly grin and I flush even though I try my absolute hardest not to. My face has been so full of blood today.

'There's nothing to talk about,' I shrug. 'He was my boyfriend, back before . . . Before I disappeared, I suppose. We didn't keep in touch.'

'Shocker.'

'Rude.'

'Were you in love?'

'I don't know, maybe? Is any teenager really "in love"? We felt really strongly about each other. But then I wanted to leave as soon as I could because of everything, and he didn't. And we emailed and things, but I don't know. Who wants to be going out with their inbox when they're eighteen? We were kids.'

I sink my fork into the tiramisu I chose from the excellent selection in the Cafe On The High Street. Less-than-innovative name, wonderful cake menu.

'So it just fizzled out?'

'I suppose. I mean, I basically told him he should just go and find someone who was nearby and not a huge downer. Maybe not in those words. But he did. I think it was the right thing. What, was he going to follow me to London so we could both be miserable?'

'But you're not miserable?'

'Just a figure of speech.' I blush.

'So, are you seeing anyone now?' Pauline asks through a mouthful of carrot cake.

'What is this, *Sex and the City*?'

Pauline indicates a seagull running away from a nearby table with half a croissant in its beak. The gull is being slowly chased by a very elderly man who doesn't stand a chance.

'Clearly not.'

We laugh and I take a fortifying sip of cappuccino.

'I am,' I concede. 'He's an architect. I met him at the gym.'

Pauline leaves a gap for more details and I don't fill it. I don't really have anything to add, but people always seem to expect more. Pauline tuts.

'And? How long have you been seeing him?'

'I dunno. Two years, I guess.'

'Oh, OK. So he's a keeper, then.'

'Yeah?'

'Are you asking me or telling me?'

'Oh, he dropped it!' I say, trying to direct her attention back to the seagull with the croissant, but Pauline will not be distracted.

'What do you love about him?'

'I don't know.'

'There must be something. How can you not know?'

'Are we supposed to *know*? I think you just choose, and then you've chosen, and then you know what you're doing. And he chose me, so I chose him, and here we are. We know where we stand.'

'But something must have *made* you choose him.'

The first time I ever saw James Hurley I was, as previously mentioned, walking on the treadmill. I had discovered over nights of testing that you couldn't stop altogether if you wanted to keep the TV screen on, but you could stroll at around two miles an hour and it would be fine.

I liked to go to the gym in the evenings, even though I didn't really like the gym itself. But knowing I was going to go meant I always had plans. At least at the gym I was on 'nodding hello' terms with a couple of people, so it felt a little bit like a social life.

One day, out of nowhere, James stood next to my treadmill and flapped his arms like a lunatic. He wasn't one of the people I was on nodding terms with, but I had seen him around. I took off my headphones.

'Hi?' It was more of a question than a greeting.

'Hi,' he grinned back. 'How are you?'

'OK . . .' I frowned and had a quick look around me to check if he might have been confusing me with somebody else. He was tall and blonde, with a strong jaw. Quite, like, traditionally handsome. I was . . . not. I don't think? I was younger then. I suppose I might have been good-looking and I just didn't realise it. Anyway, my look around the room didn't reveal anybody standing directly behind me that he might have wanted to talk to instead of me, so I carried on. 'How are you?'

'I'm good, thanks!'

'Nice.'

We paused for a minute, both feeling a bit shy. Or, at least, I was. Obviously. As far as I'd ever seen, a strange man only came up to a strange woman in the gym if he wanted to offer unsolicited (and usually incorrect) advice about her technique with weights, or if he wanted to ask her out. And I had no weights. James cleared his throat.

'So, anyway, I've seen you around a bit and I just wondered if you maybe wanted to go for a drink with me one day? We could meet here, go on somewhere?'

'Oh. Yeah, OK.'

I tried to answer slowly, aiming for nonchalance, but it was tough. I hadn't been asked out in, I mean, ever.

'Cool. Do you have a phone?'

'Yes . . .'

'Can I borrow it?'

94

'Oh, right. Here.'

I handed it over, wishing I'd upgraded when I'd had the chance and that the screen wasn't quite so cracked. He took it, dialled a number, and then held up his own ringing phone.

'Now we're connected. What's your name?'

'Charlie.'

'Nice to meet you, Charlie. I'm James.'

He held out a hand and I nearly tripped over trying to shake it. I was still strolling on the treadmill and trying to do that at the same time was a little like trying to pat your head while rubbing your tummy.

James released my hand and headed for the changing rooms. I maintained what I hoped was a cool facade until he'd disappeared, and then I looked around wide-eyed. Nobody was looking at me.

How had nobody witnessed what had just occurred? It was momentous. But they all just kept exercising like nothing earth-shattering had happened.

In five minutes I had gone from a lonely girl whose closest relationships were with a father she barely contacted and some strangers at the gym, to someone desirable. Someone with an actual plan for an actual evening actually out. I hadn't had plans since I'd graduated from university eighteen months previously. Even when I did use to have plans I always got the feeling I was only invited because I happened to be in the same house, overhearing the plans everybody else was making.

I upped the pace on the treadmill again and tried to stop myself from grinning like an idiot. I failed, of course. I had a squirming feeling in my stomach and was suddenly taken with the urge to actually run. I ramped the speed up higher than I ever had before (which, I cannot emphasise enough, was still not that high. I was very lazy).

Needless to say, after two minutes and seven seconds I had to use the emergency stop on the treadmill. There is excitement, and then there's overexertion. That day, I overexerted.

I ram a giant spoonful of tiramisu into my face so that Pauline has to stop asking me questions for a while. I wish I'd known she was such a romantic. I might have avoided getting coffee with her.

'You don't seem very excited about him, if you don't mind me saying.'

I swallow my mouthful of cream and coffee. It really is excellent. Once again, I've underestimated this village.

'You can't be excited about this stuff forever.'

'I think you can.' She shrugs. 'In fact, I think you should. If it's not exciting there's something wrong. We don't have time to waste on people who don't make our lives better.'

'It's just . . . different here.' I use my fork to embellish my point and the croissant-stealing seagull, who will apparently never be satisfied, creeps a little closer. 'London's *hard*. It gets you down. And I feel safe with him. Or, y'know, I feel like I can predict how our life is going to go, and I don't think people value that enough. *I* value that.'

Pauline's brow creases very slightly in a way I've seen a million times before. It makes me cringe.

'You don't have to feel sorry for me.' I paint a fake smile on my face to prove the point. 'I know what I'm doing. Anyway, we're getting married so it's kind of a moot point.'

'You're getting . . . Charlie, congratulations!'

'Yeah, thanks.' I never really know what to do with my face when people say that. It's just what you do, isn't it? It's not like I've won something. 'I mean, everybody else our age is doing it so I guess it makes sense. It's that time.'

'Is it quite recent? Just because you don't have a ring.'

'Oh, no, not really.' I fidget and hide my hand under the table, trying to make the movement look natural. 'I think the ring's around somewhere. You know what the house is like. It's a black hole. It'll turn up.'

It'll turn up in exactly the place I hid it, just as soon as I can bring myself to fully inhabit that part of my life again. I aim a kick at the seagull who's nearly within swooping distance, and he backs away. When I turn back to Pauline she's still looking at me with concern, so I take another heaping mouthful of tiramisu. As avoidance tactics go, this one's delightful.

We sit in silence for a little while, occasionally pulling our chairs in to let people squeeze behind us. Even though it's September the sun is warm on my back, and eventually I relax the muscles I didn't even know I'd tensed.

'I'm just saying, I reckon Adam's still holding a bit of a candle for you,' Pauline says out of nowhere.

'Pauline!'

'Sorry.'

We're silent again for a minute.

'We shouldn't be thinking about any of this, anyway,' I tell her, a chill of remorse working its way down my spine. I keep forgetting and then remembering again, and it feels like somebody's thrown a bucket of cold water over me. 'I mean, what with Dad, and—'

'Listen.' Pauline grabs my wrist just before I can shovel another spoonful of dessert into my mouth. She fixes me with a glare so fierce I quail. 'I've just lost my partner. I've had a very bad week. I'm very sad. So if I want to sit in the sunshine and gossip about boys with my could-have-been stepdaughter for a few minutes, then I will, OK?'

I nod. She releases my arm. We sit in silence for a second.

'Another round?' she asks sweetly.

CHAPTER NINE

Curiously, when I wake up on the morning of *the* day, my duvet seems to have turned into lead overnight. I simply cannot get up. I wake early. Or rather, I didn't really sleep, so I just happen to be awake anyway as it starts to get light. Every time I close my eyes I see a picture of how today might go. I still think about Mum's funeral sometimes.

Dad and I drove through the streets in a black limo. In front of us, the hearse wound its way through the narrow lanes, the windows piled high with flowers. Outside, people came to a standstill to watch us pass slowly by, and I mainly tried to hide my face.

I clung tightly onto Dad's hand as people milled around talking about me as though I wasn't even there. My early-teen bravado was suddenly nowhere to be found. They said it was a shame, so tragic to lose a parent so young. They mused about how my life had changed, seemingly oblivious to the fact that I was right there, listening to everything they said.

When it was time for Dad to help carry the coffin into the crematorium, Lowenna took me by the shoulders and steered me gently to the front row. She instructed me to save a seat for my dad, which I did very intently, happy to have been given a job, not that anybody other than Dad was about to sit next to me today of all days. I stared around the room at the green carpets, green seats, and at the green curtains at the back of the stage.

People from the village filed in behind us. It felt weird to see all these people I knew from Carncarrow in one room in the middle of a weekday. There was Mae's mum in a black dress that looked like it might burst under the strain from her pregnant belly. There was Mr Clark who ran the newsagent's and used to wink at me whenever he caught me sneaking penny sweets while whichever parent I was with bought the paper. Miss Lake, my teacher, took one look at me and burst into tears. I caught a few eyes among our friends and neighbours gathered in this room, and they all either gave me watery smiles or they shook their heads and pressed tissues to their faces. I resolved not to make any more eye contact if it was going to upset people.

A man I'd never seen before stood up and told us all about Mum's life. He talked about her as if he knew her, but he couldn't have done. Occasionally he would say something I didn't get, and a laugh would rumble around the entire audience, breaking the tension. How dare he? I tried to catch Dad's eye, so we could shake our heads in exasperation at this man who was pretending to have known Mum. But Dad simply placed a finger to his lips and carried on listening, his eyes red.

After the man had spoken they played a couple of songs from a tape Mum used to like. I stole a look around the room as the music played. People were staring ahead at Mum's coffin – some dabbed their eyes, others let their tears flow freely. Every once in a while somebody would steal a glance at me and Dad, and it made me feel self-conscious in my itchy new dress.

I didn't cry, but it wasn't because I wasn't sad. Whenever I'd bumped into anybody on the street I found they'd stroke my arm or tell me how strong I was and how things were going to get better. I knew people were looking at me, and I didn't like it. Once, I'd come barging into Lowenna's kitchen, as was my custom after a hard day at school. I found her talking in hushed tones with three ladies I vaguely recognised from seeing them hobble to and from the shops, past the school gate. They all fell quiet as soon as I entered. One of them blushed. I didn't cry at the funeral because I didn't want to give anybody anything else to talk about.

After the song, Dad stood up in front of everybody and gave a speech. He talked about how Mum had been a great mum, and how we were going to miss her, and it was all true. My eyes started to water then, but I clutched the bench as hard as I could until my knuckles went white and I stared at the floor until the feeling passed. When Dad sat back down again he was shaking, and I rested my head on his shoulder.

The coffin moved away, the curtains closed, and we all went out into the gardens so that people could mill around some more and talk behind my back about how a mother could do that to her family. I watched a bee buzzing around my sunflowers and pretended I couldn't hear.

I stare at my bedroom wall as scenes from Mum's funeral play over and over again in my head. The pillow feels damp, and I think I've probably been crying, but I'm not at the moment. Just staring. The clock ticks away while the sun comes up, and I can hear the sounds of life in the village outside. Occasional footsteps tap past on the way to buy the paper. The bin men come as well, so that's something I forgot to fucking do. The letterbox clatters downstairs, and then somebody knocks on the door.

I groan and pull my duvet over my head, and eventually whoever's at the door goes away. I know I should get up, but I'm hoping that if I don't, the rest of the day simply won't happen. It's like when you play hide-and-seek with little kids and they just stand in the middle of the room, cover their eyes, and think you can't see them. If I don't go along with it, maybe today just won't be a thing.

I must have drifted off to sleep while I was hiding from the world because the next thing I know there's a pressure on the end of the bed, which tilts me to one side. The covers are ripped away from me. I shiver, even though it's really not cold.

'Lowenna!'

I pull my knees up to my chest and Lowenna smiles at me. It's genuine, not one of the weak, sad ones I'm expecting to see a lot of today. She's wearing a black cardigan over a black dress, and has a little black pillbox hat perched jauntily on her head. It looks as jaunty as a hat clearly designed to be worn at funerals can, anyway.

'Do you like it?' she asks, touching it proudly. 'When you get to my age you end up at funerals every week so you might as well buy a proper outfit.'

'What are you doing here?'

'I let myself in, didn't I? You wouldn't answer the door and I was worried you might be up to your old tricks. I tell you what, those stairs are not easy.'

Like the gracious person I am, I decide not to point out that she shouldn't be sneaking into other people's houses if she doesn't want to be inconvenienced by their staircases.

'Oof,' she groans, pushing herself up against the soft mattress, then she falls back again.

'Are you OK?'

'Of course I am.' She dismisses my concern with a nonchalant hand. 'This is what ageing does to you. I don't recommend it.'

She pushes herself up again, and this time she stays on her feet.

'You get up. I'll go and pop some breakfast on. You should eat something. Don't want you getting all teasy before you've even got to the wake. Oh, and Charlie' – she pauses at the door – 'you can do this, OK?'

101

She shuffles out of the room. I hear creaking as she descends the stairs, and to be fair to her it does take a really long time and sound like it's a lot of effort.

It feels like almost the same amount of effort to finally drag myself out of bed. My legs really don't want to cooperate and everything aches. I stare into the bathroom mirror for a long time before I start brushing my teeth. All I can think about is the fact that the next time I stand in the bathroom and stare into this mirror it'll all be over.

I dig out what little make-up I have and try to work some magic. I'm not sure how much to put on. I'm certain that if I arrive bare-faced I'll appear to the world as if I'm either ill or stricken with grief, which is fine and not wrong. But I also haven't seen some of the people who'll be there for years, and I don't want them to think I've prematurely aged, even if I sometimes worry that I might have done.

I stand rooted to the spot with a mascara in my hand for ages. To mascara or not to mascara? That is the question. Because on the one hand, I've never seen a so-called waterproof mascara that didn't eventually end up sliding down my face when things got really bad. But on the other, I don't want to look like a bread roll when all eyes are on me. I weigh the little plastic tube in my hands as I consider my options, and eventually decide not to. Bread roll trumps panda, which is a thought I never expected to have.

Back in my room, I pull on the funeral outfit I managed to scrounge up after begging Mrs Maynard from the charity shop to let me root around in the back room unsupervised for half an hour. I found a black pencil skirt and a navy blouse, which is slightly too big for me but hopefully looks more 'artfully oversized' than 'why is she wearing a sack?'. I pair these with my work shoes, which I usually kick off under my desk as soon as I possibly can. I'm not looking forward to a full day of standing up in them, but all of the shoes at the charity shop smelled very suspicious. After all my efforts I look underdressed compared to Lowenna, but it'll do.

'Oh, you look lovely, love,' Lowenna tells me as I enter the kitchen. She's laid out a couple of boxes of cereal and a loaf of bread, as well as coffee, tea, and orange juice. Which is fine, except I have this heavy feeling in the pit of my stomach and I think it would only get in the way of anything I tried to eat.

I settle for coffee, spooning twice the amount you're supposed to have into a mug, and adding three sugars.

'How are you feeling?' Lowenna asks, cradling her own cup of tea and frowning at my coffee-making technique.

'I've been better.'

'Did you sleep well?'

'Not at all.'

Now that I'm awake I feel almost shell-shocked at how bad my night was. I can vividly remember looking at the time at least every half-hour, and if ever I started to feel drowsy a noisy seagull somewhere on the roof would get involved and make sure I couldn't actually drop off.

'Morning!'

Pauline materialises in the frame of the kitchen window wearing a black suit. She looks amazing. She joins us at the table, pouring herself a glass of orange juice. The food remains untouched by anybody.

'Full of tissues,' Pauline says, giving her handbag a pat. 'I've got us all covered. The whole crematorium, probably. How are you feeling?' she asks me.

'I don't even know,' I tell her honestly. 'I can't say "surprised" because I obviously knew this was coming, but still, surprised, maybe?'

She gives my hand a squeeze. Lowenna takes my other one in hers; her skin is papery to the touch. It feels like I'd snap a bone if I held on too hard. We sit quietly and wait for the car to arrive.

◆ ◆ ◆

The ride to the crematorium takes forever. As I stare at the coffin in the hearse in front I can't think of anything but the only time I saw Dad in the last decade – as I held his hand while the light went out of his eyes. I count up all of the milestones I reached in that time, the birthdays, house moves, getting engaged, and I imagine how excited he would have been if I'd talked to him properly about any of them.

Pauline keeps up her hold on my hand. We both get a bit clammy after a while but she never lets go. I look sideways at her and see that she's gone pale and the tears have already started. I give her hand an extra squeeze as we move slowly through the narrow streets of the village.

At one point they're a little *too* narrow. One man up a ladder, painting the front of a gift shop on a very tight bend, nearly spells disaster. The hearse in front stops just in time as the driver realises he won't get through, so our car is forced to stop quickly too, jerking Pauline and me forward. The procession sits for a little while, waiting for the painter to realise that we're there. But he's too absorbed in his work to notice us. He just sings along to the radio he's balanced in the gutter. The hearse driver beeps his horn (who knew they even had horns? Every day's a school day) and the painter jumps, stippling the shop window with cornflower blue. He flips the bird in our direction without even looking up and I must admit I stifle a giggle. Dad would dine out on this for years if he were able.

When the man finally looks up he starts like he's received an electric shock and practically jumps down from his ladder. He folds it, leans it against the side of the shop, and rushes to move his paint cans out of the middle of the tarmac. Then he removes his cap and holds it to his chest as we pass, his eyes closed ostensibly in respect, but I think it's really humiliation. I steal a glance at Pauline, she catches my eye, and we both burst into laughter.

'Bloody old codger,' the driver mutters, which just makes us giggle more.

My amusement lasts until I start seeing the crematorium appear on road signs. The swooping feeling in my stomach becomes harder to ignore, and my fingers start to tingle for some reason. My heart begins to drum somewhere in my throat. The hand that isn't holding Pauline's rises to my 'Joy' necklace, and I cling to it.

We round the last corner into the driveway. The large, manicured lawn in front of the building is studded with immature trees. Each one is marked with a plaque to commemorate someone else who's 'passed on', 'departed this life', 'been called home' – the list of ridiculous metaphors goes on. I never really understood why we can't all just agree that they've died. There are so many more trees since the last time I was here.

As we roll down the driveway the sound of crunching gravel starts to attract attention and people turn to watch our approach. A sea of black turns almost in unison to reveal basically the entire village. Some give wan smiles, some clutch tissues, and everybody looks at us. Everybody always looks.

We get out of the car and as the door closes behind us a few of the . . . guests? Would we call them 'guests'? I suppose we'll call them 'guests'. A few of the guests start to move towards us. They hold out their arms, probably in greeting, but fuck me they look a lot like zombies.

In that moment I'm transported back to Mum's funeral and I want to run away. I even look over my shoulder to make sure my path is clear. My feet practically start moving of their own accord, like in cartoons where someone moves and moves and moves, and they kick up loads of dust, but they can't get any purchase so they don't immediately manage to go anywhere. That's what I'm like. And I think Pauline can tell by my fidgeting because she grabs hold of my arm and hisses, 'Don't you dare.'

I don't think anybody's quite had the measure of me like that before (oh, whose fault is that, Charlie? Mine, because I'm too scared to let anybody get to know me, *I know*), and I'm so surprised I stay where I am. I rearrange my face and I greet the people coming towards us like an adult.

There's Mrs Trewin, who, as far as I know, is no relation, but I bet if you did a DNA test on us we'd turn out to be cousins. Which on the one hand would solve my newfound family-less-ness, but on the other hand, at what cost? She clutches a tissue as she reaches out and pats my arm. There's Mr Woods, who runs the Seafarers' Inn in the next town, where I used to do the occasional shift if he needed an extra pair of hands. Now he shakes mine, his face solemn. And there's Mae. She comes forward, slips an arm around my waist, and pulls me along to where everybody else is standing.

The group of people dressed in black opens up a little to let Pauline and me right into its heart. Around us I hear dozens of murmured platitudes:

'Good turnout.'

'What a dear man.'

'So good to see you – a shame it's under these circumstances.'

But I have trouble connecting the platitude to the person who might have said it, and I don't really feel like I want to make eye contact. I just nod in the general direction of everyone and hope that will suffice.

Mr Trelawney gently squeezes his way through the crowd until he's next to me and Pauline.

'Would you like to start making your way inside?' he asks in a low voice.

No. No, I absolutely do not want to make my way inside because if I make my way inside then eventually I have to make my way outside again, and it will all be over. Pauline slips her hand into mine.

'Yes. Thank you,' I tell him, because I am a liar.

He ushers us through the group of black-clad villagers, and they turn in our wake, following our lead. He indicates that I should walk through the double doors in front of me, but one glance at that green carpet and I can't do it. I want to run again.

If I went back to London now – as in, *right now* – I wouldn't have to tell anybody what had happened to me. I could claim it was a breakdown, rehab, anything to avoid the truth. I could let the people here carry on with Dad's funeral because they were the ones who really knew him anyway. They'd talk about what a horrible person I was for a little while, but they've probably been doing that for years. And anyway, they'd be really far away while they did it, so I wouldn't hear them, and they'd stop eventually. Because they'd forget me. Which is fine. I'm still picturing my escape when Lowenna pokes me (quite viciously, actually) in the back.

'Go on, young 'un. You can do it.'

I step over the threshold. Inoffensive cello music plays at a low volume, and the room is soon filled with the hum of chatter as people file in behind me. The stage is still the same, but the velvet curtains have changed from green to the shade of navy blue that I always fancied painting our bedroom one day, so that's ruined now. High frosted-glass windows line the walls.

I sit down at the front. Mr Trelawney gives me a little smile before giving a small nod to someone, somewhere, who I can't actually see, and the music crescendoes until people fall quiet. Everybody turns, tissues are pulled expectantly from handbags, and I am suddenly freezing. I shiver and a wrinkled hand appears over my shoulder with a shawl and a tissue. I take both gratefully and mouth my thanks to Lowenna.

The music changes to a Billy Joel song Pauline chose. Reg, Jason from the chip shop, and some of Dad's mates from the pub walk slowly down the aisle with the coffin balanced on their shoulders. It looks quite plush, so at least I did one thing right.

They put the coffin down at the front of the room and then they join the rest of us. The sound of the music slowly dips to nothing, and a vicar stands in front of us, smiling serenely. I don't recognise him, but I've never been an avid follower of the local church scene anyway. Surprising, I know.

The vicar takes a breath.

'Ladies and gentlemen, today is the day we say goodbye to—'

Out of nowhere the double doors crash open, the sound echoing around the high ceilings. Everybody wheels around to look at the intruder. There are even a few gasps.

'Wait!' the intruder cries, and I know the voice immediately. But it can't be. It really, really can't be. It can't be because I don't want it to be, but it also can't be because it *literally cannot be*.

James is standing in the doorway, scanning the crowd.

CHAPTER TEN

It feels like it takes days for the vicar to get control of the situation again. Even after the gasping and the open comments about rudeness have subsided, there's an undercurrent of muttering running through the room behind me. I grip my knees and stare at my lap, waiting for my hands to stop trembling. I. Am. Furious. I don't even know where to begin. My face is burning. I feel like any tiny amount of approval I'd earned back from the village over the past week and a half has been permanently destroyed now.

'Well, shove up, then,' James says as he appears in front of me, rolling a suitcase that would be unacceptably large even in an *actual* travel setting. It makes him look like a lunatic here. That's the problem with the front row – nowhere to hide.

Pauline shifts up and so do I, and James wriggles himself into the gap between us. He plants a kiss on my cheek and I ignore it. He tries to take my hand, but I snatch it away. I glance behind me at the rows of whispering people. Adam stands at the back, seemingly the only one not joining in with the chatter. I suppose it's because he's on duty, but still, it's nice of him.

'You OK?' he mouths over the bowed heads between us. He looks confused, but I suppose it's not too difficult to work out what the colour of my face means. I shake my head and shrug. My eyes fill with angry tears and I blink them away. Not until after my speech. Keep it together. Keep it together, keep it together, keep it together.

'Thank you for your patience, ladies and gentlemen.' The vicar raises his voice and holds up a hand, and the murmuring dies down, even if it doesn't totally stop. 'Now, where were we?'

Pauline is speaking first. We agreed we'd both say something, and she's braver than me. Plus, she has home advantage, and I feel like I lost that years ago. She shuffles a couple of pages of notes against the lectern as if she were a newsreader. I dig my nails into my palms because I don't have any notes. That's my first mistake today. Well, actually, my first mistake was agreeing to marry a man who apparently wouldn't know a boundary if it slapped him in the face. But not having notes comes a close second. But I can do this. I can do it, I can do it, I can do it. James lays a supportive hand on my knee. I deliberately fidget, crossing my legs to shrug him off. What, and I cannot stress this enough, the *fuck* is he doing here? I didn't even tell him where I live. Live*d*. Am staying. Whatever.

At the front of the room, Pauline clears her throat.

'Hello,' she says. She's too close to the microphone and it comes out way too loud. A couple of people jump. 'Sorry. You'd think I'd know how to use a mic by now with all the quiz nights, but there we go.'

The congregation laughs, and I don't get it. I thought Pauline and I had got to know each other, but I guess we haven't had that much time. I immediately feel painfully aware of my outsider-hood. It's outsider-hood I chose, yes. But it's still one that's freaking me out a bit now. What if everybody actually *does* hate me?

'I first met Martin Trewin when I moved down to Cornwall after a bit of a mid-life crisis. I'd got divorced, and I decided to use the money from that to move to the seaside and try out the lifestyle.'

'Bloody emmets!' someone yells from behind us. The crowd titters.

James sighs his disapproval next to me.

'Yes, thanks, Loic.' Pauline smiles and continues. 'I moved down, and Martin had a very similar opinion to Loic, as it happens. I took over the pub. I tried to make it nice. You know, put some cushions in and stuff. Christ on a bike, he did not like that. Sorry.'

She glances at the vicar leading the service. He looks briefly skyward and then motions for her to continue. Everybody laughs again. I am really trying to ignore the steady increase in my heart rate as my time to get up there creeps closer.

'So, one day, I've had enough, and I says to him, "Listen, Martin Trewin, you've been a pain in my arse since the day I arrived, and all I'm trying to do is keep your pub alive. What's your problem?" Well, ladies and gentlemen, he didn't even know!'

Everybody laughs again. James tuts. I fidget in my seat and move a couple of centimetres away from him. He shifts back up until our legs are pressed together. I have no space left to wriggle away again.

'I don't think he expected me to actually *ask* him what he wanted. He ended up taking me to dinner to apologise for being an arsehole. Sorry,' she says to the vicar again. He nods, tersely.

'We had such a laugh we kept on doing it, and eventually one thing led to another.'

Somebody wolf-whistles behind me. Pauline smiles. Then, her face falls. The change in her mood is echoed by the rest of the room.

'I had a wonderful time with Martin. He showed me that I didn't need to be anybody but myself. He was proof that it's never too late to find something, some*one*, very special. He'd been through so much in his life, and he had his own struggles to over-come. Anybody who's seen the state of his house probably knows that he didn't *completely* manage it.'

There's laughter again. She's going down a storm. I can't live up to this. And, like, that's totally not what it's about. But it kind of *is* what it's about. I would like people not to hate me.

'But he was a good man, and a kind man. He had an amazing sense of humour and I, for one, will miss him every day.'

Her voice cracks here, and she dabs her eyes.

'He loved his daughter—'

I'm vaguely aware that there's another couple of lines in Pauline's speech. I know, because I can see her mouth moving. But I don't hear any more because it's all drowned out by a persistent, high-pitched drone in my ears. I suddenly worry that I'm going to sweat through my blouse. At least it's dark so it won't show up. I watch her step down from the little platform and walk back over to me. She stops to let me past before she sits down. I don't realise that's what she's doing straight away. I just sit and stare at her dumbly.

'Charlie!' Lowenna hisses in a stage whisper. She jabs my shoulder and I jump. The ringing stops immediately. I can hear low-level chatter in the rows behind. The vicar stands by the lectern looking expectantly over at me.

I get to my feet, which is tricky because my legs don't seem to be under my control any more. James squeezes the fingers that hang limply at my side and I snatch my hand away.

I steal a glance towards the back of the room as I walk into position. Adam is still back there, looking at me intently, which is probably just because I'm the person he's *supposed* to be staring intently at right now. Still, he gives me a little thumbs-up, which is nice of him. I don't know what to do back so I just try not to trip up.

'Hello,' I begin when I finally make it to the stage.

The room is mainly full of faces I remember, peppered with a few I haven't seen before. And, of course, one that makes me so angry I can barely concentrate on the task in hand. Which is, like, the only thing that matters. Stop thinking about him. Stop it, stop it, stop it. I focus on the rest of the people.

Basically the entire village is staring at me. My heart hadn't even stopped pounding from humiliation at James's *insane* interruption, and now it's thumping so hard it actually hurts. And the ringing in my ears starts to get louder again, and I'm no longer worried that I might sweat through my blouse because I know without a shadow of a doubt that I already have. I touch my 'Joy' necklace with a trembling finger.

I can't—

I don't—

I feel like such a twat for not thinking of anything to say before this. But what was I supposed to come up with? Should I have planned to talk about how I'm starting to realise that I wasn't as ready to say goodbye as I thought I was when I was an idiotic teenager? Or maybe I could talk about how I pretended everybody in this room had never existed so I that I could run away from my past, and how I never even managed to be happy once I'd done it.

I'm not sure how long I stand there. I open my mouth once or twice and each time I do the congregation leans in very slightly, expecting something. Someone towards the back coughs. A baby starts fussing, and someone gets up and starts walking up and down, bouncing it. At one point Adam makes a move as if to come down the aisle. I can't work out why. Is he coming for me? He takes a couple of steps without breaking eye contact.

'You can do it!' James calls.

It echoes around the room, and Adam shakes his head and returns to his place at the back of the hall. All I want to do is curl up on this platform, in this crematorium, and die of humiliation. They could chuck me and Dad in together as a two for one.

The ringing in my ears crescendoes until I can't hear anything any more. There's a battle raging inside my brain. On the one side there's blind fury at James for turning up here and taking every opportunity to throw me off. On the other, there's blind fury at myself for failing this. For failing Dad now. For failing Dad then. The vicar approaches me and is clearly saying something. I shake my head a couple of times, hoping to clear it, but it makes no difference.

'I'm sorry,' I eventually stutter into the microphone. I'm too close and the feedback makes everybody wince. I bang my knee as I trip down from the little stage and dive gratefully back to my seat.

I cover my face with my hands as the vicar starts to talk again. The ringing is beginning to subside, and I can hear my own ragged breathing. Lowenna hands me a tissue I didn't realise I needed. I touch my forehead to my knees, giving absolutely no thought to what the rest of the crowd might think of my total lack of elegance. Pauline rubs my back.

'It's OK,' James tells me, caressing my shoulder. I shrug him off. It's all I can do not to elbow him in the ribs.

I'm vaguely aware that the vicar does a wonderful job of covering for my abject humiliation. Certainly everybody around me laughs and reaches for tissues in equal measure, which must be a good thing.

It's not the public humiliation I mind so much, although I hate it and fantasise about the floor swallowing me. It's more the *presumptuousness* of James's sudden arrival. I never said I wanted him to come here. If I remember rightly (and I do), I actually specifically said that he shouldn't. I never even told him where exactly I *was*, and he still tracked me down. I suppose he thought he was being supportive, but sometimes it's actually *not* the thought that counts. He squeezes my knee too hard and I can hear him breathing in my ear, and occasionally he fidgets and nudges me, and then he sings the hymns too loud, and who has ever *confidently* sung a hymn? Maybe it's a public-school thing. Eventually the whole thing just feels like it's all about James.

As we file out of the service I approach the coffin. In my head this is the moment I tell Dad . . . Well, I'm not really sure. But it's supposed to be just the two of us (ignoring the entire population of Carncarrow behind me), rather than our other snatched attempts at intimacy as doctors and nurses bustled in and out of his hospital cubicle.

Except that James is basically joined to me at the hip.

'Could you give me some space?' I ask through gritted teeth.

'Of course, I'm so sorry.'

He kisses me on the forehead and then moves a single step to the left. One. Fucking. Step. If I didn't know any better, I'd think he was being deliberately infuriating.

I brush the polished wood of the coffin with my fingertips, unable to summon any words, which will probably surprise nobody. There's not even a tear. My brain is too scrambled, my anger too great. In the end I move along, lured by the fresh air and the opportunity to feel the sun on my face.

It isn't until I reach the door that I realise I don't have my shadow with me any more. He's still standing by the stage, one hand on Dad's coffin, looking sombre. I stop in the doorway and nearly cause a collision with some old ladies I recognise from the church choir when we used to go to the carol concert.

'What the hell was that?' I hiss as he eventually catches up with me.

'I was just saying goodbye,' he shrugs as we head into the sunlight.

'You never even said hello.'

'And whose fault was that? He would have been my father-in-law, you know.'

And, I mean, is he . . . right? I can't even tell any more. I could be the one in the wrong. But as I watch a bumble bee buzz around the sunflowers I had added to my bouquet for Dad (don't worry, I made sure there were tasteful lilies in there as well), I don't *think* I am. The bee keeps blurring and then coming into focus as I blink the mist from my eyes and try to make sense of exactly what's happened in the last half-hour. I can't think straight.

'Look, don't feel too bad about your speech.' James tries to take my hand and I snatch it back. I try to storm away but there's nowhere to go, and I don't want to make another scene, so I end up standing a couple of paces away, shoulders hunched, arms crossed, the works. Proper 'child in a mood' stuff. But he works his way back to my side, still pulling that ridiculous case. Like, leave it by the door or something, for crying out loud.

'Where's your ring?' he asks. His voice is calm, and the logical part of my brain knows that he isn't accusing me of anything. Unfortunately, though, that part of my brain is not the one in control right now.

'I don't know,' I hiss, trying to prevent my neighbours from hearing me.

'Nice to meet you!' a couple of people call as they head off and up the driveway. James nods at them and they hurry away, giggling.

'How can you not know?'

'I just . . . It's somewhere.'

'See you at the wake, Charlie!' Loic Bennetto calls as he walks back to the cars. I raise a hand and force a smile across my face.

'Have you lost it? Do you know how much it cost?' James looks horrified.

'No, I haven't lost it.'

'Then surely you know where it is?'

He looks at me, bewildered. It really, really annoys me. Like, *really* annoys me. I can't think for the anger for a second.

116

'How can you turn up at my dad's funeral and start *questioning* me?'

I'm no longer troubling myself to keep my voice down. I feel cornered, my heart has dropped somewhere into the ground near the floral tributes, and I don't know what to do except to keep digging. This is not the time to tell him that I took it off because it was beginning to feel like a tiny shackle locking me into a future I've never been sure about. But getting the third degree in polite company is embarrassing so I don't know how to respond. So I respond by being a bitch.

'Charlie, I—'

'Come on.' Lowenna intervenes, appearing at my side and grabbing my wrist. She seems unsteady on her feet, leaning her entire (but still not much) weight on me for a moment, and I wonder if I should find her a chair.

'Lowenna? Are you alright?'

'Of course.' She relaxes her grip and stands up straight, and I wonder if maybe I'm just going mad. I probably am. I mean, I definitely am, let's be honest. 'Don't worry about me. You have to at least pretend to pay attention to everyone else. Pauline's headed off to the pub already and people want to commiserate with someone, so slap on a fake smile and stand here with me.'

She flashes her teeth at me, and I copy her, forcing my mouth up at the edges. But not up so far that it would seem disrespectful. Probably just crazed. Then she turns me around so that I face the doors again. There are still some stragglers emerging. Somewhere in the midst of her intervention James slipped away. I can see him reading the plaques against some of the immature trees, occasionally kicking a stone. The rest of the people who came are mostly dotted around the gravel pathway, clutching used tissues and orders of service, allowing the sunshine to lift their spirits.

'That was an entrance and a half,' Lowenna says in a low voice through a fixed smile. She waves at a couple of people as they head back to their cars.

'I know. I don't even . . . I didn't . . .' My voice doesn't sound like my own.

'Come on. Summon him, we've got a wake to get to.'

I really have to fight the urge to roll my eyes.

◆ ◆ ◆

Pauline has outdone herself when we arrive at the Bolster & Saint. It's the first time I've been in since I've been back and I can see why Dad might have been annoyed. I mean, it's *nice*. She hasn't completely got rid of the olde worlde charm of the place (read: old-man-pub vibes) but she's brightened it up a lot. Like, someone from out of town might actually feel comfortable spending an evening here now, which is saying something. It's amazing what washing the windows and changing the cushions can do to a place. The walls have been painted white so the whole place feels airy. She's added some magnificent plants, and I make a mental note to ask her for some tips at a more appropriate time.

All of the tables have been pushed against the wall, and one of the greatest buffets I think I've ever seen has been laid across them. There is so much stuff in pastry I can't even figure out where I'm going to start.

'I'm sorry, is there a vegan option?' James asks Pauline as she hands him a plate.

'A what, love?'

'A— Ow!'

Pauline looks startled as I punch James in the shoulder. I pull him away from the table, throwing Pauline an exaggerated smile. She frowns back.

'You could be non-vegan for one day, couldn't you?'

'Not really, no.'

'I very much doubt there is a vegan option.'

'Well, that's not very good, is it?'

'Why? We know every single person who might come to this and nobody's a vegan. Why would Pauline waste a load of money on tofu if nobody's going to eat it?'

'You can't know everybody.'

'I literally do.'

I prove it by pointing at everyone in the room in turn and reeling off their name and dietary requirements.

'Actually, dairy gives me the shits now,' Reg pipes up as I proclaim him free of any allergies.

'Thanks, Reg.' I glance at his plate. 'You might want to lay off the sour cream in that case, though.'

'Nah, it's worth it,' he tells us through a mouthful of nachos. 'It's what your dad would have wanted.'

'See?' I say, turning back to James with triumph in my eyes. I've even surprised myself by how many details I remember.

'Do you not see how incestuous that is?' he shoots back, picking up a celery stick and giving it a suspicious sniff.

'Now you know why I never told you about my childhood.'

Rather than responding, he picks up a whole bowl of crudités and stalks away to take a position on one of the window seats. I stare around me, and it feels like I'm coming back to the room after being hypnotised. It's filled up a lot. I suppose there are those people who think it's rude to turn up before the family. I can just picture them sitting in their cars outside the pub, cursing the amount of time it took me to arrive.

'Alright, Charlie?' Pauline comes over, wiping her hands on a tea towel. She has a floral apron tied over her black suit, and her hair has started to come loose from the bun she had it in earlier. She looks so at ease here. And still maddeningly chic.

'Oh, Reg, I wouldn't eat that if I were you!' she calls, as he shovels a nacho loaded with sour cream and cheese into his mouth.

'Thank you, Pauline, but it's worth the risk.' He waves her away, nacho still in hand, dropping sour cream on the floor as he does so.

'That man is going to destroy my toilet later,' she sighs.

She scans the room, taking in the groups of people dotted around clutching paper plates piled high with food. Then she catches sight of James slumped in the corner with his bowl of vegetables.

'Are you ready to talk about Himself yet?' she asks with a nod towards you-know-who. He's still picking at his celery sticks, but I guess the food smells are getting to him now because he's started to eye up nearby sausage rolls with envy. I know it's not very loyal, but I feel a desperate need to ~~bitch~~ express my emotions, so I nod, relieved.

Pauline ducks behind the bar and grabs a half-full bottle of wine. I glance over at James, who's being absorbed against his will into a group of pub regulars who've all loosened their black ties. They're good people, so I know they'll look after him. I grab a bowl of crisps from the table and head to the door.

We take our stolen goods and cross the road, perching on the steps of the harbour. The granite is cold. Once upon a time Mum would have suggested I'd get piles for sitting here. Pauline passes me the wine bottle and I take a swig.

Behind us, I can hear chit-chat and the occasional laugh from inside the pub. I haven't paid much attention before but I look back now. Pauline's smashed it with the exterior too. The mucky, seagull-shitty walls have had a fresh coat of blue paint and each of the windowsills holds a box full of bright-yellow flowers. More grow in pots on the pavement, dotted the entire length of the building. And even more have been placed on top of the outdoor tables there's probably not really enough space for. When we get to sorting out Dad's garden, Pauline is *definitely* taking charge.

The sun is just starting to go down, and the pink of the sky is reflected in the water of the harbour. The sea beyond the entrance looks choppy, but the boats moored here barely move. A couple of children investigate a tower of lobster pots and buoys on the opposite wall.

'Go on, then.' Pauline nudges me, bringing my attention back to the wine bottle in my hand. I pass it to her.

'I just . . . I mean, what the hell is he *doing* here? I didn't want him to come. I actually directly told him not to.'

'It's kind of sweet, though. He seems nice. Picky eater, maybe.'

'He just wants to be able to brag about how much of a hero he is when we get back upcountry. How he came after me in my time of need.'

I know I'm being a bit unfair, but frankly my feet are killing me, it has been A Day, and I couldn't care less.

'Do you think you're being a *bit* unfair?'

'No.'

Pauline hands me back the bottle and I take another swig.

'Do you want me to tell him he has to leave before we do the lock-in?'

I feel another rush of affection for Pauline that might be down to the Pinot Grigio, but which is lovely nonetheless.

'It's OK,' I tell her. 'I'm an adult, I'll . . . deal with it.'

I gesture with the wine bottle, which I guess looks a little bit like I plan to deal with it violently. Not my intention.

'Charlie, I really don't think—'

Before Pauline can get any further we're interrupted by the clip-clopping of high heels on granite. A risky move, because that shit gets *slippery*. So something must be urgent. The sound recedes, before getting louder again. We can hear someone breathing as well, hard and ragged, and then—

'There you are!' Mae appears at the top of the steps.

She stops, leaning against the railings to catch her breath, kneading her side.

'It's Lowenna,' she pants, and my heart jumps into my throat. 'She's had a funny turn.'

CHAPTER ELEVEN

I knock over the wine bottle as Pauline and I jump up from the steps. It smashes onto the granite, sending a little tsunami of crisp white flowing down to the water, but I don't stop to do anything about the mess.

My heart climbs from my throat to my mouth as we enter the pub and faces turn to look at us, pale and panicked. Loic is on the phone behind the bar, and everybody else stands on the fringes of the room, paper plates full of Scotch eggs still in hand, but totally forgotten and drooping precariously. Reg crouches in the centre of the floor. One of the tablecloths has been pulled nearly clean off. The floor is littered with chipsticks and olives. That jaunty black hat has fallen off and come to rest against one of the table legs. I search the room for James out of habit, and he's standing in the corner, eyes wide and one hand to his mouth. Pauline gives me a firm shove into the room.

'You're blocking the door,' she barks.

The jolt from her pushing me is enough to kick my brain into gear again. I cross over to Lowenna in two paces and throw myself onto the flagstones, barely registering the pain in my knees as I land. Pauline takes a little more time to get down, which is fair.

I take Lowenna's hand in mine and it's cold and clammy where it would normally be warm and dry. She's shivering on the cold stone floor, so I tug the fallen cloth completely off the table to cover her. A silver platter comes tumbling with it, sending chicken skewers flying.

'The ambulance is on its way,' Loic calls to us, the phone still pressed to his ear. He listens to some instructions from the other end of the line. 'They say to keep her talking.'

'Well, that's not going to be a problem, is it?' I say. It's too loud, and too cheerful, and everybody can probably tell. I drape the tablecloth over Lowenna, tucking it in at the sides. She's too light. She looks so tiny and weak. I catch Pauline's eye and she looks away, pressing her apron to her forehead.

'What are you playing at, Lowenna, eh?' I ask her, raising myself up onto my heels so that I can make her look into my eyes. 'What was it? One too many mini pasties?'

She doesn't answer.

'It's OK,' I tell her, too loudly again. My face feels hot and I worry that I sound angry, but I can't really moderate my tone. 'The ambulance is coming, and they'll sort you out.'

Her eyes flutter closed.

'Lowenna, don't go to sleep, please!' I call, not sure if I'm getting through to her. 'Is Adam here?'

People on the edge of the room look at me blankly.

'*Is. Adam. Here?*' I ask again.

Adam should *be* here. He could keep her talking. Heads turn around the room as the message gets passed back, but it's no good.

'I think he stayed back at the crem,' somebody pipes up.

I tap Lowenna gently on the side of the face and she opens her eyes and then narrows them at me. I'll pay for that one day. I hope.

'Hey, Lowenna,' I say with my voice low. 'If you stay awake right now I'll stay in Carncarrow and look after you until you're better. Whatever you need.'

'And I'll be there to help,' Pauline chimes in. 'And you'll have all the cider tops you can drink. On the house.'

Lowenna smiles and squeezes my hand as her eyes flutter closed again.

'Lowenna? Lowenna!' My voice cracks as I call her name and for once I'm not embarrassed about the eyes that might be on me.

'Loic, where's that ambulance?' Pauline calls. Loic jumps and lifts the phone back to his ear.

''Bout ten minutes.'

It's the longest ten minutes of my life. Lowenna's chest moves up and down as she takes shallow breaths, but it's moving fast. I don't know how fast it's supposed to be going. Another thing they should have taught us in school. Honestly, what was the point?

When the paramedics finally arrive the entire wake must look like we're in some weird cult, silently sitting in concentric circles arranged around an unconscious woman. One kneels down next to me.

'Excuse me,' he says, 'I need a bit of room.'

But I don't move. I'm too relieved to see the bright-green jacket and the gigantic bag of tricks. Somewhere in there he must have something that can fix all of this. He gently prises my hands away from Lowenna's.

'We'll do what we can.'

Pauline clamps her hands to my shoulders and pulls me away. We watch as they get to work. They unbutton her clothes and stick things to her crêpe-paper skin. They switch on a machine which beeps at them. All the while Pauline holds on to me, and I hang on to her. I'm vaguely aware of James out of the corner of my eye. He inches into my line of sight, looking unsure. At one point he reaches for me as well, but he doesn't get close enough to touch me and I don't make any effort to move towards him. The other paramedic stands up with a crack of knee joints and leaves the pub.

125

She returns a minute later with a stretcher on wheels, struggling to get it over the doorstep. Several of the villagers dart to the doors, holding them open and helping to lift the stainless steel, happy to have something to do.

'We're going to have to take her in,' the paramedic tells us once she's safely inside with her guard of honour. 'Does somebody want to come too?'

I glance at Pauline.

'You go,' she tells me. 'I need to get things tidied up here. I'll try to get hold of Adam as well. Let him know what's happened.'

I hug her quickly, and I'm halfway to the door before I realise I'm being followed.

'Do you want—' But I forget what I was about to say when I realise it's James hovering at my shoulder, rather than somebody useful.

'I'll come too.'

'Oh, I don't think—'

'No, don't be silly. I *want* to come. Lorraine is your friend so I should be there.'

'It's *Lowenna*.'

'Whoever.'

Pure rage hits me as he dismisses her with one word, but there's no time for an outburst.

'We won't have enough space for two.' The paramedic starts to usher me out of the door. The stretcher bearing Lowenna is already in the ambulance.

'Fine.' James relents and takes a step away from me. I allow myself to be bundled into the back, where I am immediately afraid to move in case I accidentally touch anything I shouldn't.

'Hold her hand,' the paramedic tells me. 'Keep talking to her.'

He turns around and begins to busy himself over Lowenna. She looks tiny in comparison to him. Like a little grey alien, all wrinkled skin and bony limbs. I can scarcely believe this is the same woman who used to crawl around on the floor with me and slice butter onto the bread for my sandwiches instead of bothering to spread it.

'Come on, Lowenna,' I whisper.

◆ ◆ ◆

As soon as we arrive at the hospital Lowenna is whisked away and I'm not allowed to go too.

'Come with me, love.' A nurse smiles warmly and steers me towards a waiting room. I find a seat as far away from other people as I can. The thin, wipe-clean cushion gives a little sigh as I squash the air out of it. But I can't sit still for too long. After a while I jump up and pace the shiny floor. But my feet are killing me so I sit down again.

I can't believe I'm back. I'm still dressed in the black I had to wear after my last foray here, for crying out loud. The ridiculousness overwhelms me and I laugh. The lady in the seat opposite me looks up with a tear-streaked face.

'Sorry,' I tell her. I get up and begin pacing the room again.

Eventually I hear shoes squeaking and stop moving to see who could be coming. The tearful lady does the same. We just want it to be someone who can tell us everything's going to be OK in our particular drama. James appears in the doorway and we visibly deflate.

'Charlie, there you are,' he says, rushing over and putting an arm around me so roughly that I somehow end up with my face directly in his armpit. 'How's Rowena?'

'*Lowenna*,' I correct him, pushing him away from me.

'Sorry.'

He sits down in silence, suitably chastised, and I go back to pacing until my blood stops boiling. I'm still fuming about his sudden appearance at the funeral, and his sudden appearance *here* has reminded me of his sudden appearance *there*. Ultimately, I suppose, I wish he'd just stop *appearing* at places I haven't invited him to. But he's only being nice. He's being nice, nice, nice. Once I've got my feelings back under control, I sit down next to him.

'They don't know anything yet,' I concede.

'Well, I'm sure they'll let you know as soon as they do.'

'Did you get here OK?' I ask, genuinely curious.

'Just about,' he huffs. 'I got the bus and we got stuck for ages behind a tractor actually *carrying* a boat which, like, just pick one stereotype and stick to it, you know?'

I nod. Now that my fury has subsided again I just feel exhausted. My night without sleep is catching up with me. Plus, there was the wine and not enough food. I rest my head on his shoulder. After a couple of seconds he takes my hand and I let him. His skin feels warm against mine, and in this moment that alone is comforting enough to make me forget everything else.

I think I drift off to sleep for a little while. I can't be sure, but I blink and the light doesn't seem the same any more.

'Alright, sleepyhead?' James smiles.

I nod. I stretch and my body clicks in about fifteen different places.

'Did anyone come to find me?'

'Not yet. Shall I go and find us a coffee?'

I nod gratefully. He wanders off in completely the opposite direction to the one on the sign pointing towards the cafe. I let him go anyway, because I figure he'll make it eventually.

When he disappears I close my eyes and take a couple of deep breaths. The disinfectant tang is hitting the back of my throat and, now that I've noticed it, it's making me queasy. The nylon lining of my skirt has stuck to the backs of my legs and the swampy situation is made worse by the vinyl cushion on the chair. I fidget. With my eyes still closed I can focus more on the sounds in my immediate area. Somebody in the waiting room is drumming their fingertips on the arm of a seat, while somebody else turns the pages of a magazine far too loudly and far too fast. Running footsteps fade into prominence and then back out again as whoever they belong to rushes past.

It's starting to hit me just how much this speckled lino floor has become a feature of my life in recent weeks. It will doubtless appear prominently in the 'highlights reel' of my life one day when I'm old and it all flashes before my eyes.

When I arrived here on my own, desperate to find Dad, there was a queue of at least ten people in front of me. I am staunchly 'pro' everybody getting in line and waiting their turn, but it turns out that those are actually only my personal values as long as I don't want to get somewhere in a hurry. I stood at the back of the queue picking my cuticles and imagining all the ways I'd murder each of the people in front of me, all the while keeping my face completely neutral. Friendly. Cheerful, even. As the line moved, but not fast enough, I started tapping my feet and sighing quite loudly, becoming the kind of person I cannot stand to have anywhere near me in a queue.

'Hello, my love, how can I help?' a cheery receptionist asked as I finally (finally!) made it to the front of the line.

'Martin Trewin?' I banged my entire lower half against the desk, I was so keen to finally reach it. I tried to pretend it didn't hurt but honestly the bruises only just disappeared in time for the funeral.

The receptionist tapped away on the computer for a couple of seconds and then pointed me in the right direction.

'Go down this corridor, then turn left, and then walk for a couple of minutes, go past two doors next to each other, second right, you'll see a pot plant, take the lift opposite that . . .'

I stared at her mouth as it kept moving, listing off directions when I'd already forgotten the first ones she'd said, thus rendering the later ones useless.

'Got it?' she eventually asked, brightly.

I nodded dumbly and we both knew I was lying.

'Look,' the receptionist said, picking up the phone, 'follow the signs to the third floor. When you get to the desk there, tell them Saz sent you. They'll show you where to go. I'll call them now.'

She brandished the receiver and gave me an encouraging nod.

'Thank you. So where's—'

'That way.'

I wound my way through pale-blue corridor after pale-blue corridor, my shoes squeaking away on that same shiny, speckled floor.

I'm aware of someone sitting down heavily in the seat next to me. I can hear the air sighing out of the vinyl cushion. I open my eyes.

'Hi,' Adam says.

He looks terrible. He's still in his black suit from the funeral, but he's crammed his tie into the pocket of his shirt and loosened his top button. His shirt and his jacket are both creased. There's a stain on his jacket.

'Are you OK?' I ask him. I know the answer is 'no', and I also know that he'll say 'yes'.

'Yep.'

The phone rings at the nurse's station outside and we both hold our breath. But nobody comes into the room.

'She'll be OK, you know,' I tell him, as we deflate.

'If you say so.' He gives me a wan smile. 'I don't know what I'll do if she's not, though.' He adds this almost as an afterthought.

There's nothing I can say to make this better. I don't know what else to do so I slide my hand into Adam's, lacing my fingers with

130

his. He looks at me in surprise, but I read the posters on the wall opposite us instead of looking at him. He brushes my thumb with his like he always used to.

I don't know how long we sit there together but it can't be a huge amount of time. A new family comes in, looking worried. One red-eyed child drops a bottle of something on the floor and it leaks bright sugary pink all over the lino. An older man, who I decide is the boy's granddad, takes his sweet time searching through the stack of tattered magazines in the corner. He picks up three issues of *Home & Garden* but puts them all down after five minutes. A small girl toddles among the seats for a little while before getting sick of the whole situation. She plonks herself down at the feet of a startled middle-aged woman and screams. I flinch as she does. The sound goes right through me. I don't understand what people see in children.

The family leave shortly afterwards, and everybody in the waiting room shares a moment of relief before we all remember why we're here. I notice the tension return to the shoulders in front of us.

What I don't immediately notice, however, is that James has returned, laden with two paper cups and a little packet of Hobnobs. In fact, I don't see him until he's standing directly in front of us.

'What the fuck is going on here?'

CHAPTER TWELVE

'Excuse me!' squawks a lady in the row of chairs behind us, pressing her hands against the ears of a small boy who's so absorbed watching *Peppa Pig* that I doubt he's even noticed we exist.

'Sorry,' James tells her. He turns to us. 'What the fuck is going on here?' he asks again in a whisper, except that his whisper is so full of venom it still comes out louder than I think he intended. The lady huffs, grabs the boy by the hand, and pulls him as far away as possible within the confines of the waiting room.

I'd sort of forgotten that I'm even holding Adam's hand, so it takes a moment to figure out what James is talking about. Then I drop it as if I've been burned. Adam shifts in his seat, bristling.

'James.' I smile, wide-eyed. I will my face to just look normal, to stop making me look like we were up to anything. Because we weren't. We weren't, we weren't, we weren't. I can tell it's not working by the way James frowns. 'This is Adam. Remember? I told you about—'

'This is Adam? Fucking *Adam*?'

'Um, I'm Adam.' Adam bristles, shifting in his seat. 'Who the fuck are you?'

'Shitting Jesus, could you all please watch your language?' the angry woman interjects from the other side of the room.

'Sorry,' we tell her in unison. She stares at us and taps her foot briskly. I take the hint.

'Come with me,' I say, and both Adam and James follow me down several corridors, and some steps, until we end up outside the front of the hospital, more by luck than judgement. The air has the very first hint of autumn in it. On any other day it might be lovely.

The hospital is an older building that must have been something else once upon a time, because it's way too nice to be a hospital. The door is flanked by a couple of ornamental stone planters, neat gravel beds line the space in front of the building, and the car park beyond is packed. A barrier sticks up in the air, and cars rush down an actually busy road on the other side. The bright street lamps and multiple lanes of traffic feel alien after a few days of winding lanes and pitch-dark nights, and it puts me on edge. I focus on taking deep gulps of air that doesn't smell like disinfectant.

Except I'm so busy taking deep gulps of air that doesn't smell like disinfectant that I don't hear the sounds of a scuffle until it's too late. I wheel around in time to see James give Adam a shove so hard it sends him reeling backwards. There's a moment where it looks like he might actually topple over, but he catches himself at the last minute, clinging to the branches of a small tree in one of the planters by the door.

'James!' I yell.

Adam regains his balance and stands up straight, brushing non-existent dust from his suit. He takes a couple of prowling steps forward, looking for all the world like something you might see on a nature documentary. James makes a detour over to me and tries to hand me his watch.

'Fuck off,' I tell him. 'I'm not helping you.'

'Oh, so you're helping him?'

'I'm not helping either of you. You're both being idiots. Stop it.'

'But he pushed me,' Adam protests.

'And now you're *both* acting like five-year-olds.'

I shouldn't have said anything. As Adam pauses to let my words sink in, James catches him across the jaw with a fist. I jump up a couple of steps to get out of the way of what I know is going to happen next.

It's like a red mist descends over Adam. He narrows his eyes, lets out a cry and launches himself at James. They both tumble to the floor and roll around there, a whirl of fists and kicking feet. I haven't seen a proper fight since the school playground and it doesn't look like anything's become more sophisticated. It's a little bit . . . pathetic?

I stand, a bit gormless, on the steps for a minute or so. I mean, I don't know what to do. There's no danger of either of them seriously hurting the other one because they're really bad at this, so I'm not especially worried. I figure they'll probably tire themselves out before long and stop of their own accord. And then maybe I'll be able to get a word in edgeways, who knows?

'Hey. Hey!'

A couple of security guards walk towards us from an alley down the side of the building. They break into a run as they catch sight of James and Adam, still rolling around on the ground, snarling and kicking out without really achieving much.

The security guards throw themselves into the melee, and for a second it's a tangle of arms and legs and I'm not totally sure who's trying to stop whom. But the guards get a firm grip each on James and Adam and manage to pull them apart. They both strain against them, but after a few seconds all the fight (if we're even calling it that) drains out of them and they slump to the floor.

The security guards stand up and dust themselves off.

'These belong to you?' one of them asks me.

'I suppose,' I tell him.

'Good luck.'

They both head back inside and are not quite out of earshot when they start laughing. I know it's not aimed at me but my face still burns for about the ninetieth time today. I wouldn't be surprised if it was actively glowing in the dark.

'What the hell are you playing at?' I demand as James and Adam both stand up. They're covered in dusty patches from the gravel, James has a graze on his cheek, and Adam's shirt pocket hangs forlornly from his chest where it's been torn away. His tie lies trampled on the ground. They both shrug, suddenly sullen. It's like I'm scolding two overtired children. Which I basically am, except both of the 'children' are in their thirties. James climbs up the steps and reaches for my hand. I can't decide whether to give it to him or not. I catch Adam's eye and he frowns.

Somebody in scrubs appears at the top of the steps, framed in the light that spills from the reception area. 'Are you all here for Lowenna Murphy?'

'Yes,' Adam and I tell him, suddenly alert.

'Maybe?' says James. I hit him and make contact with his ribs. He grunts.

'Would you all come with me, please?'

'What on *earth* are you playing at?' Lowenna demands, gesticulating with a pot of strawberry jelly. 'I'm in this room in peace and quiet, *dying* for all you know, and suddenly I'm asked if I know I have visitors and whether I know how to stop them from knocking seven bells out of each other in the entrance!'

She turns her gaze onto a very young nurse who can't long have finished her training. The nurse flinches as Lowenna frowns at her.

'Sorry, Mrs Murphy,' she practically whispers. 'We didn't know what to do.'

'That's OK, love, I'm only playing with you.' Lowenna chuckles. The young nurse looks slightly relieved but mainly very uncomfortable. She more or less runs away. I can hear her hospital-issue trainers squeaking on the floor as she goes.

'Now, then,' Lowenna begins.

I was so relieved to come into the room and find her sitting up and making nurses uncomfortable that I completely forgot the fight, even though it happened only moments ago. James hung back in the reception area, probably not keen on watching the final moments of a stranger. I was so convinced that we were being brought upstairs to say goodbye. I have a hundred per cent record for it here, after all, and I could still see the frighteningly quiet bag of bones who'd been stretchered out of the pub a few hours earlier.

But when we came in Lowenna was propped up on pillows, complaining in no uncertain terms about having a drip stuck in her arm. She was already developing a vicious bruise. But she had some colour back in her cheeks and she looked bright-eyed. I could have cried with relief.

'Charlie, are you with us?' she demands now. I force myself to pay attention.

'Yes. Sorry.'

'Good. First things first. My unruly grandson.' She turns her focus on Adam, and I think I see him quail under her stare. 'What on earth do you think you're playing at, fighting? At your age? And in a hospital, of all places?'

'It wasn't *in* the—'

'No, no, of course, you're right, how silly of me. It was only *outside* the hospital, where anybody with their window open could hear you and then get a really good view of what was going on. Not to *mention* the fact that you could have hit someone in a delicate condition! Do you think a woman in labour needs to be clobbered by a fully-grown man having a fight?'

'I would never—'

'No, I know you wouldn't *on purpose*, but accidents happen and you should be old enough to know better.'

'I am—'

'Then act like it!' shrieks Lowenna. A nurse sticks her head around the door and looks reproachfully at her. Lowenna ignores her.

'But he started it!'

'Adam Michael Murphy, is that acting like an adult?'

'Mrs Murphy, you really should try to calm down,' the nurse tries to interject. 'In your condition—'

'My condition is called "old age", darling, and it'll get me whether or not I tell my grandson he's an idiot first. And I'd prefer that he know.'

Lowenna doesn't take her eyes off Adam. The nurse pauses in the doorway until the younger nurse from earlier appears beside her, pulling her away with a wary shake of the head.

'And you.' She turns her attention to me, and I somehow lose sensation in all of my fingers. 'What were you doing while all of this was going on?'

'I was just . . . standing there,' I tell her after a pause.

'And do you think that "just standing there" is helpful?'

'No?' I venture.

'Exactly. No. No, it is not. So next time, I urge you to find a modicum of courage and put them in their places. Not that there'll be a "next time",' she adds threateningly, looking at Adam again.

'But he—'

'I don't care what "he" did or said, young man. I expect *you* to behave.'

'Yes, Grandma.'

'Lowenna, I—'

'Yes?' She looks ferocious again and I falter under her glare. Any thought of defending James's honour disappears.

'Nothing.'

'Good. Now, would somebody get that boy in here?'

I look at Adam and he looks back at me. We both just stand there, each regarding the other one coolly, neither one of us wanting to be the first to move.

'Well, I'm not gonna go and get your fucking fiancé for you, am I?' he says eventually. Apparently word gets around.

'Adam.'

'Sorry, Grandma.'

I sigh and leave the room. Outside in the corridor the strip lights on the ceiling are reflected in the floor, making me feel like I'm inside an optical illusion. A man pushes a floor polisher around at the other end, the whirring filling the silence like a white-noise machine. It's making me a bit dizzy, and James is nowhere to be seen.

I almost miss him when I walk past a room near the end of the corridor. He's standing next to the bedside of a man in his fifties or thereabouts, having an animated discussion. I do a double take.

'James?'

'Here she is! We were just talking about you.' James greets me with open arms and no hint of shame, and it immediately annoys me.

I take another look at the man in the bed. His leg is wrapped in plaster and suspended from the ceiling, in the kind of contraption I thought they only had in films. His hair is a mess, salt and pepper spread across the pillow.

'Oh, Mr Matthews, hi,' I say when I recognise my old English teacher. I can't believe I'm seeing one of my teachers in pyjamas. 'Can I please borrow my . . . James?'

I grab James by the arm without waiting for a reply and pull him from the room. We squeak our way along the quiet corridor, the floor polisher having moved on to duties elsewhere.

'Are we leaving?' James asks me brightly.

'No.'

'Have we got time for a quick pit stop in the shop?'

'No.'

He comes to a stop in the corridor, looking at me closely.

'Are you mad at me?'

'No.'

I make us start walking again, until we turn into Lowenna's room.

'Here she is!' Lowenna cries. I've only been gone two minutes but she's somehow got three members of the nursing staff gathered around her bedside and is handing out a packet of biscuits she definitely didn't have before.

'Now, then,' Lowenna begins, after she offers both James and me a garibaldi. It has no flavour, but I haven't eaten anything since a couple of stolen crisps at the wake, so in this moment it's delicious.

'What did *you* think you were playing at, young man?'

James is staring around the room, a sprinkling of garibaldi crumbs on his jumper, and he doesn't immediately realise she's talking to him. He jumps as he notices everybody's eyes on him.

'Oh. Um, nothing?'

'Nothing? Why would you start a fight over nothing?'

'I didn't start it!'

'I have it on good authority that you did.'

'I never—'

'James,' I interject. 'Come on.'

He pauses and then sighs heavily. A couple of the garibaldi crumbs float to the floor.

'Fine,' he concedes. 'But those two were all over each other.'

'We were not!' Adam beats me to it.

'Well, you were sitting there holding hands and looking all cosy. I've come all this way and she's barely even looked at me. And I know about their past, and—'

'We were just . . . comforting each other because we were scared!' I protest.

'I was here! I could have comforted you. I came a long way to do that,' he says, and it's really sweet, but it also makes me want to scream. I dig my nails into my palm and fight to swallow a surge of anger before I can answer.

'Well, that wouldn't have helped Adam, now, would it?'

'I couldn't give a shit about helping Adam.'

For a moment there's silence in the room. We all stare at each other. James looks hurt and a little bit bewildered. Adam glares. Lowenna looks like she knows exactly what she wants to happen now but would find it far too easy to just give us that information. The nurses who were in here earlier have backed as far into the corner as they can, half-eaten biscuits in hand, staring at us in horror.

'I think you can go.' I smile at them and they run out of the room. They don't even try to disguise it. They literally run.

'And, look,' I tell everybody else. 'Shall we just pretend none of this ever happened? I wasn't doing anything, Adam wasn't doing anything, nobody should have got into a fight' – at this point James and Adam both start to protest loudly, and I raise my voice over both of them – 'but now we just need to accept that it happened and move on.'

'Well done, that young lady.' Lowenna claps approvingly. James and Adam don't look so keen, but they both nod their assent anyway.

'Have they told you I can go home, by the way?' Lowenna asks brightly.

'Really?' Adam asks. 'Nobody mentioned it to us.'

'No, well, I expect you were too busy rolling around on the floor outside,' Lowenna says lightly, picking a raisin out of her biscuit. 'I'm a bit bruised, but they say I'm fine otherwise so I might as well go home.'

'And then *we* can go home?' James slips his hand into mine.

'Yep,' I say, my voice strained.

CHAPTER THIRTEEN

'It's not like Transport for London, is it?' James huffs, as we huddle at the bus stop outside the hospital to wait for the hourly service, and I know he's only trying to fill the silence but it still annoys me. Adam's driving Lowenna home. There was one more seat in the car, but James was not invited to take it for obvious reasons. And while I'm not sure exactly what the protocol is for this kind of situation, I think my travelling back with Adam and leaving James to fend for himself might break it.

'Nope. Because it's not London.'

I actually think the buses are pretty shit too, but my response to James's disparagement is to wildly overplay how much I love every little quirk of life in the middle of nowhere. James playfully nudges me, trying to get me to smile, maybe to offer him a hand, but I can't bring myself to do it.

'What do you want to do first when we get home?'

'Sleep. Then go for a swim.'

'Where will you swim? The leisure centre? Isn't it a bit—'

'In the sea.'

I look at him, lit up harshly by the fluorescent bulb of the bus shelter, which I suspect is doing me no favours either. A frown puckers his forehead. Then, after a few seconds, his face drops. And at about the same moment he realises I'm talking about staying in the village, I realise he was talking about going back to London.

'Oh,' he says.

'Oh,' I say.

We sit in silence for a really long time. At one point a seagull comes past to investigate whether we have anything it could steal. James kicks out at it, and it jumps into the road to avoid his trainer and is very nearly hit by a van.

'Don't do that!' I scold.

'It's vermin.'

'Not very vegan, though, is it?'

He gives me A Look, and then tuts and glares down at his shoes. He scuffs at one of the wheels of the case.

'I brought you some clothes, by the way,' he mutters at his feet.

'Thanks,' I sigh to the ceiling of the bus stop.

When the bus finally turns up we still haven't addressed the cloud of disagreement hanging over us. We never have been very good at talking about our problems. I can never face it, personally. I don't know what James's issue with it is because, well, that would involve talking about our problems and, famously, we don't do that.

We sit stiffly next to each other. I try not to let any part of my body brush against his. There's nothing to see out the window. It's pitch black and there are no street lights along the little lanes. The driver seems to have no sense of danger, so we hurtle along, branches whipping into view at the last minute and scraping the sides with an almighty noise.

I press the bell when it's getting towards our stop. James looks at me.

'Are you coming?' I ask.

'I don't see where else I'd go,' he replies with a shrug. He's trying to seem nonchalant, but I can see all the hurt and frustration rising up his neck in the form of a bright-pink flush. It's reached the tips of his ears too. That's how you know it's really bad.

The great thing about James in the early days was that he provided me with a ready-made social life. I really couldn't believe my luck. For starters, I had become convinced, as I spent every night on my own, that there was something wrong with me. Or rather, that the normal life lived by my flatmates and neighbours, who stumbled home laughing on Saturday nights or disappeared with a rumble of suitcase wheels in the early hours of the morning, just wasn't going to be for me. And I wasn't upset about it. I was fine. The understanding that I might never have what everybody else had crystallised inside me, and I got on with life.

But the first thing James did when he asked me out was to destroy that understanding. Every few days I would go out with him, come home tipsy in the small hours, and finally feel like I always imagined other people felt as they drunkenly tried to aim keys into front door locks.

'Tell me about your ex,' he breathed at me over a sticky table in a grotty bar one night. I choked on my drink. I guess maybe it's an innocuous enough question if you're not dating an actual emotional minefield. He wasn't to know.

'Sorry?' I played for time while coughing up vodka and Diet Coke.

'Why'd you break up?'

'Oh. I moved away. And we tried to do the long-distance thing but he had stuff on, and I . . . also had stuff on, and it was just too hard, you know? So I called it off.'

'In person?'

'Email.'

'Wow. That's cold.'

'No! I—' It was a tricky one, because how do you say 'The last time I was in any kind of relationship WhatsApp hadn't been invented and

I didn't own a mobile phone' without looking like there's something wrong with you? Which there isn't. There isn't, there isn't, there isn't. In the end I just lied.

'I meant that I, um, sent him an email asking if we could meet up and then we did, and then I told him. I did the decent thing. 'Course I did.'

'Good. I was all ready to defend . . . what's his name?'

'Adam.'

'I was all ready to defend Adam's honour and call you a monster.'

'Well, no need!' I tried to look cheery but I think it came out wrong.

'Sorry, joking.'

'No, I just . . .' I sighed and chewed the inside of my cheek for a moment. 'He was a really great guy and I messed it up.'

'Jeez, it actually sounds like I should be jealous. I take it all back. Screw Adam's honour.'

'What?' I flushed. I could feel it happening. I laughed and hoped he wouldn't notice. 'Don't be silly.'

'Uh-huh. Well. Another drink?'

James also started inviting me out with his mates. We were very different people. They were a rugby crowd, and I don't think it would surprise anybody to learn that I know nothing about that. Or about how to hang out with a crowd of mostly blonde, rugby-shirted men, yelling at the screen and laughing. But they were kind enough, they explained what the hell was going on, and I didn't get in their way.

In the space of a couple of months the calendar I kept on the wall actually started to fill up with stuff. Weddings, work drinks, Six Nations fixtures . . . It didn't matter what the stuff was. It mattered that there was stuff at all.

We didn't have a lot in common. James is career-driven and sporty, he's a social butterfly, and his family is well-off. To this day, I don't really know what I am. But how boring would life be if our interests were exactly the same? I wasn't going to be shallow enough to let a few little differences get in the way of the Great New Thing I had got myself into.

Sure, nobody was going to write any great love stories about our relationship, but we both realised that, and we were fine with it. I certainly was. My dad had been head over heels in love with my mum and losing her nearly destroyed him. Suffice it to say that, with James, the stakes were not that high, which is exactly how I wanted them.

By coincidence, both my and James's flat contracts came up at around the same time, a few months after we started dating. I couldn't face the idea of moving in with yet another group of strangers and becoming the awkward quiet one in the shittest room of another leaky-roofed semi in South London. So when he suggested we move in together instead, I jumped at it. We might not have been on the same page all the time but better the devil you know, right? Not that James was a devil. Just different. And we could split the rent and we didn't hate each other. Winner, winner, chicken dinner.

It's probably reasonable to wonder what James saw in me. His mum wasn't impressed with me when we met. She asked me about my parents and I made it weird. I stuttered about my mum not being with us any more (ew), turned bright red, and stared desperately around the room for anything I could use to change the subject. I ended up asking James's parents their opinion on fishing policies because it happened to be on the front page of the Daily Mail that lay folded on the coffee table. His mum thought I was a lunatic, which was entirely fair.

'Darling, I'm just not—'

'Well, I am.'

I was about to offer to help wash up when hushed-but-not-that-hushed voices stopped me in my tracks outside the kitchen after dinner.

'She doesn't seem very . . .'

I mean, friendly? Confident? Able to do small talk like a functioning human? That sentence could have ended a hundred different ways.

'Mum, would you just stop? This is what I want.'

'But, I don't—'

'Not that I have to justify myself to you, but Charlie makes me happy, OK? It's nice having someone to come home to, and she gets on well with my friends. She wants something stable, so do I, and I don't think that's such a bad thing. At least we're not just in it for the sex or the jokes, or whatever, you know? We're going to build something together. That's exciting.'

I tiptoed away. James's dad had fallen asleep in front of the telly, so I watched the football scores roll in because I didn't want to wake him by changing the channel, and waited until the discussion had played itself out. It felt weird to hear James talk to his mum about me. I suppose I should have been offended to hear that the thing he seemed to like most about me was that I probably wasn't going anywhere. Maybe a little bit sad to discover that he apparently didn't think of me as sexy or funny. But, to be fair, he wasn't wrong. I did get the uncomfortable feeling that what he wanted to 'build together' was children, but I figured maybe all the magazines and the yummy mummy influencers would be right, and my biological clock really would start ticking one day. Even if it was a little late. At least he'd never go anywhere either.

He follows me wordlessly off the bus and along the high street. I don't have anything to say to him either. I can see the lights in the windows of the Bolster & Saint. They must be mid-lock-in. I glance at James, and then look back in the direction of the pub. I'm pretty sure I can hear laughter. It would be wonderful to be there instead of in this crushing silence. Just for a minute.

I stalk down the high street, and he stays a couple of paces behind me. I occasionally hear scuffing noises as the cobbles trip him up. Where there are alleyways leading to the harbour the lights just completely disappear, giving the impression of a black curtain hung to our left. I wonder if James has noticed the stars. I wonder if he's noticed how clean the air smells, or the salt tang to it, or if he's registered the sound of the sea carried over by the breeze. But I think I know the answer.

We're back at the house all too soon. James raises an eyebrow as I give the door a push and walk straight in without unlocking anything. He probably thinks I could have been murdered by now. Or it could be a reaction to all the knockers, which do look a *bit* mental.

'Tea?' I ask when we get inside. I throw my keys onto the shelf above the radiator with the practised ease you can only build up over time. I deliberately ignore his horrified look when he sees the mess.

'Am I allowed one?'

'Don't be stupid. Go and sit down.'

I point him through to the living room and race upstairs.

'You OK?' he yells.

'Just need a piss!' I call back.

'Charming.'

I yank open the drawer I hid my ring in and jam it onto my finger. It feels as if I'd never taken it off. A constant shiny reminder of how my life is set in stone.

With that done, I dash back downstairs and busy myself in the kitchen. Tea for James, neat gin for me. When I go back into the living room, drinks in hand, James looks up from a book he's been flicking through. He spies my glass and raises an eyebrow.

'Please don't start,' I tell him.

To his credit, he says nothing.

'I found my ring,' I add after a minute. I flash my finger at him and force my mouth up at the corners.

'That's good. Where was it?'

'Windowsill, upstairs. I must have taken it off while I was cleaning.'

'Ah. Well, mystery solved.'

We both sit on the sofa and I know it's a cliché, but you could absolutely cut the tension with a knife. I don't know what to say and it isn't until James puts an arm around me and pulls me into him that I realise I'm crying.

'Hey,' he croons as I cry onto his shoulder. 'What's all this?'

'What do you *think* it is?' I sob, plucking at my black skirt. The nylon lining is still sticking to my skin, and the fabric strains against my thighs. My bra is digging into my back. I want to be in my pyjamas immediately.

'No, sorry, of course.'

James continues to hold me as I weep onto his shoulder. I slowly but surely soak his jumper, and he strokes my hair. When the tears have slowed and eventually stopped, he hands me my glass and picks up his now-only-lukewarm tea.

'To be fair, I actually do think you need that,' he tells me with a shrug.

We sit quietly again for a couple of minutes. There's less tension now. It feels like a barrier's broken down.

James is the first one to break the silence. 'I don't understand why you never told me.'

'Told you what?'

'Everything.'

'There was nothing t—'

'Don't do that. Don't play it down. You make it seem like I'm being unreasonable. I'm not. There was loads.'

I am absolutely certain that I'm:

A) going to cry again, and

B) completely incapable of explaining the last twenty years of my choices.

'I just . . . can't. Not now,' I whisper, my eyes threatening to brim over again, which I would not have thought was possible.

'OK. But we have to have a conversation about this. At some point.'

I nod.

He feels around in the cushions of the sofa. He's looking for the remote because that's how we mark the end of all awkward conversations.

'You have to push the button,' I sniffle, pointing at the TV.

'Oh, wow.'

'You don't have to be a twat about it.'

'I just said . . . Never mind.'

He gets up and switches the TV on with a sigh. The flickering light from the screen hurts my swollen eyes, but it's better than sitting in silence. I glance over at James. He watches the screen, expressionless. I take a sip of my drink.

'I should have,' I tell him, eventually. 'Told you, I mean.'

He raises an eyebrow, but doesn't look away from the TV. We both know I'll tell him everything, but he can't push me or I'll clam up. I'm such a catch, honestly.

'There's a lot I should have told you. I think living in London is a mistake, for one thing. I hate getting up every morning and fighting to get on the train that takes me to an office I hate being in. I hate my job. I should never have gone up there. But I couldn't stay here either. So where does that leave me? And now I've been too miserable for too long, and I don't know how to get out of it any more. There's too much to change. I can't do it. And I should have told you what this place was like, and about how I grew up, and about my mum, but I didn't want to because it's painful and you never pushed it, so I guess I thought I got away with it.'

James opens his mouth, and for a moment I wonder if he's going to find a way to argue, but he concedes with a shrug. Silence takes over. I notice his hand twitch on the sofa next to me, but he decides against reaching for mine. On the TV an audience cheers about something.

'I always got the feeling there was something, you know? You always looked like a rabbit in the headlights when I asked about your childhood, and I guess I gave up in the end. Why put you through it? There was definitely something going on.'

'I'm going to bed.'

'Charlie.'

I don't look back as I go. But I stop halfway up the stairs, suddenly paralysed. I don't want to leave things the way I have. It's just that I also can't breathe in that room any more. James lets out a sigh in the living room, and the dodgy spring in the sofa creaks as he stands up. The glow from the TV goes out, and the hallway is plunged into darkness. These are the same signs I used to watch out for shortly before sneaking out to go and see Adam. Except, for crying out loud, don't think about Adam right now.

James sticks his head around the door frame and catches me frozen on the steps.

'Mind if I join you?'

'Whatever.'

I dither on the landing. The only double bed in the house is in Dad's room. *I* haven't even been in there yet. And he's not sleeping in Dad's bed, that's for sure. But he'll expect to be in with me. Which I guess means we're stuck sharing my teenage single.

We undress silently. I trip over my jeans as I pull them off and swear under my breath as I try to find my faded old nightie. James doesn't say anything, but I can't be sure whether that's because he hasn't heard or because he's ignoring me. And I can't ask because of that whole 'we don't talk about our feelings' thing. I've overdone it today already. It's exhausting.

I climb into the single bed and shift right across until I'm pressed up against the wall. James pulls the duvet mostly off me without realising and wraps a habitual arm around my waist.

''Night,' he mumbles into my neck. Outside the window a seagull lets out a squawk. James snores. I try those useless mindfulness breaths.

CHAPTER FOURTEEN

The next morning it's as if nothing ever happened. James slips out of bed when his usual alarm goes off at 6 a.m., and I'm finally able to release my death grip on the side of the mattress, which has been all that's prevented me from rolling into the ditch in the middle for the past seven hours. My hands ache. I can finally get some sleep.

Of course, it's short-lived. I wake up to the mattress sagging as James perches on the side. He strokes my hair, but he does it too hard and kind of squashes my eyeball. I try to blink away the splotches that suddenly appear in my vision.

'I made breakfast,' he says.

'Be there in a minute,' I groan. We both know I'm going back to sleep.

I feel the mattress lift again as he stands up, and the door clicks shut. I'm just drifting off as my phone buzzes on the bedside table and I nearly jump out of my skin. My half-asleep brain hasn't quite caught up with the present moment, so for a minute I think I need to turn it off to avoid James. Except that he's pointedly clanging pans downstairs, which he will continue to do until he hears me get up, and then deny if I mention it.

'Hello?'

'Charlie. It's Adam.'

'Oh. Hi.'

'Hi. Listen, Charlie. It's about Grandma.'

And, just like that, all I can hear is my heart pounding.

'Is she OK?'

'Yes! God, it's nothing like that. No. It's just that she needs to take it easy. I'll be over there when I can, but would you mind popping your head in sometimes? For however long you're here, anyway. You must have to get back soon.'

'Of course!' I promise, only hearing what I want to hear. 'I'll go and say hello later.'

'Thank you. You know she loves you.'

I feel a bit flustered for no particular reason so I can't think of anything else to say.

'I'm sorry,' Adam eventually sighs.

'You have nothing to be sorry for.'

'OK, but I am, though.'

'Thanks. Me too.'

'You don't have to be either.'

'No, I know. I am, though.'

'Bye.'

'Bye.'

There's no going to sleep now because I have phone anxiety coursing through me, so I get up. As I sit on the side of the bed searching for my slippers, my ring catches the light that streams through the curtains. It glints at me accusingly.

I sigh and kneel on the floor next to the suitcase James brought with him. It looks even bigger in my tiny room. You could probably rent it out as holiday accommodation. I flip open the lid and dig eagerly through his selections. And then I dig some more, hoping to find something I can actually wear.

I mean, Jesus Christ. Look, it was a very nice idea, but half of the clothes in there are the workwear that always feels like a costume that doesn't quite fit me, and half of them are – not to put too fine a point on it – scruffy AF. What am I going to do, wear a three-sizes-too-big, faded-after-years-of-washing Mickey Mouse T-shirt with a nice black pencil skirt? Pair a chiffon blouse with my daytime pyjama bottoms? Just walk around the village dressed fully corporate or fully ready for bed? Why doesn't he want me to look *normal*? My kingdom for a pair of jeans. I pull on a pair of tracksuit bottoms and then steal his sweatshirt.

James looks genuinely surprised to see me walk through the door only maybe twenty minutes after he first came to wake me up. A stack of pancakes is piled on a plate in the middle of the table. I don't know where he found half the ingredients with all of the junk in the cupboards. But then, I don't know what half the ingredients even are.

He frowns. 'I brought you your own clothes.'

'I'm wearing them.' I kick a leg to highlight my trousers. Could I take the time to explain to him what was wrong with his choices? Sure. Would it make any difference at this stage? Definitely not. Also, I do think a fashion lecture would be a *bit* rich coming from me.

'Coffee?' he asks, shaking his head.

'Please.'

Some of the awkwardness from last night has lifted. I still feel on edge, but it's my usual level, so in a way it's comforting. Shit but familiar.

'Listen,' he says as he hands me a mug. 'I'm really sorry about yesterday. If I was arsey. And for the hospital. I just had to be up so early to make the train and then it was so much to take in. I was just tired, and I felt kind of out of place, and I didn't deal with it very well.'

'It's not me you have to apologise to.'

'Well, I would still like to, if you'll accept it.'

He reaches over to touch my hand and I grit my teeth, because what is wrong with me? He's being nice, any idiot can see that. I force my face into a smile and nod. He looks relieved.

'What's the plan for today?' James asks, just as I shovel a huge forkful of pancake into my mouth. I hold up a finger and chew hard. It takes longer than I expect.

'I don't know,' I tell him eventually. What a build-up for nothing.

'Oh, OK.'

'I mean, Lowenna's home so I'm going to drop in and check she's OK, and I need to properly concentrate on clearing out the house. Pauline said she'd help. We could have a go at the garage today.'

'And what happens when you get everything cleared out?'

I open my mouth to answer and then stop short. I actually . . . don't know. I've been thinking so much about my arbitrary task that I haven't stopped to consider what will happen afterwards.

'I dunno.' I can feel myself getting defensive and I try to bury the instinct. There's no reason. I know there's no reason. 'I guess, it gets sold?'

'Oh, cool. You know, maybe we should buy somewhere. We could use the money for a deposit once you sell. What do you think?'

I stare at my coffee. I didn't stir the milk so it billows like clouds. I frown and pretend to examine a chip in the rim of my cup.

◆ ◆ ◆

I've been avoiding thinking about the future for months on end. In fact, ever since James showed up at my office on Valentine's Day to ask me to marry him.

My colleagues were lovely and bought me wedding magazines and adverts for wedding fairs they'd torn out of the *Evening Standard*. They volunteered to come shopping with me if I wanted to go and look at dresses or choose coloured ribbon, for reasons I'm unclear on. Invitations, maybe? To go around flowers? I always politely declined.

On the train to and from work I would scroll through engagement hashtags on Instagram, flicking through happy couples and trying to inspire in myself any of the joy these people flashing rings on sun-drenched beaches seemed to feel. I tried to imagine it happening somewhere other than the marble floor in front of the security guard's desk as all my colleagues were leaving work for the day. Maybe I'd feel differently if it had been private and Mabel the receptionist hadn't started snapping photos for the next issue of the employee newsletter. I wasn't sure, though. All I knew was that I didn't think I felt the way I was supposed to feel.

But, I mean, why not? I'd levelled up. It's exactly what we're all put on the earth to do. You meet someone, you go out with them for a couple of years, you move in together, and then you get engaged. And then you never have to go on another date as long as you live, not that I'd been on any before James came along, but still. That's the prize. You are locked in. And they are locked in for you, as well. They're never going anywhere. That's the idea, anyway. And the hamster wheel goes round.

I was so busy rationalising it all that I forgot to make a start on planning anything. And James didn't exactly spring into action either. I went to a wedding fair, but I got so overwhelmed the second I walked through the door that I turned around and left again. I told myself it was because it was too crowded, but it was really because I couldn't see myself in any of the dresses, at any of the venues, with any of the today-only-special-offer photobooth packages at the reception. I couldn't picture my wedding at all. Later, when I opened my goody bag, it was one third leaflets, one third chocolate bars, and one third weight-loss tea. I kept the chocolate.

Considering I can't even imagine buying a wedding dress, the idea of buying a house together is ludicrous. For a start, I don't know how any of that works. For another thing, it's terrifying to think that I'd be tying myself to another person for the rest of my life. With money, not just words. I'd need to check exactly how it all works when you get divorced as well, but that doesn't seem like a very strong start. And lastly, and *very* crucially, I don't even know if I have any right to the house.

Dad could have left it to Pauline. He could have left it to Lowenna, or Reg, or someone he knew from the pub. He could even have left it to charity. They could save themselves a ton of mileage from coming to collect all the bric-a-brac, and just open up the living room as a jumble sale. I probably should try to find out what his wishes were, but it's a door I'm not ready to open at the minute.

I worry at the chip in the rim of my mug. My vision swims in front of my eyes. James is still staring at me, expectant.

'Mmhmm,' I tell him, unable to form actual, human words.

'Good! We should sit down one day and talk about it, properly. Do some maths. When things have settled down a bit.'

He beams at me. I've made his day.

'Is there somewhere I can set up my computer?' he continues.

'Your— Why?'

'Well.' He takes a dramatic pause. He *bloody* loves a dramatic pause. 'I had a little chat with work when I came down here and they've been very supportive, and I'm going to stay here with you and work remotely!'

My mouth drops open. I really have to fight to keep my face from doing anything that might suggest that I'm not happy with this arrangement. Because that's not even correct. I *am* happy. I am happy, happy, happy. My fiancé is a wonderful, supportive man, and I don't find him overbearing at all. I know objectively that it's lovely for him to want to stay and support me through this difficult time. So an open mouth is fine. A raised eyebrow is OK. Wide eyes could mean I'm excited. Just stick with that. He frowns as I fight to bring my expression under control.

'Do you not . . . *want* me here?'

'No! It's not that!' My voice is way too loud and way too cheery, and he looks terrified for a second. I clear my throat. Get it together. 'No, I'm pleased. That's . . . really nice of you.'

I don't think I sound very believable, so I lean forward and take his hand. He looks delighted. It's very rare that I'm the one to initiate any kind of contact, and his obvious gratification makes me feel terrible. He's so good to me.

'And you're not worried that you'll miss out if you're not at the office?' I ask in a last-ditch attempt to change his mind.

'Charlie, you are so much more important than a job.' He brushes his lips against my knuckles. 'And besides, they gave me a new laptop and we just got this amazing new productivity suite, so, if anything, it might actually help me.'

'Oh, cool.'

'I just think we should be together at a time like this, you know?' He strokes my hand.

'Yep.'

My voice sounds strangled but he's so happy.

◆ ◆ ◆

Over the next couple of days, I think we actually settle into a nice little routine. James wakes up and seems to enjoy strolling into the village to buy eggs, cereal, and orange juice from Karnkarrow

Konveniences. Mrs Rowe is, by all accounts, thrilled to have a new customer out of nowhere.

'She keeps trying to get me to buy all of this extra stuff,' James tells me one day while we're having lunch. 'And, I mean, it's fine but I only came in for toilet paper so she must realise that doesn't mean I want a vape as well, y'know?'

I shrug. 'She's just making the most out of you coming in.'

'Yesterday she asked me if I wanted her to order in some sushi specially. She said I looked like I'd be into that kind of thing, and she knew a guy who'd do it cheap.'

When I generally roll out of bed an hour later, breakfast is usually laid out on the table. Thankfully, it is never the questionable sushi that Mrs Rowe promised James. That has yet to appear, and I can only hope it never does. I eat with a side order of guilt that I could ever have been unhappy when the man I'm due to marry is always so good to me.

We get to work on the house after breakfast. Or rather, I do. It becomes clear after about the first hour on the first day that it's a job best done by myself, with Pauline when available. James keeps trying to help, but he doesn't understand what's important and what can be thrown away.

He shows me some beautiful pieces of jewellery tucked away in a box, but I know deep down that I'm wearing the only one that really matters. On the other hand, there are floods of tears when James empties a cupboard and out tumbles the shoe brush Dad used to use on my Kickers every Sunday night before school. We hit a particular low when he uncovers a ball of grubby fabric stuffed behind some books on a shelf.

'What do you think this is?' He holds it up, revealing lace along one edge. 'Net curtain?'

'Put that down.'

'But what—'

'Put it down!'

'What's this?'

I danced around my parents' bedroom with a bright-white piece of tulle, having directly disobeyed an order not to touch anything.

'Charlie, what did I just say?'

'But what is it?'

I threw it in the air and watched as it floated back down. One end was lined with white lace, the other gathered, and it seemed to take ages to come back to earth.

'I said "leave things alone".' Mum snatched it out of the air and laid it out on the bed.

'But it's pretty. What is it?'

'For crying out loud, it's a veil.'

'What's a veil?'

'Charlie, I'm a bit busy here.'

I should mention that Mum was trying to put make-up on while I was being kind of a pest. And this was the nineties so, I mean, the lipstick alone had three separate stages.

'I just want to know.'

'I wore it when I married your dad. In my hair, like this.'

She pulled me in front of her, grabbed a couple of hair grips from the dish full of little messy bits on the bedside table (we've surely all got one of those) and pinned the veil into my hair. It dragged on the ground behind me.

'There. But we need to put it away in two minutes so that you can go to Lowenna's.'

'Why?'

'Because you can't turn up at Lowenna's house in my old veil.'

'But why do I have to go?'

'Because your dad's work is having a party, and I have to go to that.'

'Why do you have to go?'

'Believe me, I don't want to.' Mum tried to speak and apply lip liner at the same time, and you have to applaud the effort.

'What?'

'Don't say "what", say "pardon". Come on, take that off now, I'll be late.'

'No.'

'Don't make me count, Charlie. I'm not in the mood.'

She unhooked a satiny black dress from the wardrobe door, unzipped it and stepped in. She fought valiantly with the zip, but it wouldn't do up.

'For fu—' She made a noise of frustration and gave up halfway. 'Charlie, please.'

She tried a second time, but the zip wouldn't move. She tore dresses out of the wardrobe with another noise of frustration, flinging them onto the floor. She finally pulled a plain navy one over her head. It was nowhere near as glamorous as the satiny one, and she sighed as she smoothed it over her stomach.

'Come on, Charlie.'

But I was too busy twirling in front of the mirror, thinking I looked like Rapunzel.

'Now, Charlie.'

And still I twirled.

'Charlie!'

She grabbed the end of the veil as it whipped past her and, of course, I know now that she just didn't anticipate how well she'd fixed it into my hair. It was an accident.

At the time, however, I felt a sharp tug on my hair, tripped over, and burst into tears on the floor. Mum froze, looking horrified. Then she let her end of the veil drop and scooped me off the floor.

I'm pretty sure she must have been late to the party. She freed me from the veil but still had it in her grip while she was doing up my coat and looking for my other shoe. She ducked into the living room and suddenly she didn't have it any more. I didn't really think about it after that.

Lowenna let me wave goodbye from the front door after I finally made it to her house. Mum turned around halfway down the path, and the make-up she'd tried so hard to do nicely was already running down her face.

I get into the habit of checking on Lowenna during the morning and stopping in again in the afternoon. We talk about everything and nothing, and I'm starting to wonder if a woman in her nineties might actually turn out to be my best friend. Or maybe second best, after Pauline.

'Hi, Charlie,' Adam says as we cross paths at her front door one day.

'Hi.'

He pulls me into a hug and it lasts a smidgen too long before Lowenna interrupts.

'Charlie Trewin, were you born in a barn?'

'You're in trouble,' Adam singsongs.

'Yeah, because you're *getting* me in trouble.'

'I can still feel a draft,' Lowenna calls. 'I'd hate to catch pneumonia after everything I've been through.'

After a day of clearing out the house we generally stop into the Bolster & Saint for a drink. Or three. James would be perfectly happy to just stay at the house and watch TV, but I don't really want to fall into that habit – I don't want to let TV carry our relationship because we can't make conversation. Just because it's been working for years doesn't mean we should do it forever.

The trick, I soon remember, is to talk about absolutely nothing. I went in *way* too heavy on his first night here. It was uncharted territory. Favourite foods, places we'd like to go one day, the weather. That is where I can relax. It's like one of those electrical games where if you touch the loop to the wire a buzzer goes off. If we stray too close to a big topic of conversation, we lose our easy flow and I start willing a hole to open up under my seat. We stray dangerously close to talking about children and future homes once, before I remember to derail the conversation with a joke.

We natter idly about everything and nothing, but mainly nothing, and then we head back home. We switch on the TV and watch whatever James is trying to keep up with. I'm sure he'd watch something I wanted to watch if I brought it up. Except I'm not actually sure at all, so I save face by not even asking. I claim to enjoy whatever he likes and we pass the rest of the night in peace.

He gives it a couple of days out of respect before he tries to get me to have sex. And I go along with it to a point because I don't want him to feel discouraged. I don't want him to think I'm rude. But all the positive thinking in the world won't change the fact that I don't feel ready for that just yet. Maybe I won't feel ready while we're under Dad's roof. It just feels so seedy.

So I lie in bed (still my childhood single) and let James do what he wants for a little while. He kisses me, squeezes my breasts. He does it too hard, but he's been doing that for years. I was too embarrassed to tell him he was hurting me on our first night together and now I'm too embarrassed to tell him about being too embarrassed to tell him, and now we're getting married, so I might as well get used to it forever.

After a little while I yawn performatively and he asks me if I'm tired. I confirm that I am, so he kisses me on the forehead, wraps himself around me, and we fall asleep. Well, he falls asleep. I lie awake, staring at the ceiling. I can tell he's really dropping off when he starts to twitch – his leg against mine here, a hand against my stomach there.

A week goes by in more or less the same vein and I could swear that James is actually starting to enjoy it. There are a couple of men he says hello to at the pub. He even goes for a swim in a pair of trunks Pauline finds in Dad's drawer while sorting through his clothes. I decided to leave that task to her because I very much doubt that Dad would like to think of me rifling through his Y-fronts. James lasts about five seconds in the sea and doesn't even get his shoulders under, but that's beside the point.

Pauline's around most days to help work through the piles of junk. Some days are slow going. We unearth things that make one or other or both of us cry, and we can't bring ourselves to throw anything away. Some days we have a phenomenal burst of progress and manage to unearth a whole new patch of floor or a bit of wall that hasn't seen the light of day for years. The carpet and the paintwork have faded in patches where Dad's stuff sat for God knows how long without being moved. The patchy colours make me unutterably sad if I think too much about them.

'There's some more of it over there,' Lowenna points. For some reason, today I thought it was a good idea to set her up in a folding chair while Pauline and I try to clear the garden. I figured it might be nice. The sun's out, it feels autumnal, she could be out in the fresh air. Lovely. That was before I discovered that she's some kind of gardening dictator.

'Not there!'

I freeze, my hand hovering over a plant. I'd love to be more specific, but I famously live in a flat in London. I don't even *see* gardens, let alone do actual gardening. I know fuck all about plants.

Is that stopping Lowenna from scolding me when I nearly pull up the wrong thing every five minutes? You would think. But apparently not.

'Don't you even know what mind-your-own-business looks like?'

'Is it a plant?'

Lowenna tuts and shakes her head. I bet people don't have to put up with this kind of treatment on *Gardeners' World*. I suppress a smile and take a breath of the air. I can smell salt and maybe a couple of the plants and/or weeds. There's dirt under my fingernails and a bead of sweat rolling down my back. I kind of love it?

'Can I help with anything?'

James appears in the doorway. He holds a tray laden with glasses and a jug of water. All very civilised. Pauline stands up and stretches her back. I reach towards a couple of stems in the flower bed, but Pauline catches my eye and ever so subtly shakes her head. I withdraw my hand.

'Actually, young man, now that you mention it, we want to move those stumps over to the wall.' Lowenna points at a couple of rotting chunks of wood in the overgrown grass towards the end of the garden.

'I could do that!' I chip in, and I don't even know why. If I see so much as a woodlouse on one of those stumps I will scream, drop it on my foot, and break my toe. But I selfishly don't want James to play with us.

'Well, now you don't have to, do you?' Lowenna says. 'We have a strapping man here to do it for us.'

James visibly puffs up upon being described as a strapping man. He scoops up the biggest stump like it's nothing, tossing it in the air ever so slightly to get a better grip. To show off, more like. He dumps the tree stump next to the wall and raises a cocky eyebrow at me as he walks back across the garden. And, like, what does he want? Am I supposed to be impressed? He walks to the next stump, picks it up like it's nothing, and puts it with the first one. And he does the same another five times, like he thinks he's in a Coke advert or something.

He heads back to us with dirt smeared down his T-shirt. He picks up a glass, fills it with water, and downs it. I am amazed he doesn't tip it over his head and toss his hair.

'Anything else?'

'Well, you could always help us with a bit of w—'

'No, thank you,' I cut across Pauline. 'We're fine.'

I give him a smile so that it doesn't seem like I'm being mean, even though that's exactly what I'm being.

'Oh. OK. Well, you know where I am if you need anything.'

He salutes – *salutes!* – and heads back to the house.

Lowenna and Pauline very slowly turn to look at me. I am determined to avoid their gaze, so I reach for something in the flower bed and tug it as hard as I can, trying to distract them with my ineptitude again. I feel the roots give way, and they're *still* looking at me. Maybe I guessed a weed right? First time for everything. But they're still staring.

'*What?*'

'That wasn't very nice,' Lowenna says simply. 'And that's a primrose. We want those.'

'It's a bit late now.'

'You could just go up there and apologise,' Pauline weighs in.

'No, I meant . . .' I hold up the bundle of leaves in my hand. I shrug and throw it on the weed heap anyway. 'I don't need to apologise.'

'I saw you rolling your eyes at him.' Pauline peers at me.

'He was making a meal of it!'

'He wanted to impress you. Is that the worst thing in the world?'

'No, it's not, it's just . . . It's annoying.'

Lowenna tuts.

'What?' I'm trying too hard to sound jovial and it comes out too high-pitched.

'If he's getting on your nerves that much when he's being perfectly nice and helpful, don't you think you ought to say something?'

'Look, he's not *annoying* me—'

'That's funny, because that was the exact word you used, but OK.'

'I'm just achy and mucky, you know? It's me.'

I'm keen for Lowenna to go back to shouting at me about plants now. Those were the days. I turn back to the flower bed.

'It's not just today, though, is it?' Now Pauline's joining in as well. It's like I'm the *only* one who cares about this garden.

'Sorry?'

'Well, I've seen you before. Just little looks, here and there. I don't think you're as subtle as you think you are.'

Ah.

'Listen, Charlie.' Pauline sits on the grass next to me. Her knees crack as she stretches her legs out in front of her. I stare resolutely at a worm making a break for it across the hole where one of the maybe-weeds once grew. 'I'm not trying to make you feel bad. But take it from a divorced person. It's best to deal with your problems head-on, or you might end up – well – a divorced person.'

'I didn't realise that was what happened.'

'Well, it wasn't *quite* the same. He was the one with the problem in my case. But if he'd just sat down and said to me, "Pauline, I'm not happy" . . . I mean, I still couldn't have magicked myself into being twenty years younger and nor would I have wanted to, but I would have been well out of there a lot sooner and I wouldn't have wasted so much time. I could have had five more years with your father, for all I know.'

'I don't want—'

'And I'm not saying you're in that much trouble, obviously, but it's better to talk things through.'

'She's right.' Lowenna shades her eyes with her hand and looks down at me. For a moment I feel like I'm in infant school, sitting at her feet. Except I'm definitely a sussed adult woman, with everything under control. We know this. It's fine.

'And, look. You didn't have a very good example when you grew up,' Lowenna continues. 'It's understandable if you feel like you have something stable and you don't want to rock the boat. But you know what? You can be better than your parents. If you have a problem with that boy, you march in there and you tell him. And then you can work on it.'

'But I don't have—'

'And if you don't have a problem with *him* but you have a different problem, you march in there and you tell him that. Or tell me that. Or tell Pauline that. Anyone, OK? You're allowed to admit when things aren't good.'

'OK?' I give her a look like she's the crazy one even though it sounds an awful lot like she's saying *I* am. Which is crazy in itself because I am fine.

'Promise me.' Her tone is threatening and suddenly I'm a teenager again.

'I promise.'

'Good. Now, Pauline, love? You get weeding that bed. Charlie, go and find the lawnmower, you can't be trusted.'

◆ ◆ ◆

One day, after work halts because we no longer have space to move, Pauline brings her tiny blue hatchback and we pack it full of black bag after black bag on journey after journey to the dump.

Sometime around mid-afternoon the nice men whose job it is to watch over everybody as they throw things away share their biscuits with us and offer us cups of tea. We pass twenty minutes like old friends. Well, Pauline does, and I am also there.

After that we settle into a routine of cleaning most of the day, and then trips to charity shops and the dump just before it closes. Over time, the house I remember from my childhood starts to emerge from the chaos. It's bittersweet – there's the wall where Mum used to measure my height every month, a column of little pencil dashes marking the passage of time until I started Big School. And there's the stain on the living room carpet where I accidentally kicked over a glass of red wine. Mum was 'having a hard time' that day and screamed at me. Only now do I realise it probably wasn't actually about me.

There's a sense of triumph at the visible improvements to the house.

'We're making headway. We'll be finished soon,' Pauline says one day as we clink our glasses across the bar of the Bolster. But our visible progress means that Dad is slowly ceasing to be such a prominent part of our lives. It's work that needs to be done, of course it is, but it does feel a little bit like we're erasing him. And, on a personal note, I don't know how much longer I can get away with keeping London, James, work, life generally, on hold.

One day I head out for a walk and when I get back home – wait, I mean 'to Dad's', obviously – Lowenna is standing in the front garden peering into the living room window.

'Are you OK?' I call, and she jumps.

'You should be careful, young lady, scaring an old woman like that' – she clutches her chest for effect – at least, I *hope* it's for effect – 'you'll give somebody a heart attack.'

'But, to be clear, you're not actually having one now, are you?'

'No. But you should be more careful. I came to see if you wanted to join me in a chippy tea,' she tells me. 'My treat, but you'll need to go and get it because I can't carry very much these days. You can invite that man of yours too.'

'Oh, Lowenna, that's really kind, but . . .'

She totters over to me and grabs my wrist. The intensity in her eyes scares me a bit.

'Please say yes. You have no idea how long it's been since I had a battered sausage.'

'It's a date, then.'

CHAPTER FIFTEEN

'Well, you don't have to come, do you?' I hiss at James as we sit on the bench in the chip shop, waiting for our order. Miracle of miracles, they do a vegan option. I had expected to have an argument. 'Take yours home, she won't mind.'

'No, but I—'

'So come, then!' I'm losing patience. 'Do what you want.'

'You going to Lowenna's, by any chance?' Jason asks, distracting us from our bickering as he shovels chips into three paper bags.

'How'd you know?'

'She's the only person I've ever met who can live in a fine Cornish fishing village and still go for a sausage every time.' He tuts.

Still, he chucks in a pot of mushy peas for free, so he can't be too offended.

I tell Lowenna what he said as I divvy up the food. We've overdone it. There's at least the same amount of chips again still sitting on the kitchen counter wrapped in vinegar-flecked paper.

'Oh, what does Jason Cardew know, anyway?' Lowenna scoffs. 'I'm not about to start eating slimy alien *things* just because they happen to live near me. By that logic I should be eating *you* for dinner. And anyway, if he doesn't want my money he doesn't have to sell battered sausages now, do 'e?'

Lowenna's house hasn't changed a bit. In the living room, shelves on either side of the fireplace are dotted with ornaments of men fishing, woodland animals, and a collection of those roosters you apparently get everywhere when you go to Portugal. One shelf is filled with photos in mismatched frames. There are distant nephews on their wedding days, photos of various babies, and several charting Adam's development over the years. I try not to look too hard. Which is easy because I don't *want* to look anyway. One of the frames is smaller than the others, plain silver, and it holds a photo of my mum and dad.

'That's from before you were born.' Lowenna sat with me on the rug in front of the fire and handed the frame to me.

'Why's their hair funny?'

'It was all the rage. You should have seen the perm on me back then.'

I stared at the photo. It only showed Mum and Dad's faces mashed together. They were both grinning, eyes screwed up against the sun behind the camera. Mum's hair was being blown across Dad's face. I touched Mum's face and bit my lip.

'Charlie, look at me.' Lowenna laid a hand over mine. 'Your mum's having a hard time at the moment, but she's going to be OK. OK?'

I shrugged.

'You know your dad's going to look after her, right?'

'Right.'

I looked down at the photo again.

'And I'll be better too.'

'You don't need *to be better, you sausage. It's not your fault. And you don't need to worry, either. That's all. Shall we put the telly on?'*

We eat our chippy tea in companionable silence as *The One Show* wraps up and makes way for *EastEnders*. I forgot how good chips could be. So often now I end up with the thin, floppy burger-chain fries – too salty and gone too quickly. But these are pillowy inside with just a little crunch the first time you take a bite. Lowenna's detested fish is crispy in a way that I'd forgotten fish could even be – on the rare occasion I've had fish and chips in London it's always gone a bit soggy by the time I get it home.

I suddenly become aware that Lowenna has been talking while I've been gazing lovingly at my plate. James is looking at me for help. He doesn't seem to realise he can talk to her without my support.

'Sorry?'

'I *said*, do you want to come to the quiz at the Bolster & Saint tomorrow night?'

'Oh, Lowenna. I don't know. I'm not really sure if I feel up to it, you know?'

'I will accept that answer, young lady, if you can promise me that you're genuinely going to spend the time sitting at home and weeping over your dear departed father.'

I blush – although that could be something to do with the large amount of potato I've just eaten and the carb sweats I can feel coming on. I chase a stubborn scrap of batter around my chip paper with my little wooden fork and avoid eye contact as if I were a teenager half my actual, adult age. Sensing a vulnerable moment, and possibly one where he can score a few points with Lowenna, James slips his hand into mine and caresses my knuckles. His fingers are greasy, and I pull my hand away and wipe it on my jeans.

'A quiz night does sound fun,' he says.

'Oh. Yeah, you can come too,' Lowenna replies. 'The more the merrier.'

She turns her attention back to the TV for a while. I get up and start collecting the fish and chip detritus. I walk past James on the way out of the room and he makes a desperate grab for my hand, flashing me panicked eyes.

'Do you need a hand?' he asks.

'No, all under control,' I trill back. I get a sick kind of pleasure from thinking of him squirming in front of *EastEnders*, trying to decide what to say next, or whether he should say anything at all.

I take the pile of chip papers to the kitchen and 'do the washing-up'. I basically snaffle half of the leftover chips, then screw up the wrappings into a big ball and throw it into the recycling.

'And then I got down on one knee and she said yes,' James is telling Lowenna as I return.

'What's this?'

'Oh, Lowenna was just asking how I proposed to you.'

'Was she, indeed?' I eye her suspiciously and she looks back like butter wouldn't melt. But Lowenna is not a romantic woman so she's definitely up to something.

'At work,' she says, her tone cynical. 'In front of a ton of people.'

'Yes, I remember.' I try to keep my voice neutral.

'I wanted Charlie to be surrounded by people she knew when it happened,' James smiles. He hasn't picked up on Lowenna's sarcasm. He was never very good at reading a room. 'But then, well, I couldn't really think who Charlie's friends were so I figured, she spends the most time at the office, we'll plump for that.'

I feel my face colouring, and this time it's not the chip sweats. I always try to brush off the fact that I don't have many (fine, any) friends, but it's tough to avoid when someone says it out loud. Lowenna frowns at me.

'Well, it's a very interesting story, James, thank you for sharing. I've learned a lot.'

There's something in her tone that makes me think this conversation might not be over, but I'm probably being paranoid. No, I'm definitely being paranoid. I hope I'm being paranoid.

'Have you two thought much about the wedding?' she asks innocently as we all stare at the TV.

'Not—'

'Well, we'll probably do it quite soon after we get back up to London,' James announces, which is news to me.

'*Will* we?'

'I thought so, yeah. All of this just makes you think, doesn't it? How precious life is, y'know?'

'Sure.' My voice is strained. Strained with excitement, though. I'm happy. Happy, happy, happy. I mean, yes, I have a headache and a shooting pain in my sternum all of a sudden, but that is because of all the fried food.

'Sounds like a plan, young man.' Lowenna nods, and I can't figure out what she's thinking. 'I don't know why these people think we'd want to watch them watching TV,' she continues, shaking her head as she changes the channel. 'Look at the state of this wazzock – what's he done to his living room?'

I'm still getting to grips with a Carncarrow that has all the mod cons, so I'm surprised when Pauline asks if I want to get a manicure the morning after the Grand Chippy Tea with Lowenna. I'm also a little bit worried they might find flakes of cod still under my nails.

'Where?'

'Just at the place on the high street?'

'There's a place on the high street?'

'I mean, yeah. There has been for years.'

'Oh.'

'You really have to get rid of the notion that this is some hinterland with nothing to do, Charlie.'

As the manicurists get to work, I remember that I bloody hate manicures. I sit and do as I'm told, trying desperately to think how to fill the silence. But then, do I need to? It kind of feels like I do. But I don't know what to say. Luckily, Pauline does a lot of the heavy lifting, chatting about how she's coping without Dad. She even gets everybody at the salon opening up about their feelings. I suppose it would be quite liberating if it wasn't for the fact that it's absolutely mortifying. I feel like I should be saying this kind of stuff as well, but I have nothing to add. Which I know can't be healthy. Maybe Mum was the same and that's why she ended up . . . Well.

'You're all done,' my manicurist tells me. My nails look great. I look forward to forgetting that they're still tacky in fifteen minutes and ruining them. I've gone for a bright red which, I only now realise, I felt drawn to because it's basically the same colour Mum used to wear.

She always used to tap her nails against her coffee cup while I ate breakfast. They were long, and red, and I thought they were very glamorous indeed, which they were in comparison to my bitten nails, or Dad's, which were often caked with mud from the garden.

One morning she chewed one as she stood leaning against the kitchen counter. I dug around in a very unappetising bowl of soggy Weetabix, hoping to find something I might actually want to put in my mouth. Her eyes were red, and the kitchen was silent, apart from the clink of my spoon against the bowl.

'Have you been crying?'

I broke the silence, because once upon a time I did things like that. It was mainly a diversionary tactic to get out of eating my bowl of mush. Mum took a gulp of coffee, throwing it back like you might down a shot.

'No, Charlie.'

'Why have you been crying?'

'I haven't. Eat your breakfast.'

'I'm not hungry. And you have been crying. Grown-ups don't cry.'

She dropped into the seat next to me. I was right. She had definitely been crying. I took a triumphant mouthful of Weetabix (top marks for empathy) and then spat it straight back into the bowl (top marks for table manners).

'Where did you get that from?'

'What from?'

'That grown-ups don't cry.'

'Dunno.'

She reached over and placed a hand on my arm. The nail she'd been chewing was far more ragged than the others, the cuticle red and sore.

'Charlie, I don't know how to break this to you. Grown-ups cry. Everybody cries.'

'Even Dad?'

'Even Dad. It's healthy. It doesn't feel *healthy,' she sighed. 'But they say it's healthy.'*

'I don't think I want to be healthy, if there's crying.'

'Honestly? Me neither.' She tapped the side of her nose, then she smiled, and it felt like the room got a little bit brighter. She scooped me onto her lap and pulled my bowl of – frankly, by this point, wheat soup – in front of her. She pushed it around with the spoon.

'Do you know what? You're right. Being healthy is awful. Shall we go to the beach and get an ice cream for breakfast?'

'Yes!'

'Alright, go and put your shoes on. I'll see if Dad wants to come.'

I destroy one of my lovely new nails as I take my shoes off in the hallway when I get home. You can really see the difference we're making when you go away and come back with fresh eyes. Pauline's decided that we should extend our break into a full day and I'm inclined to agree with her. So I have some free time.

There's much more space to walk down the hall as I go to the kitchen and flick on the kettle. The kitchen has a ton more room. We spent a day working through the dates on all of the packets. Anything in date went to Pauline's friend who volunteers at the food bank. Anything out of date went to the dump. The food bank did not benefit hugely, and for the millionth time I tried to imagine what Dad thought he was gaining by hanging on to this stuff. But it just ended up breaking my heart all over again. I had to accept that it was going on the list of Things I'll Never Get To Ask.

I can hear James in the living room, strolling around, talking to someone. He's incapable of sitting still when he's on the phone. I should probably offer him a tea too, I suppose.

'Oh God, look, I don't know.'

He sounds so agitated as I reach the door that I don't want to go in. I also shouldn't be listening on the other side, but it's too late now. I run a finger over the ruined nail polish on my thumb, trying to push the creases flat again.

'It's just a process, isn't it?' he continues. 'It's a pain in the arse, and I want to ask, but I think it's one of those things where you sort of just have to see how it all shakes out.'

I'm intrigued. Maybe he's pitched some new idea and he's waiting to hear back. We don't really discuss the minutiae of our work. Or at least, I don't like to talk about mine so I don't ask about his, and that's the pattern we've fallen into. Another topic of conversation off limits.

'It had better be soon, though, I can tell you that much. I can't take much more time in this fucking backwater. Are you all out tonight?'

I feel the 'backwater' comment as if it were an actual slap in the face. I push the door open slowly. James spots me standing there. I can hear whoever he's talking to laughing down the phone.

'Yeah, mate, I have to go.'

We stand on either side of the open door, just looking at each other. He eyes me warily, waiting to see how I'm going to react. And, actually, so am I.

'Nobody's *making* you be here, you know?' is all I say in the end. I stalk back up the hall to make my tea. I'm no longer doing a round. He follows me into the kitchen. I flick the kettle back on and slam the teabag jar on the side.

'That's not true,' he shoots back. 'You're making me.'

'Oh, OK. That's easy, then, you can go.'

I push past him to get the milk out of the fridge. He slams the door shut as I try to open it and grabs my wrist.

'You don't get to just shrug me off like that, OK? I love you. I'm not going to leave you alone at a time like this.'

I shake him off and retrieve the milk.

'I don't need you here,' I reply sullenly.

'Do you think I'm fucking stupid? I know you don't *need* me here, Charlie. But I still *want* you. I want to be *with* you.' I pull a mug from the cupboard. James takes it away. 'Would you pay attention when I'm talking to you, please? This is serious. Because, honestly, I wonder if I'd even see you again if I left now. Apparently you make a habit of cutting people out of your life when it's convenient to you. I never put two and two together before now, but you're flaky, Charlie.'

'What?'

'You're a fucking flake. You flake on people. You flaked on your dad, and you flaked on this place, and then you flaked on me to come *back* to this place. You've flaked on your job, you've flaked on our life. You're a massive fucking flake.'

He clenches his mouth shut and looks at me, suddenly wary. Very slowly, he hands me back the mug he stole. I turn it over in my hands a couple of times, and then I throw it at the wall behind him. It explodes in a shower of bright-yellow ceramic.

'Jesus Christ.' He shakes his head at me and then storms out of the room.

The front door slams.

CHAPTER SIXTEEN

'So, I think tomorrow you can start checking through those policy documents, and then maybe start collating figures for the update meeting,
OK?'

I tried to avoid leaving work at the same time as Magdalena,
because she always did this to me. Who gives their employees a to-do
list when they're in a lift and have nowhere to write anything down?

'Sure thing,' I said, trying to keep it non-committal so she wouldn't
be surprised when I forgot tomorrow.

The lift pinged and the doors slid open. I stepped out and then
paused to scrabble around in my bag for my lanyard. I heard the first
chords of a song. For a second I was worried my music was playing
through my headphones in my handbag, but no. It was 'All You Need
Is Love', which was much more James's style than mine. He was the
secret Love Actually fan.

So maybe it shouldn't have come as a surprise that, when I finally
unravelled my lanyard from everything else in my bag and looked up,
I saw James standing on the other side of the barriers holding a tiny
Bluetooth speaker aloft.

'What are you playing at?' I hissed as I darted through the barrier
and grabbed his arm, hoping he'd make it all stop. It was home time
for everybody, and all of my colleagues should have been pouring across
the atrium, but James was in the middle, causing a scene. Basically

everybody had stopped in their tracks, foot traffic backing up all the way to the lifts. Magdalena looked bemused, but maybe not surprised? She and James had hit it off at the Christmas party so they were all pally. He might even have got her blessing for whatever the hell this was.

He turned the music up as loud as it would go and I suddenly realised, with a jolt, what was probably happening. But surely not here? And surely not now?

'Charlie.' He had to yell over the song.

'Shall we go somewhere else?' I shouted as well. My face burned and I felt the eyes of every one of my colleagues on me.

'No, Charlie. We're doing this here.'

'I'd really rather go somewhere else.'

'Charlie.'

He turned the music off, and you could suddenly hear a pin drop. There was the odd rustle as somebody shifted a bag from one shoulder to the other but, aside from that, everybody waited in silent expectation.

'Charlie, I love you. I couldn't believe my luck when you said you'd go out with me. You're funny, you're sarcastic, and you're basically the complete opposite of me. But in a good way. The yin to my yang. We complement each other. I'm loud, you're quiet. I'm romantic, you're hating every minute of this' – I did want to ask why he was doing it if he knew I was going to hate it but I reminded myself to be nice. Be nice, be nice, be nice – 'You play things close to the vest, I like to think I bring you out of your shell. I want to settle down, start a family, all of that stuff. And I think you want that too. So . . .' He shuffled from foot to foot for a moment, looking around. Then, after a pause, he held the speaker out to me and nodded to indicate that I should take it. I did. He got down on one knee, and a ripple of whispers moved through the people gathered behind us. 'Charlie Trewin, will you marry me?'

There was a collective intake of breath around the atrium. My stomach did a funny thing that felt like when you're at the top of a rollercoaster and you leave it hanging in mid-air. But, I reasoned, that *was probably what butterflies in your stomach felt like. That was what happy felt like. I just wasn't very familiar with it. But it was fine, and I was happy. I was happy, happy, happy. This was good. A Very Good Thing.*

I nodded, unable to find the words. James jumped up and kissed me, and everybody around us burst into applause.

OK, 'burst' is strong. Nobody really knew me that well, but people gave us a polite clap, and a couple of them said 'Congratulations' as they left for the night. As they left to meet their friends and tell them about the insane spectacle they'd just witnessed, probably.

James pulled me into a hug and then tried to kiss me again, which was where I drew the line. We had to get out of there. I handed the speaker back to him so he wouldn't feel like I was actively trying to push him away. He put it back in his bag and threw an arm around my shoulders to steer me outside.

'Congratulations, Charlie!' Magdalena called as we headed for the exit. I gave her a thumbs-up and kept telling myself how excited I was.

I end up letting the kitchen get dark around me as I sit at the table, paralysed. I remember Mum sitting here like this sometimes, in rooms that got dark around her. But this is not the same. It's not, it's not, it's not. The kettle I boiled twice cools completely, water still unused. When I'm finally roused, it's by the front door opening again.

'James?'

'Not this time, dearie,' Lowenna cackles. 'Bloody Norah, you've made some good progress in here! Are you about ready to go?'

She appears in the doorway of the kitchen and I frown. What does she—

'To the quiz?'

'Oh, shit, yeah.'

'Less of that, thank you. It's alright when you're my age, but people still pay attention to you.'

'Sorry.'

I don't get up, and Lowenna taps a foot impatiently.

'Are you coming, or are you going to let a very old lady in poor health stand around waiting all day?'

'Sorry' – I pull out a chair for her – 'I don't think I'm in the mood.'

She snaps on the light before she sits down. She is dressed To. The. Nines.

'What have you done? Where's James, if he's coming?'

'Why would I have done anything?'

'*Did* you do something?'

'No, actually. We just had an argument.'

'I'm sorry to hear that.'

'Thanks.'

'So, are we off, then, or what?'

'Lowenna!'

'Look, you did promise and I *have* been ill, and you wouldn't want the last thing I ever feel to be disappointment, would you?'

'Fine.'

People look up from their pints and peanuts as Lowenna and I enter. Lowenna gives the whole room a triumphant wave like she's just returned from war.

'Are you finished?'

'What? This is my comeback tour. I *did* nearly die on this floor not that long ago.'

'But—'

'Just let me have my moment.'

I usher her over to a seat and head to the bar.

'Alright, Charlie?'

Loic Bennetto greets me with a smile. I didn't get the chance to see him much at the wake, between one drama and another. Time has added to the wrinkles around his eyes and his hair has gone totally white, but aside from that he hasn't changed at all. Literally. I think he might be wearing the same shirt he always used to.

'The usual?' he asks.

'I think my usual's probably changed since the last time you served me, actually,' I smile.

'What you on about? You was just here on . . .'

I watch the cogs turn as he performs goodness knows what feats of mental arithmetic. He moves a finger through the air as if he's writing out equations.

'Bloody hell,' he eventually breathes. 'So no pineapple juice and lemonade, then?'

'No, thank you. A cider top, and a G&T with extra G please.'

'Coming right up, young 'un.'

Behind me, Lowenna holds court where I left her, directly under one of the lights which dot the walls. It looks like a halo. People approach her and she smiles beatifically at them.

I thank Loic and turn around to run the drinks back to the table.

'Watch it!'

Adam is suddenly about three inches from my face and I think I'm going to topple over. Half of the G from my G&T slops over the flagstones. He deftly grabs hold of both glasses to prevent any further disasters. His hands are warm over my own. I let go and stagger sideways.

'What are you standing right behind people for?' I demand.

'I was going to the *loo*, if you must know. But thanks for the drink.'

He pretends to take a sip.

'Adam Murphy, that had better not be my drink you're holding,' Lowenna calls from her corner. I think I see him go a tiny bit paler.

'She's your *grandma*,' I whisper, arching an eyebrow.

'Doesn't mean she's not scary.'

I leave Adam holding my drink and run Lowenna's over to her to avoid any further incidents. She pats me gently on the arm.

When I return to the bar Adam is getting Loic to top my glass back up.

'It's on me,' he says, when he sees me looking.

'I suppose it's the least you can do considering it is *literally* on me,' I show him my splattered shoes. He feigns fear.

'You're a big scary Londoner now as well, you'll probably sue me or something.'

'Bloody right I will.'

'Oh hi, *Adam*.' Mae, of florist fame, sidles up to us and winks at me. 'Fancy seeing you two together!'

'Hello, Mae, how's things?' Adam asks with a weary smile.

Someone laughs somewhere behind me and I whip my head around because it sounds so much like James. We've never argued before and – I don't know. I thought the whole point of getting engaged was so that someone couldn't just disappear on you. Which, to be fair, wasn't true for Mum and Dad either. I just thought . . . But everybody has their line, right? What if I blew it? But no, stop thinking about James right now. Stop it, stop it, stop it. If Lowenna thinks I'm moping there'll be hell to pay.

I force my attention back to the here and now, and realise I don't know what's happening any more. What I *do* know is that Mae is looking at me expectantly and Adam is looking at me with a raised eyebrow, which I *think* is supposed to mean something, but I don't know what.

'Sorry, I didn't catch that.'

'I *said*, are you two on a date? You know, for old times' sake? Your boyfriend is refusing to confirm or deny. And I won't judge you, obviously. Grief is a spectrum, as I'm sure you've discovered lately.'

'Mae, you do know she had already discovered that before—'

'Yes, thank you!' I interject, desperate to get us off the 'dead parents' path. 'No, obviously not a date, just a chance meeting. Old friends. Catching up. Etcetera, etcetera. Anyway, you've met my fiancé.'

I flash my ring at her as a reminder and I could swear a cloud passes over Adam's face, but it's gone before I can tell if I even really saw it.

'OK, ladies and gentlemen, please take your seats, the first round of BolsterMind is about to start!' Pauline saves us any more awkwardness.

I'm really impressed with BolsterMind. Is the punny title a little bit dodgy? Sure. And admittedly the only pub quizzes I've been to before have been when I was needed to make up the numbers, rather than really get involved, but still. The atmosphere is great, the in-jokes fly, and my cheeks hurt from smiling, except for in the moments when I remember that Dad should be here too.

I go outside during a break because my face feels hot, and it's pretty much just me and the village. It's breezy, and I turn my face into it, letting it cool my cheeks. I can hear the sea but I can't really see it, despite it being so close. I cross the road, and with the lights from the pub behind me I can make out the boats, and the moon's rippled reflection. I can smell salt, and the seaweed dried to the walls. I don't want to get too close to the edge for fear of falling in, since I can't totally make out where granite gives way to water. So I turn back to face the pub. There are lights in the neighbouring shopfronts and a group of women laugh together a few doors down.

They're illuminated by a string of lights marking out the edge of a seating area. Their table is littered with empty plates and half-full glasses of wine. The sound of their laughter disrupts the peace, but it's kind of nice. I wonder what that must feel like. I wonder if—

'Charlie.' Adam materialises at my side.

'Sorry, I'll be right there.'

'I should hope so too. London landmarks up next – you're our golden goose.'

I smile, but I guess I'm not that convincing.

'Everything OK?'

I shake my head, banishing everything apart from being here now, in the nice breeze, with the sound of the sea, and Adam next to me.

Or . . . no. Just the 'here, now, breeze, sea' bit. End of sentence.

'Yep, I'm right behind you.'

In the end we don't quite manage to scoop the win, but we do finish as runners-up. The round that scoops it for us is 'Cheeses of the South-West'. I'm so glad I never let James persuade me to go dairy-free because I smashed it. We receive an extremely dusty bottle of Bristol Cream sherry as a prize. Lowenna's eyes light up and Adam and I are more than happy for her to take our share too.

As we walk home after another cider top and G&T&G, Lowenna and I are silent. Or rather, I'm silent and she can't stop yawning. She told anybody who would listen from about eight thirty onwards that it was past her bedtime, so at least she was telling the truth.

'Goodnight,' she yawns as I drop her at her front door and shine the torch on my phone to help her see the lock. 'I'm glad you decided to come.'

'Me too,' I smile. And I think I mean it.

◆ ◆ ◆

I sneak upstairs when I get inside and find James already fast asleep in my room. There's no space to get into bed too because he's spread-eagled across it. He shifts in his sleep and gives a little snort. I leave the room and close the door silently behind me. I creep back downstairs and into the living room, where I lie down on the sofa.

Even though the curtains are as flimsy as anything and no contest for the moonlight outside, I start to feel drowsy as soon as I rest my head on a cushion. I'm not sure if it's Loic's insane measures of gin, or the luxury of not having an arm draped over me for the first time in over a week, but I nod off almost immediately.

CHAPTER SEVENTEEN

When I wake up the next morning it sounds like a pile of junk is toppling down the stairs, except they've mostly been cleared at this point so it can't be. Running feet head down the hallway, and then turn into more of a slapping sound on the tiles in the kitchen. Then they become ordinary running feet again. The living room door flies open and James's dishevelled head appears over the back of the sofa. I sit up and rub my eyes.

'Oh my God, you're here, thank fuck for that.' James clings to the terracotta velvet of the sofa for support.

'Well, I couldn't exactly get in with you last night, you didn't leave me any room.'

And, honestly, thank goodness for that because I slept *fantastically*.

We regard each other awkwardly for a minute. I wonder which way this is going to go. We don't usually make it to a full-on fight, managing instead to spend hour upon hour in each other's company feeling totally on edge and not sure how to change the atmosphere. I wonder if things will be better or worse considering the yelling, and the storming out, and the – oh God – mug-throwing. I close my eyes as the memory comes back properly.

'Coffee?' James's question brings me back to the present.

'Um, yeah. Please. Thanks.'

He disappears to the kitchen, and I follow him, keen to establish how we're going to be behaving towards each other today. Are we still going to be arsey, or are we going to pretend all is forgiven? I'll follow James's lead because I'll do basically anything for an easy life.

'So, are we . . . alright?' I ask.

James puts the jar of coffee down on the worktop, takes a breath, and then sighs.

'Yes. We're OK. I'm sorry I said what I said. About this place. And about you.'

He continues to make drinks and I sit down at the table. I feel . . . Is that *disappointment?*

For one brief, shining moment, I think I thought maybe he'd end things with me. I already know that I could never do it if the roles were reversed. I'm in too deep to give up now. Although we could both probably do better. James could go off with some driven career woman he finds mentally stimulating, and I'd . . . I don't even know what I'd do. I suppose I'd mainly have to figure out how to get by on my own in a city that basically demands you join forces with others to survive. I'd have to get very rich, very fast. Or at least get better at talking to strangers. The former is probably more likely.

James places a mug in front of me and snaps me out of it.

'What are you smiling about?'

'Oh, nothing, I was . . . Yeah. Nothing.'

'Was Adam there last night? I assume you went to the quiz without me.'

I open my mouth but I'm pulled up short.

'Did you *want* to go?'

'Well, it would have been nice to meet your friends.'

'But you were so . . . Never mind. I'm sorry. But you *had* disappeared.'

'And you never tried to find me.'

'I thought you might want to be left alone.'

We look at each other and both take a slow sip of coffee. My stomach feels weird. I can't read James's mood any more.

'You *did* storm out,' I reiterate, just so we're definitely clear who's in the wrong here.

He's silent for a minute. Considering my words, maybe?

'I'm so sorry' – there are tears in his eyes – 'I never want to argue like that again.'

'It's fine, it's—'

'It's *not* fine.' He starts properly sobbing. Which is absolutely his prerogative as a man who is in touch with his emotions. But, I admit, I do have a *little* cringe, even as I support his right to shrug off the shackles of toxic masculinity and express his feelings. 'I should never have been talking about you behind your back and I certainly shouldn't have used a very traumatic part of your life against you. Can you forgive me?'

He throws himself off his chair, onto the floor, and puts his head in my actual lap. I want to recoil, but I can't imagine he'd take that very well, so I just place a hand on his hair as lightly as I can get away with. Because I am *fucking* uncomfortable.

'Well, can you?' He looks up at me from my lap, his eyes red. This would be the window for me to open up. I should tell him about how my heart leapt when I briefly wondered if we'd break up. I should tell him how uncomfortable he's making me. I should tell him I'm not sure if I ever want to see London again.

Oh wow, that one came out of nowhere.

Anyway, we've all met me, so we know I don't tell him any of that.

'Yes,' I tell him. And he pulls me to my feet and kisses me as my heart sinks.

◆ ◆ ◆

James shuts himself in the living room and starts work for the day, and I wander around the house trying to settle on a task. There's a lot to be getting on with but, I don't know, I just feel restless. Like, what if that was my chance and I blew it? I keep replaying our fight in my head, and the conversation this morning, and thinking about all the wasted opportunities I missed to tell him I wish it was over. I'm such a coward.

Except I'm *not*. I'm just committed to making this work. That's all it is. I've made my decision, and I am *not* trapped, I'm just doing the thing that makes sense. I'm fine, I'm fine, I'm fine.

Pauline sends me a text and stops me from spiralling further than normal.

Fancy a swim?

The weather's turned overnight. The warm sunshine and dazzling turquoise water have been replaced by steely sky and a mercurial sea. A breeze blows a wisp of hair into my eye, and I shiver a little bit. I don't feel like I'm on a nice summer holiday any more. This suddenly seems like a ridiculous idea. There are still a few people sitting on the cafe terrace, but they're bundled up in borrowed blankets, cagoules hanging on the backs of several chairs. The horizon is blurred by distant rain that will, no doubt, be making its way here very shortly. A couple of passing ships far out to sea look like they've been partially erased by the downpour in the distance. A group of paddleboarders bob much closer to shore, but nobody's mad enough to submerge themselves. Until now.

Pauline jumps straight into the water when we're ready to go. She looks pale and sad today, and I feel guilty. I'm not the only one working through stuff, and I haven't asked her how she's been doing. Whenever she's come over in the past couple of days, we've just got straight to work without a lot of chatter. I've started building my walls again.

I'm feeling a little more reticent than Pauline when it comes to getting in the water. I mean, I cannot emphasise enough that it is *grey*. It's going to be chilly. I cross my arms over my chest as if that's going to offer me any protection at all, and watch Pauline, who got straight in and has already managed a good few strokes of breaststroke.

'You can do it,' someone whispers, and there's suddenly a hand on the small of my back.

I thrust my elbow back as hard as I can without even thinking about it. It makes contact with soft flesh and Adam falls into the sand with a grunt.

'Oh shit, sorry!'

I crouch behind him as he coughs, scattering a couple of twigs of dry seaweed with each staccato exhalation. Pauline climbs out of the sea just behind where he writhes on the sand in pain. I assume she's going to come over to help, but she actually gives us a wide berth, tiptoeing in an exaggerated circle up the beach. I look at her, signalling for backup with my eyes, but she just winks at me. She gathers up her clothes and leaves the beach without so much as a glance back. I still feel guilty that we haven't been able to talk, but now I also curse her.

Adam doesn't seem to be in as much pain any more so I think it's safe to assume I haven't ruptured anything. So I sit down next to him, feeling the chilly dampness of the sand soaking into the bottom of my swimming costume.

'Where the hell did that come from?' Adam groans. It's kind of muffled because he has his face in the sand.

'Krav Maga, sorry.'

'Since when do you know Krav Maga?'

'I don't. Not really. Or not much. One of the interns at work got beaten up outside a pub once, so they put on a couple of classes.'

'Well, it's pretty effective.'

'Thanks, that's the only move I remember.'

'You'll get by,' Adam wheezes, shifting to an upright position.

We sit side by side on the sand in silence for a couple of minutes. I stare out at the drizzle on the horizon. Watery sunlight tries desperately to break through but I don't think it's going to succeed today. The clouds are marbled with light. Beside me, Adam draws little patterns with a piece of dried-out seaweed. I try to focus on the here and now and let go of the knot of tension in my chest from my talk with James.

'So, we swimming, then, or what?' Adam eventually asks.

I stretch out my legs so that the very tips of my toes make contact with the tiniest ripples at the water's edge. It's probably no colder than it is on any other day, but the absence of sunshine and blue sky, and the addition of a stiff breeze, makes it suddenly seem a whole lot worse.

'No, thanks.'

'Go on.' Adam nudges me. 'You'll feel better if you do it.'

I groan, but then stand up and wade in up to my knees before I can change my mind. Jesus Christ, it's even worse than I thought. Back on the beach, Adam strips down to his trunks and then gets in next to me.

I take a few more steps until I'm up to my stomach, and Adam walks beside me. I take a sharp breath in as a wave pushes the cold water further up my midriff. Adam is fronting it out, pretending to be tough, but there's a tension in his shoulders that tells me he's holding his breath, and he's coming out in goosebumps on his chest.

Emboldened by the knowledge that he's not actually superhuman either, I pinch my nose and duck under the surface. The water hurts my shoulders, but after a couple of seconds the sensation ebbs away. But then my head starts to ache and it gets stronger, and stronger, and stronger, until I can't take it any more. I burst upwards and break the surface with a grimace. The headache subsides a couple of seconds after I come up for air.

Adam regards me from where he still stands waist-deep in the water. Then he dives with surprising grace and materialises at my side.

He splashes me and I shriek, even though I'm already in. Look, it's cold, alright?

'I thought you were Cornwall born and bred! As if you can't handle being in the sea.'

'Hey!' I splash him back.

He floats on his back next to me, and I copy him. The sky swims above me as the headache takes hold again, and I briefly lose the ability to see. But then it starts to abate. The image of the clouds above me sharpens and I can think straight.

'Speaking of things that make you uncomfortable.' Adam's voice drifts back to me from wherever he's floating. I put my feet down to look at him. 'Do you fancy coming out tonight? I was talking to Mae after you left the quiz' – is that a flicker of *jealousy*? I mean, stop that *immediately*, Charlie. 'Since you're back, we thought we should do a proper little reunion. Get some people from school together, go out, like we used to.'

'But I never used to do that.'

'So you'll get the chance to give it a go, won't you? It'll probably be better now because I don't think they make Bacardi Breezers any more.'

I lie on my back again, trusting the water to support my weight, hoping that if I don't mention the idea any further he might just drop it. I don't have anything against the people I went to school with, particularly. I just have a lot against making small talk with people I don't really know, and also crowded, loud places. On the other hand, I can't imagine anywhere in off-season Carncarrow is going to be packed to the rafters. Still, I feel nervous at the idea of a night out. I don't know what to do on one. Plus, it doesn't feel right so soon after Dad. I should still be wearing black and gnashing my teeth. But then again, haven't I done enough of that already? It might give me something else to—

My runaway train of thought is interrupted by a tug on my foot which pulls me forward through the water. My feet bump into Adam's shoulders, and I stand up to face him.

'Hey. Just come, OK? This might surprise you, but it's not actually something you need to overthink.'

I nod, if only because the sudden proximity of Adam means I can't quite think straight.

CHAPTER EIGHTEEN

When Pauline lets herself into the house later, I give her a piece of my mind before I even see her.

'I can't believe you did that!'

'Bloody hell, Charlie, can I at least shut the door?'

'Do you want a tea?' I snap, because I'm indignant but I'm not a monster.

'Go on, then.'

I hear her kicking off her shoes as I click the kettle on and fish two teabags out of the jar.

'OK, carry on.' She appears in the doorway and sits down at the now-quite-clear table. 'You were saying?'

'I can't believe you just left me there with him like that.' I try not to spill tea on the floor as I carry both mugs to the table. 'I needed backup.'

'Funny, I thought you were getting on just fine on your own.' She smiles, blowing across the top of her mug.

I narrow my eyes. 'Well, I . . .'

Honestly, if I could think of a single answer in this moment I would never wish for anything ever again. My face is getting hot, and I kind of want to roll my sleeves up, but I don't want Pauline to know I've gone all flustered. For no actual reason, by the way. She's just making it weird.

'To tell you the truth, Charlie, I think he's good for you. You're different around him.' She glances back down the hallway. 'Is James here?'

I shake my head.

'He went to the shop.'

'Right, well, in that case, OK. There's nothing *wrong* with James. But with Adam you seem lighter. You smile.'

'I don't—'

'Listen, I'm not sorry. I think it's nice. You deserve to be happy. Actually happy.'

'I am!' It comes out very high-pitched, which isn't ideal, but I can't help it if that's my voice.

Pauline raises an eyebrow. 'Charlie, come on.'

'I mean, Dad found someone who made him happy and it still all got taken away from him, didn't it? And he made *you* happy, and then what happened?'

'That is *not* the right way to look at—'

'I'm going to make a start on the cupboard under the stairs.'

My chair scrapes against the tiles on the floor as I push it back, and I leave her sitting in the kitchen.

'What do you think this is?' Pauline pulls a red metal box out from under the stairs later. It has a combination lock. We're both sitting on the carpet next to the open cupboard, surrounded by piles but with no actual plan of action.

'Dunno, I guess we won't find out, though,' I say, like a quitter.

Pauline tries to open the lid and proves my point immediately. She tries again, and then stands up with a sigh.

'But if it's locked, don't you think it must mean something? Or it could be cash? Or something valuable.'

'Actually, we haven't seen the family jewels yet – maybe they're in there. Doesn't look big enough, though, the crowns would never fit.'

'Hilarious.'

Pauline takes the box away and sits on the sofa. She turns the dial a few times, but has no luck. I turn back to the cupboard, which seems to have spilled twice the amount of stuff it could possibly have held.

'What's your birthday?' Pauline calls.

'Tenth of July.'

'What was your mum's?'

I brace my hands on my knees as I stand up. My knees click more than anybody's should in their early thirties. I stand behind Pauline and look over her shoulder.

'Fourteenth. Also July.'

'Wow, close together.'

'We shared a birthday party once. Pirates. Dad dressed as Captain Hook.'

I smile at the memory while Pauline tries the lock, but it still doesn't budge. Something suddenly occurs to me.

'Try 1234.'

'Really?'

'I bet he won't have changed it when he bought it.'

I feel tense as the dial clicks next to each of those numbers. Which is dumb, because what does it prove if it does or doesn't turn out to be the right answer? But somehow I feel like my entire understanding of Dad is riding on it. There's a click. Pauline raises her eyebrows.

'Lazy bugger.'

A glow of pride and affection spreads in my chest. Which, again, is ridiculous.

The box seems to just be cards. Pauline tips it upside down so that they form a stack, and we each take one. The one I pick has a picture of a vase of flowers on it when I turn it over.

> Happy birthday Martin! Sorry it's late and a bit girlie
> – stole it off Ruth! Reg

Judging by some of the others in the box, I don't think Reg ever managed to send a card that was on time or not stolen from his wife. We look at a few each, tutting affectionately at Reg, Loic, Jay . . . basically all the village's men of a certain age stealing cards from their wives to send greetings to their friends in a time before text messaging was invented. It's kind of sweet.

> Joy, sorry to hear you're having a hard time again.
> Remember, things get better! I'm here if you ever want
> to talk, just pop by the shop. Love Selena x

OK, that one stings. I've piled the other cards up on the sofa cushion next to me. But this one, with its black-and-white photo of a tree in the snow, goes into my lap.

'Look at this.' Pauline makes me jump. She hands me a card with a picture of a duck in a bucket. The handwriting inside is loopy and slanted, I have to squint to read it.

> Martin, I'm sorry for how our conversation ended the
> other day. I hope you can see that I really do want
> to help. If there's anything I can do always let me
> know. But please think about what I said, it might
> help Charlie to adjust if nothing else. All my love,
> Lowenna xx

I frown and look up at Pauline. She's frowning and looking back at me. And then, without discussing it, we stand up simultaneously and head to the front door.

◆　◆　◆

'Lowenna?' Pauline calls as we let ourselves in. We show ourselves into her living room. Our arrangement so far has been that we'll make her a cup of tea every time we arrive as long as she doesn't get up to greet us.

'Don't tell me you need another break already.' Lowenna sits regally in her armchair, her feet up on a small pink pouffe. 'You've got no staying power, either of you. I think you need to let me come and be foreman again. Stick the kettle on if you want, though.'

I thrust the card at her, and then Pauline and I both sit on her sofa and wait. I watch her frown and then open it. There's a flash of recognition in her eyes.

'Bloody Norah, I forgot,' she breathes. 'Fat lot of good that did, eh?'

'What was this all about?' Pauline asks.

'It must have been a year after Joy passed away,' Lowenna says, frowning again. 'Maybe a little less. He just would not put her stuff away. Which was understandable, but Charlie was spending more and more time at my house.'

She glances at me. Maybe she thinks I'll be offended. But I give her a wan smile and nod for her to continue.

'I didn't begrudge it, of course, spend all the time here you like, but it's not right to see a kid avoiding her own home, you know? So, I had a word.'

'So, any plans to put any of Joy's things away, do you think?' Lowenna asked, gently. I stared at my lap and tried to shrink into the sofa cushions. As if she'd marched me back over here for this. We didn't talk about her any more. That was the unspoken rule. We couldn't.

'What?'

'I don't mean to rush you, Martin. God knows it's lovely to see you back on your feet a little, but I just wonder whether it might be better for both of you to clear— No, not "clear". To throw— No, not "throw". Oh, look. I mean no disrespect, but it's like this house is still stuck in . . . that *day*. I come in and I expect her to be the next one through the door.'

Dad just looked at Lowenna, his face inscrutable. He'd been so hard to read for so long. Maybe he always had been and I'd never really noticed. If I'd learned anything it's that you can't ever tell what anybody else is thinking, even if you love them.

'It's not healthy. It's not good for Charlie. I just wonder if it might help you both to adjust if you got rid— No, not "got rid". Moved. Just moved some of her stuff. You could put it in the loft. Or I could keep it in mine if you're struggling for space.'

'We're not getting rid of anything.'

'But, look, for example, you have a pile of her washing still on the chair. That doesn't need to be there, does it? I've forgotten what the room looks like without it. You don't need her old post. And those stained-glass things in the window that you never liked. Nobody's actually enjoying them now, so—'

'Charlie, go and do your homework.'

'I don't have—'

'Go upstairs, Charlie. Please.'

Dad's face had drained of colour, aside from one pink spot in the middle of each cheek. I looked from him to Lowenna. She folded her lips together and gave me a little nod. And I left them in the living room.

I obviously didn't do my homework. Instead, I lay on my bedroom floor, trying to listen through it. But the carpet was too thick to get much. I was about to try my luck on the stairs when they began raising their voices.

'Because I can't! I don't want to! I've got so little left, I—'

'You have Charlie! You have your friends! You've got so many people who could help you if you'd just let them. It's not right, Martin.'

'I need you to leave.'

'But I—'

I opened my bedroom door a crack, just in time to hear the footsteps in the hallway.

'Martin, please, I didn't mean anything by it, it's for Charlie's sake, I just—'

'I'm sorry, I just can't.'

I heard the door slam and raced to the window in time to see Lowenna hopping over the flower bed between our front gardens. She looked up at the house and caught me staring. She held up a hand for a moment before she disappeared from view.

'Charlie?'

I look up and Pauline's standing over me, hands on hips.

'Sorry?'

'I said, do you want a tea?'

'Oh, no, thanks. All tea-d out.'

Pauline leaves the room and I sit quietly on Lowenna's sofa. I'm not sure if we're not talking because we're both so comfortable, or because we're both thinking about that day. Well, I know I'm option B.

'So, he just kicked you out?' Pauline asks, when she comes back with two mugs. She puts one down on the table next to Lowenna.

'I shouldn't have pushed him on it,' Lowenna shrugs. 'It wasn't his fault. It wasn't anybody's, I know that. It was the height of Kim and Aggie and I got ahead of myself. But I should have taken "no" for an answer. Been a bit more gentle.'

She takes a sip of tea, and then takes a breath like she's about to say something else. She opens her mouth and then closes it again.

'What?' I ask.

'It's just . . . I mean, sometimes I wonder if maybe the house wouldn't be like it is now if I hadn't done that.'

She suddenly looks really small in her armchair.

'Oh, Lowenna.'

'You just wonder these things, don't you?'

I glance at Pauline, unsure what to say. She looks at Lowenna.

'I think it always would have come out somehow. Everything with Joy was so traumatic and he never could express himself very well, could he? If it hadn't been the hoarding it might have been something worse, you know?'

Dad never spoke about shouting at Lowenna. And I didn't think he'd shout at me, necessarily, but I wasn't keen to bring it up again because . . . Well, why would you? Things were hard enough.

But anyway, one day I came home from school and the house was clearer. It was nothing mad, but the pile of Mum's washing was gone, some old magazines, a few ornaments and things that had always made the place look a little untidy. All of the things that used to be innocent but then they got left behind and suddenly they made every room feel claustrophobic. Lowenna was right. It didn't feel like she'd been erased, but I guess it was nice not to have constant reminders everywhere you looked. I could breathe. We still had some photos up, and it's not like things bring people back anyway.

It wasn't that often I went in my parents' room any more. When I was younger I used to jump into their bed on a Saturday morning to watch Live & Kicking on their staticky TV, but I had passed the age where that would be weird, and that TV was no longer with us anyway. All of which to say, it was probably a good couple of weeks before I actually went into their – well, Dad's at that point, I suppose – room again.

I can't even remember what I wanted. Probably, like, a plaster or paracetamol or something. The kind of things Mum always kept in a box in her wardrobe. I was halfway up the stairs, running on muscle memory as much as anything else, before it even occurred to me that the supply might have run out and there was nobody to restock it. I stopped right there until the pain in my chest subsided. And then I carried on and let myself in.

I didn't know where I was for a second. The dressing table was piled with the folded laundry, the magazines, and everything else that had disappeared from the house after Lowenna's visit. Mum's shopping list pad sat on the windowsill, alongside her toiletries from the bathroom and the handbag she'd left sitting in the hall. A stack of trashy novels sat on her bedside table, looming over her side of the bed.

'What are you doing?'

I whipped round to find Dad hovering in the doorway looking – I don't even know. Ashamed? Annoyed? A bit of both?

'What is all this?' I finally asked after the silence had stretched between us for long enough.

'Charlie.'

'No, seriously. What is it?'

'It's her.'

'But I thought you got rid of it.'

'You can't just get rid of someone, Charlie. I won't. I already failed her, she deserves better than being erased.'

'No, but . . .'

I honestly don't know quite what came over me. It might have been that old feeling of claustrophobia that I thought was gone, or the fact that Dad had been lying to me. Or, not lying? But making me think things were one way when they were actually something else. I don't know. It was super-confusing, and weird, and I just—

'Why can't this family ever just be fucking normal?' *I shouted.*

'Charlie.'

'I mean it. We have everything with Mum, and then maybe we're starting to get used to it, and now there's this? Why can't I just have one day where I have a normal life in a normal house like everybody else?'

I hadn't ever seen Dad crumple like he did then. I never saw it again, either. But in that moment his body folded forward and he threw his hands over his face. His shoulders shook, and he stood on the landing audibly sobbing.

I could hear my heart beating inside my head because I didn't know how to deal with that. Where was Lowenna when you needed her? Where was any *adult? In the end, I walked over to him and folded my arms around him, and he squeezed me back and wept into my shoulder.*

Maybe the weirdest thing is that we never mentioned it again. Because you're never going to say, 'Hey, Dad, remember when you cried so much you actually scared me?' Not a fun anecdote. So, after that I never questioned the compulsion to keep hanging on to stuff, even when there didn't seem to be a link back to Mum any more. Not worth it. I just let him do what he needed to do.

CHAPTER NINETEEN

When it's time to get ready to go out I sit at the desk in my bedroom staring at myself in the mirror. I look tired. I probably would have looked tired before everything I heard about today. I don't know when all of these lines appeared on my face, and is that an actual *pockmark*? My eyes are red from the seawater earlier, and the cry I may or may not have had in secret when I got back from Lowenna's. All in all, not ideal.

I've laid out all of the make-up I brought with me. I mean, I say 'brought with me', but 'dug out from the bottom of my bag in pieces' is probably more accurate. There's the world's dullest brown eyeshadow, a purple glitter one which has crumbled into dust, my mascara (waterproof but unfortunately not Charlie-proof), and a lipstick which is the same colour as my lips, so I'm not even sure why I bought it in the first place.

James appears at the door. 'Remind me where you're going?'

'Just to a bar. Maybe a club.'

I smear some purple on my eyes and instantly regret it. I scrub it with my sleeve.

'Is the bar the Bolster?'

'No, a different bar. People don't go to this bar unless they're on, like, a Night Out. A proper one.'

'Then how come you are?'

''Cos it's people from school and it's for old times' sake. I don't know. I didn't choose it.'

James spins my chair around, just as I'm trying to put eyeliner on, and I draw across my face.

'Hey!'

'Is *he* going to be there?' he asks me, significantly.

'Yes.' I stick my chin out defiantly, daring him to say something. I turn back to my desk and try to rub out the eyeliner line that now extends to my temple, and not in a sexy 'professional make-up artist' kind of way.

'But—'

'He's never done anything.'

'Except date you, and beat me up.'

'A decade ago, and you started it. And you barely scratched each other. Where is this coming from?'

'I don't know, it's just weird, isn't it? Things here are weird.'

'I'm sorry you don't like my backwater.'

'That's not funny.'

James hangs around for a little while longer. I feel like he's waiting for me to say something, but I have nothing else to offer. I make very close inspections of my fragments of make-up. I keep purposefully silent, and he does the same, and we have a stand-off right here in my childhood bedroom. He stares intently at me, and I stare intently at anything but him, until . . .

'Fine,' he sighs, and leaves. I don't hear him go downstairs for ages, so I know he's just waiting out on the landing for me to change my mind and call him back. I grind my teeth and keep absolutely still, until I hear the creak of him actually going downstairs.

I have to put down the eyeliner I'm about to have a second go at because my hand is trembling too much. I shake it out. I really don't know why I feel so nervous. I'm only going out with people I know. Just because I haven't seen them for years doesn't make them scary. If anything, *I'm* the one who went off and got successful and interesting, or so (incorrect) local rumour would have it, anyway. *They* should be scared of *me*.

I run a brush through my hair and do the best I can with my face given my limited resources. I have to change out of my first-choice top because I'm left with a thin film of glitter all the way down my chest from my eyeshadow. I end up in the blouse I was wearing when I rushed here from work on that first, terrible day. It doesn't feel like a *great* omen, but I'm really trying not to be the kind of person who scans the world for omens every time they're unsure about something, so I stick with it.

We've arranged to meet at the bar at 7 p.m. before we go on to the 'club', such as it is. It's really just an old warehouse on the out-skirts of the village where they put all the ugly buildings. Someone's stuck up a few lights, added a sound system, and covered the ceiling with some cheap velvet drapes that soak up all the sweat and send it raining down on you from about 2 a.m. onwards. Or so I've heard. It was never really my scene. Probably because of the whole 'sweat shower' thing.

I have to go to the loo about four times while I'm getting ready. I'm tired too. And I'm not just making excuses. My head feels a bit spinny. It would be so much easier, so much *better*, to just call Adam now and tell him I can't make it. I'm not up to seeing people, and I'm never up to small talk. They wouldn't miss me.

'No,' I tell myself sternly in the mirror. Actually out loud, I would add, so I'm definitely going a bit mad. 'Stop being negative. It's just drinks. Just nice drinks with nice people. It's going to be fun. Fun, fun, fun.'

'Pardon?' James yells from downstairs.

'I didn't say anything!' I shout back.

I'm the first person to arrive at the bar, after all my resistance to coming at all. 'Razz' is a different kettle of fish to the Bolster & Saint. Their USP seems to be that they offer myriad violently coloured vodka shots. This makes them a Very Cool Bar.

I treat myself to a luminous-blue shot and a glass of white wine. Dinner of champions. I down the shot quickly to get rid of the evidence, and it burns. A warmth spreads to my extremities and I finally start feeling ready for the evening ahead. I briefly wonder if this means I have a problem. But I think I'm allowed one after the last couple of weeks.

A fire crackles in the hearth, which is a bit much. It might be raining but it's not exactly winter. So now I can't tell if my sweating is a result of nerves or actual overheating. The room is dotted with leather couches, but I opt for a high table ringed with plastic stools and positioned in the bay window. The only problem is that the ceiling's quite low, so once I've sat down I'm not sure I'll be able to get up again without bumping my head.

There's one other person in the place when I sit down to cradle my wine, and that's the surly teenager behind the bar, who I'm not totally convinced is legally allowed to sell me anything. This is so pathetic. I twitch every time I hear car doors slamming, even though it happens a lot because Razz is right next door to a Domino's. That's new. What a time to be alive.

Adam is the first person to arrive and my stomach does a funny jump when I see him, which I choose to believe is nothing more than relief that he turned up. He raises a hand and mouths, 'Drink?' I look down at my glass. I don't remember finishing the entire thing, but that would appear to be what's happened. I nod.

He brings over two glasses of wine and two acid-green shots.

'Sour apple,' he tells me as he pushes one towards me. 'A classic. I thought you might want a sharpener.'

We 'cheers' and down them. The aftertaste might stick around forever. It's not long before we're interrupted by a squeal.

'Oh my *God*, Charlie Trewin! I thought you were well out of here. I couldn't believe it when Mae said you were in town.'

Claire Robinson, who was in my year at school and spent the entire time winning the cross-country races I walked at the back of, pulls me into a one-armed hug and kisses the air just above each cheek. She was always surrounded by a gaggle of adoring fans, so I didn't even realise she knew who I was, let alone that she would be pleased to see me. That she would have *any* emotions about seeing me, in fact.

'Matt's sorry he couldn't come,' she tells Adam. 'He's got an extra shift at the warehouse, couldn't turn down the money, obviously. So, it'll just be you and the girls.'

She laughs lightly and squeezes his arm. My throat tightens. For no reason. No reason at all.

We're joined in no time by Billie-Joe and Emma, who I was very intimidated by at school, but who both seem to remember me as if we were there yesterday. Next, there's Rosenwyn from the year above us – she was always showing off prizes she'd won for dance in assembly, so we did not move in the same circles. Mae arrives last, dressed in a sparkly top which puts my last-worn-on-the-tube-and-smells-like-it blouse to shame. She sits next to me and gives my leg a squeeze.

'How's it going?' she asks me quietly as the others chatter.

'Up and down,' I tell her honestly. Adam shifts in his seat and his leg comes to rest against mine, the warm weight of it reassuring. I can't tell if it's deliberate or not. I try to catch his eye, but he avoids looking at me. Or maybe he just has nothing to look at me *about* in the first place. HOW ARE YOU EVER MEANT TO KNOW?

During the first bottle of wine and most of the second, our motley crew chatters mindlessly about who said what at school, which teachers we thought were having affairs, and how little we'd actually been prepared for life as adults. We go around the table and gossip about everybody we ever dated, or slept with, from school. Or, most of them do. Adam and I stare at our drinks as if staring really hard at a glass of house white might transport a person out of an awkward situation.

'And of course you two don't need to mention each other!' Claire laughs as the chatter reaches us.

Adam suddenly becomes very interested in what's happening out of the window. (Nothing. Obviously nothing. Apart from people with pizza boxes.) A furious red flush rises up his face even in the weak light of the cheap candles. Which are, by the way, definitely a fire hazard when the soft furnishings are presumably saturated with quite a lot of vodka.

Our group gets louder and more high-pitched the more wine arrives at the table. I feel a little bit sorry for the boy behind the bar. Except he's deeply absorbed in his phone and clearly not worried as long as we keep ordering drinks. Which we do.

The chat turns to work. I can feel the alcohol seeping into my brain. I shouldn't have started before everyone else.

'I don't even know if I have a job any more,' I laugh nervously. Oh God, did I just *slur* my words? 'I do HR, and it's definitely not policy to leave before lunchtime on a Wednesday, not tell anybody, and then just not turn up again for a couple of weeks. I think I might be out on my arse.'

The thought is so huge and scary that it's basically stopped feeling real, which is how I can joke about it in Cornwall's saddest bar with a group of people I mostly don't know very well. They don't seem to find it funny, though. I'm the only one who laughs. Everybody else shifts in their seats. Mae leans over to top up my glass.

'So, Emma, how are the wedding plans coming along?' she asks after a moment, probably keen to avoid any further awkwardness from me. Emma's eyes light up.

'Oh my God. It's *so* exciting. We're doing the ceremony at St Piran's, and then having the reception at the Bolster, and it's *so* nice to be able to do it in our hometown, you know? We'll have all the photos taken on the beach, and then it'll be a seafood supper for everybody, and . . . Yeah. I just love all the planning.' She glows as she talks about it, and I wonder what that must feel like. 'Of course, Charlie, if you're around next July you should come!'

'Cool.' I try to smile, but it doesn't quite reach my eyes. Everything I've drunk is preventing me from figuring out why I'm turning into a bitch, when she's being lovely. Her smile wavers.

'Are you . . . excited about *your* wedding?' Rosenwyn asks me, uncertain. I'm desperate to stop being weird, but it's a question I could never answer like a normal human being, even without garishly coloured vodka in the equation. I always say 'yes', because I know that's what people want to hear, but my voice, and my eyes, and my body language, always say 'no'. Because the answer is 'no'.

In the end, I settle for a shrug, a non-committal nod, and a silent plea that nobody wants me to go into any more detail. My reaction is lacklustre enough that it actually triggers another uncomfortable silence, and I feel a frisson of panic move through the group. I catch Billie-Joe as she shrugs at Adam, and I feel that spark of envy again. I grip my empty glass tighter. What *is* it?

'I'm going to get another round!' Adam announces to the silent group.

It's enough to get everybody chattering again. When he returns from the bar he pointedly puts a glass of water in front of me. Mae gets the conversation back on track.

'Enough of the coupled-up people, am I right, ladies? Single mum over here!' Mae throws her head back and laughs, then holds up her glass for us all to cheers her. I do so gratefully.

'Mae, your littlest one can't even be that little any more, can he?' someone asks. I'm a lot of wines deep now and they're all blonde people I used to go to school with, so they've started to blur into one. One of them refills my glass, so that one's my favourite. The water Adam got me remains untouched.

'He's four.' Mae smiles, eyes shining. Her whole demeanour changes when she talks about him. I try to imagine having that strength of feeling about anything, but I can't. 'How about yours?'

'I've got an eight-year-old and a two-year-old,' Emma replies. I think it's Emma, but I'm only forty per cent sure. The safest thing to do is to stop addressing anybody by their names. Everybody coos as she passes her phone around to show us the screen saver featuring her two children.

'Any luck, Billie?' someone pipes up.

'Not yet, but you know how it is, it's early days.' She seems subdued.

'It'll happen, Bill.' Emma squeezes her shoulder. 'How about you, Charlie?'

'Hmm?'

'Any kids?'

I laugh, but it's a bit too raucous. Adam fidgets next to me.

'No. God, no. Can you imagine?' I should stop there, and yet I carry on, and I don't know why. 'I'm just really busy with – um – my career, and you know what London's like, it's just so non-stop, I don't think I'd have time to look after some parasite demanding all of my attention, you know?'

Everybody around the table falls silent again.

'Charlie, can I see you outside for a bit?' Adam asks.

◆ ◆ ◆

He grabs my hand and pulls me past the toilets and out of the fire escape, into an alleyway. It's pissing it down with rain so we try to huddle under the overhang of the roof, dodging little waterfalls where the gutters have been choked with weeds.

'What's going on?' Adam asks.

'What do you mean?'

'What do you mean, "What do you mean"? You know what I mean.'

I suspect I *might* know what he means, but he's dragged me out here in the rain, so I don't feel inclined to play along.

'Sorry, you'll have to catch me up.'

'You!' he explodes. 'You're being so . . . I just . . . What's *with* you tonight?'

'Nothing!' I snap.

'I know you weren't keen to come, but—'

'I didn't want to come at all. You *made* me.'

'Yeah, and now you're being really judgemental. This isn't you.'

'That's really not—'

'Just because *you* chose to pretend this place never existed, doesn't make you better than us. It's nobody's fault that the life you ran away for isn't the one you wanted.'

I open my mouth and then close it again. He's absolutely right, and I know that, but I don't like how easily he got to the root of the problem. Even *I* haven't managed that, and it's *my* problem. I pick at the skin around my nails and try to centre myself, to remember my official party line. I am happy with my choices. I am happy, happy, hap—

'Are you actually happy, Charlie?'

Adam isn't even looking at me, he's staring at a cascade of water flowing down the side of the building. I could probably go back to the table now and we could pretend he'd never asked.

'Seriously? What do you think?'

'I don't mean right now. With your dad and everything. I mean all the time. Before this happened. Are you happy when you wake up every day?'

I feel a flare of annoyance, and I kick at a puddle. All it really achieves is that now I'm annoyed and I have a wet toe.

'Why's everyone so obsessed with the idea that you have to be happy all the time? It's unrealistic. Nobody's happy *all the time*.'

'Are you happy any of the time?'

'That's not . . . I don't . . . No, OK? No, I'm not happy. Any of the time. And I wish everyone would let me get on with it.'

'Don't you think your mum would want—'

'Don't you *dare* bring her into it.'

'You know I'm only asking because I care about you.'

'Yeah, right.'

I take a couple of steps back towards the door.

'You're the one who *left*. I still care about you. You seem to think that you're unlovable, Charlie, but you're not. Believe me.'

There's a silence then. Adam shrugs. And then we just look at each other, neither of us sure what to say. Somewhere off to one side the water continues to patter down from the gutter over our heads. Adam looks crestfallen, and all I can think to do is reach out and touch his hand. He looks down at my finger tracing a pattern over his, and then back at me. And I *swear* I do not know where it comes from (OK, fine, it mainly comes from vodka) but I launch myself at him out of nowhere.

It feels so familiar – he kisses me back for a moment, playing with my hair like he used to when we were sitting on the sea wall halfway up the cliff.

'Wait' – he pushes me back – 'I can't do this.'

'You could, though.'

'No, Charlie. You're drunk. It's not right.'

I take a step back. The whole alleyway's spinning so I end up losing the shelter of the roof and standing directly in the rain.

'But—'

'And you're getting married! We're not doing this.'

I look back towards the door, but I can't go in and face everybody again. For one thing, I look like a drowned rat. And for another, I've maxed out my ability to sit in a social group and pretend everything's fine. At least for today. I take a step towards the end of the alleyway, the road, and, eventually, home. I mean, Dad's house. Not *home* home. Obviously. Because that is where your heart is and that is famously London, and I'm happy with that, and . . .

'I wish I hadn't left.' I shrug.

'But you did.'

'But—'

'There's not much else to say, is there?'

I can't think of a single thing to do except to turn around and run. So I do.

CHAPTER TWENTY

I'm woken up by a pressure on the side of the sofa. I couldn't even face trying the stairs last night so I just collapsed in the living room again. Frankly, it's a miracle I didn't fall asleep in the flower bed outside. When I finally lay down, the entire room kept lurching from side to side, and I kept replaying everything that had happened with Adam in the alley. It obviously wasn't ideal, but under the influence of adrenaline and *quite* a lot of alcohol, it felt like a nice thing in the moment. Now, however, with the cold light of day shining through my eyelids even though I would really like it not to, and when I know exactly what that pressure on the edge of the sofa is, I'm wracked with guilt. Should I tell James? He deserves to know the kind of woman he's marrying. He also loves nothing more than getting mad at me for stuff, so he'd have a field day. Although it's no laughing matter. The thinking is hurting my head.

I open my eyes one at a time. The curtains are closed but it's still too bright in here. James is leaning so close to me that his forehead is practically resting on mine. I recoil as far as the cushion will allow. My head is *pounding*. It's like everything I drank last night has combined into one, developed a physical form, and is now trying to bash its way out of my skull. And the room is spinning, so I'm pretty sure I'm still drunk, which means it's only downhill from here.

'Good morning!' James shouts into my face with a grin, and I throw a blanket over my head, which sets off the Booze Monster in my skull again.

He pulls the blanket away from me and in that moment I know I'm going to be sick. I think James can see the green rising in my face because he jumps away just in time for me to free myself from the brightly coloured crochet blanket and race to the toilet.

I puke up an entire spectrum of colourful vodka (which does not look so attractive when it's going in the other direction) and then slide onto the bathroom floor because the Booze Monster has caught up with me after my sprint and sapped the last of my energy. The avocado tiles feel cool against my sweaty back.

'Is it over?' James calls from somewhere.

I groan in response because I've forgotten how to do words. He sticks a head around the toilet door and hands me a glass of water. He's made an ice pack out of a bag of frozen peas covered with a tea towel. He crouches next to me and holds it against my forehead.

When I'm ready to move he guides me to my room, holds back the covers while I climb into bed, and then actually tucks me in. He draws the curtains and sits on the side of the bed. Throughout these manoeuvres I sweat pure vodka and come to the chilling conclusion that James is a saint, certainly far too good for me, and I am the worst person in the world.

'Listen, I'm really sorry I was weird about Hospital Guy yesterday. I was being a dick. If you say there's nothing there, there's nothing there. Did you have a good night?' he asks, stroking my hair.

I shrug, and then my chin trembles. The Booze Monster shoulder-charges my forehead and tears spill down my cheeks. My eyes burn. James sits on the side of the bed and rubs my back until I fall asleep.

◆ ◆ ◆

When I wake up hours later the Booze Monster seems to have quietened down. He's still there, but he's tiptoeing around my skull instead of tap dancing. It's a struggle to open my eyes because they've been glued shut with tears of shame and manky old mascara.

'Charlie!' James calls from the hall.

I hear running feet pounding up the stairs, two at a time, and then James materialises at the door. He passes my handbag to me. It is vibrating insistently.

'Too early,' I groan.

'It's three in the afternoon.'

'Oh.'

He shakes his head, I *think* affectionately, and leaves me with my buzzing bag. As I fumble around inside, my phone stops ringing. Then it starts up again, which would be unusually persistent for the scammers who are often the only people to call me.

Oh fuck. Work.

'H— Hello?' I croak.

'Hello, is that Charlie?'

'Speaking,' I say as my stomach drops.

It's Magdalena. I wonder briefly if I'm going to throw up again, but I decide to be a grown-up. I am in control of this situation. It's fine, it's fine, it's fine.

'Charlie? You sound terrible.'

'Oh. Yeah, I've been ill' – which is *not* a lie, because even if your illness is caused by drinking an entire bottle of wine and a plethora of sugary vodka shots, it's still an illness.

'Well, that's not surprising, you've obviously been through the mill.'

'Sure.'

'James told me what happened,' she adds. 'Charlie?'

'Hmm? Sorry. Yes, I know, I asked him to.'

'And how are you now?'

'Oh. Yeah. I'm fine. I've been better, but I'm . . . fine.' I'm so grateful we're not on FaceTime.

'I was phoning to talk about whether you knew when you might be ready to come back.'

'Oh,' I say. I start to sweat, so I throw the duvet off, but then I immediately start shivering.

'I'm . . . I'm not really sure.'

I close my eyes and I can see people in business suits milling around in the shiny atrium. I can picture the same faces getting into the lift with me every day, after we spent the entire tube journey studiously ignoring each other. I can picture the whiteboard in our office with the list of major projects we have coming up in the next few years. I would rather die than be around to see any of the major projects we have coming up in the next few years.

'Charlie, I'm afraid I really need to press you for an answer. I think we've been very lenient, all things considered. But you must understand that it's not a free pass. We do need to know we're working towards a date here. Maybe you could look to come back part-time and work up from there?'

My breathing starts to get quicker, and shallower, and my knees have gone weak, even though I'm still horizontal.

'I can't give you an answer, I'm afraid. Not right now. I'm still away, and there are a lot of loose ends to tie up.'

'I understand. But, Charlie, I really do need to hear something by the end of the week.'

Magdalena hangs up without even saying goodbye, and I bury my phone under my pillow, then punch that pillow for emphasis. My initial panic at having been tracked down starts to give way to anger. It's all very well for work to invade every aspect of my life

223

when I'm in London, but I resent it encroaching here. Work swallows the mornings I spend dreading going in, and the evenings I spend stewing over some terrible meeting or other. It even invades most of my weekends, what with the Sunday Scaries that usually start on a Friday evening. But, I decide, it does not get to take over home too. Not *home* home.

I've reached under the pillow and dialled again before I've quite connected my brain.

'Hello?'

'Hi, Magdalena, it's Charlie again.'

'Oh, Charlie, I—'

'Listen, Magdalena,' I say sweetly, through gritted teeth. 'I've been giving it a lot of thought' – well, all of about twenty seconds, she can easily do the maths on that – 'and I've decided that I won't be coming back. At all.'

There's silence on the other end. The practical part of my brain is screaming at me to fill it, to make some joke, to tell her I didn't mean it. Instead, I sit and dig my fingernails into my knees to keep my heart from leaping out of my chest.

'I'm sorry, are you—'

'Yes, sorry, I quit. This is me handing in my resignation.'

'Charlie, you work in HR, you know that's not how it—'

'OK, bye then!'

I hang up the phone before I can change my mind and throw it to the edge of the bed in triumph. I throw too hard and it tumbles to the floor, where it rings once. Then it rings again. And then it doesn't ring any more.

I sit dead still. The pounding in my heart has made the pounding in my head worse. Adrenaline courses through my body and the silence of the room presses against me. A seagull shrieks outside and I jump.

I cannot *believe* I just did that. I could count on one hand the number of times I've stood up for myself before today, and I would have five fingers left to count something different. A grin spreads over my face as I imagine Magdalena trying to get her head around what's just happened. She'll sit in the HR office, where we have the privilege of a door, unlike the rest of the company. She'll close that door, and she will *bitch*. And I don't have to listen to it! And at 5.30 p.m. today (contractually, but it'll really be 7 p.m. because it always is, because you have to show willing) I should be getting into the lift, and then cramming myself onto the tube. And I never have to do that again either.

And, sure. The idea of not getting paid again for a long time is pretty terrifying, and I'll never get a reference, but, I mean . . . A bubble of laughter rises in my throat, and I can't hold it back. I start to giggle. And then the giggles turn into hysterics. Tears stream down my face, and I've woken my hangover up again, but I don't even care.

'What's going on?' James appears in the room, looking concerned. 'Are you—'

'I did it!' I practically squeal. There's zero decorum in any of this, I hope I'm making that very clear.

'You did what?'

'I quit my job.'

I widen my eyes at him. He widens his at me. I screech. I can't help it. But as it turns out, he wasn't widening his with joy.

'What? That's insane.'

'Don't call me insane.'

'But you just . . . Charlie, were you even going to talk to me about it first?'

'I told you how unhappy I've been.'

'Yeah, but I didn't think you were going to *do* anything about it, y'know? There's unhappy and then there's *unhappy* and you weren't *unhappy*.'

'I fucking was. I'm sick of it. Life's too short. Too. Fucking. Short.'

'Are you still drunk?'

He looks at me with narrowed eyes, searching my face for an answer that isn't the one he's already been given.

'Honestly? I think I might just be growing a backbone.'

I say it quietly so as not to scare away this new development.

'I think I preferred you before.'

He shrugs. I shrug. I mean, what are you supposed to say to that? It certainly takes some of the shine off my moment of triumph, but I refuse to let it dampen my spirits completely. Absolutely not. No, no, no.

James picks up my phone and holds it out to me.

'You can still undo it,' he says, and there's desperation in his voice. He tries to press the phone into my hand but I refuse to take hold of it. 'Please.'

'No.' I shake my head and laugh. This feels so weird. 'I'll find something else.'

'What am I going to say to Magdalena?'

'Do you know what? I really don't care. She's not my problem any more.'

James regards me for a couple more seconds, then stalks out of the room and down the stairs. I hear the living room door slam. I'm willing to bet he's calling Magdalena right now to try to smooth things over. It won't do any good, though. She can't take me back when I've been as insubordinate as I've just been.

I feel weird. I'm still getting over the world's worst hangover and now I'm all keyed up from the phone call. But I think I feel . . . sure? No. I know. I feel sure.

I sink back onto the bed, squeeze a pillow tight, and smile. The Booze Monster high-fives my brain in triumph.

◆ ◆ ◆

I've washed my face, changed into some fresh (not *nice*, but at least not actively gross) clothes, and even managed to manoeuvre myself into an upright position at the kitchen table by the time James finally emerges. I could hear him talking quickly as I shuffled, zombie-like, past the living room door, but I couldn't make out what he was saying.

In any case, when the door finally opens I am nursing a cup of tea the size of a small bucket. The steam curls up to my face, and I let it because I feel like there's probably some kind of skincare benefit. Like, it'll purge the last traces of rainbow vodka from my pores or something, I dunno.

'You're up.' James moves towards the window to raise the blind.

'Don't,' I say, too desperately. Get it together, Charlie.

'Wow.'

He raises an eyebrow and reboils the kettle. I don't say anything, he doesn't say anything, and eventually I can't stand the silence any more.

'Can you please not judge me?'

'I'm not judging you.'

He moves towards the fridge, and I *promise* you there's something judgemental about the way he does it.

'Look, I know you don't agree with this.'

I watch him pour milk, stir his tea, and put his cup down on the table. I'm sure he's moving slowly to make it seem like he's a normal, rational person and I'm an irrational screw-up. Or maybe that's the hangxiety talking.

'You know what? You're right. I don't agree,' he says eventually, when he's taken a seat and considered what to say, because I guess that's what sensible people are supposed to do. 'It's very sudden.'

'I—'

'And fine, if you were unhappy you shouldn't stay, but you've *never* mentioned it before. It's all very out of the blue.'

'I know, and I—'

'And I don't think it's unreasonable for me to be worried about how we're going to pay the rent now. Or what about how we're going to pay for the wedding?' There's an ever-so-slight increase in pitch and his eyes widen. 'The insurance is coming up soon as well. It's so reckless, Charlie.'

'You can't keep being so reckless, Joy!'

I was lying on the grass in the garden, minding my own business, when I first heard my dad shout at my mum. It was breezy but warm, and the clouds were scudding across the sky at a rate of knots. If I stared long enough and softened my focus it felt like the world was about to tip onto its side. I was vaguely aware of a whispered conversation before that, but talk between grown-ups didn't really interest me, and I didn't notice the whispers becoming hisses, and the scrape of chair legs on paving slabs as Dad pushed his chair back.

'I'm sorry, you know I love you, but you need to think about Charlie. Think about me.'

I sat up, startled, just in time to see him disappear into the house, leaving half a gin and tonic sitting on the table.

Mum gave me a watery smile that I didn't believe for a second, drained her glass, and came to lie next to me. I settled back onto the ground, blades of grass tickling my bare arms. Mum let out a sound that might have been a sob. I slipped my hand into hers and rested my head on her shoulder.

228

And this time I am an adult. I don't throw anything. I don't even raise my voice. In fact, I don't say anything. I know James is still talking because his mouth is still moving, but all I can hear is a high-pitched whine.

I've pushed myself up to standing and am out of the room before I even realise I've moved. I feel a hand on my shoulder, but I shrug it off, and then I've slammed the front door behind me and am taking huge breaths of fresh air. I pause at the garden gate. I don't know where to go now. I look back at Lowenna's house, but I'm really not sure where I'd start. I fish my phone from my back pocket and write a text.

Meet me on the wall?

I head for the beach. Except I don't step onto the sand. Instead I follow the path that runs the length of it until it climbs up the hill. I pass the cafe, with its blackboard advertising 'Fresh Cornish Lobster' and customers competing for space to sit on the terrace. I pass the lifeguard hut, which is all shuttered up now that it's off-season. A dog runs up to me and sniffs my knee, and I barely crack a smile as its owner calls it back.

I follow the path as it slopes sharply upwards. Off to the left, a set of stairs has been cut into the rock. It's a much more complicated and, frankly, dangerous route to the same place, so I've never understood the point of them. Nevertheless, I grip the railing and descend. About halfway down, the steps pass a sea wall which is wide enough to sit on. You can climb over the handrail, walk along the wall, and have a panoramic view of the bay, usually all to yourself. Unless you're, I don't know, a shy teenager looking for secret places to meet her boyfriend, and then I *imagine* that you might invite him along too.

Adam is already sitting on the concrete and kicking his legs over the side when I get to our old meeting place. He's found the exact spot we always used to come to, even before hormones and feelings and all those teenage things turned a friendship into something else. We did carve our initials into the wall, so I guess it's not *that* difficult to find. They're still there. Maybe a little weathered. Aren't we all? He's wearing a full suit and I realise, with a twisting sensation in my stomach, that I've probably pulled him out of work. How quickly I forget that other people aren't skivers like me.

'First of all, I'm really sorry,' I say, holding a hand up to stop him from speaking. 'I don't know what got into me last night.'

'I think it was mainly blue raspberry vodka.' He gives me a wry smile. 'A lot of it.'

'Well, it was a shitty thing to do and I'm sorry.'

'It was. Thank you.'

For a second, his face is impassive. Then he smiles and pats the patch of concrete next to him. I sit down. We don't need to be this close. After last night we probably *shouldn't* be this close. But I like the feeling of his leg pressed against the entire length of mine. I don't wriggle away, and not only because I would risk falling to my death if I did.

The wall cuts the cliff pretty much in half. Seams of different-coloured rock fold into one another to form a sheer face behind us. In some places it's tufted with grass and stubby little plants that have managed to survive being exposed to the elements. Where it remains bare, lichen studs the surface in splodges of yellow, grey, and blue-green. Somewhere above us the coast road continues to rise out of the village. People will be walking past right now with no idea we're here.

Below us, the reef is exposed by the low tide. Hundreds of rock pools of all shapes and sizes shine up at us, reflecting the light from the overcast sky. A big black cormorant stands near the edge of the water, holding its wings open to dry. A couple of children in bright-yellow raincoats pick their way over the rocks below us, nets and buckets in hand. That was us in a previous life.

I'm not really sure when I rest my head on Adam's shoulder, but suddenly it's there, and then my hand is in his again. I don't know why I'm doing this. It's wrong, it's wrong, it's wrong. Is it wrong?

I trace the lines of the initials I carved back when things felt difficult, before I had any idea. They've been smoothed by time and rain, but they're still there.

'So, was there something else, or did you just want me to ruin a perfectly good suit?'

'Shit, really?'

Adam laughs. 'Please. You can chuck this thing in the machine, it's fine. Don't avoid the question.'

I sigh. I'm struggling to string a thought together now that I'm here and I kind of can't tell if that's the last vestiges of my hangover or because, well, I'm here.

'I don't know, I just . . . Do you think I'm reckless?'

'What?'

'Reckless? Me?'

He puffs out his cheeks while he considers.

'No . . .' he says slowly, considering. Considering more than I hoped he would, to be perfectly honest. 'I wouldn't have said that. Or, not before, anyway. But then there was last night.'

'I said I'm sorry.' My face suddenly feels hot.

'I know, I'm just saying. I don't think you're *naturally* reckless. But I guess I don't think you're yourself, either. D'you see what I mean?'

'I—'

'Because I don't think you *want* to hurt anybody, but I think James would be hurt if he heard about last night. And it wasn't exactly fair on me either.'

He shifts and removes his hand from mine. I don't know what to say, so I don't say anything.

231

'Look. All I'm saying is you need to figure out what you actually – as in, *actually* – want. You're kind of flailing.'

'And you think I'm a bad person?'

'No comment.'

I look at him in dismay and he laughs.

'Sorry. Bad joke. No, I don't. I think you need to get it together, and I think you will. Eventually.'

We sit in silence for a while. I kick my feet and watch the sun shimmer on the water. Adam starts throwing stones over the edge of the cliff.

'I quit my job.' It suddenly feels very important that he know this. It's not like I need his approval but, well, *somebody's* approval would be nice.

'That's awesome!'

The enthusiasm of his reaction alarms us both, as well as a couple of seagulls who'd been slowly edging closer to us. They take off and I watch them land on the sea, two little dots in the shining expanse. It's nice, though.

'Sorry' – Adam eventually breaks the silence again – 'I mean, it's awesome if you think it's awesome.'

I smile.

'It's pretty awesome.'

'Charlie Trewin: Free Agent. A decisive move, I like it.'

'Something like that.'

CHAPTER
TWENTY-ONE

Over the following days I boomerang between giddy joy at never needing to go back to the office and look interested again, and heart-stopping terror about, well, the same thing. It's all very well to prioritise being happy but happiness doesn't pay the bills. And there are a lot of bills. But if I wait a little while the pendulum swings back to joy again and I know – *I know* – I've done the right thing.

And yes, fine, things are a little frosty with James. And my stomach lurches when I see Adam. But I lock those feelings away and try to focus on the task at hand.

Pauline and I uncover mountains of paperwork in the chests and boxes dotted throughout the house. They'd previously been buried by heaps of other stuff. But we're getting there now. Some particular highlights include a signed photo of Kevin Keegan, a hand-whittled spoon, and a receipt for a budgie. We never had any pets. I spend the next few hours incredibly paranoid that we're about to uncover a tiny bird skeleton.

We sort through at least twelve tool chests, keeping one of everything, along with a few spares. We send everything else to the charity shop. On our fifth visit within twenty-four hours I can no longer tell whether Ethel Maynard is going to kiss us or beg us to stop. Our visits start off with her trilling her thanks while she battles to find space in the stockroom for everything. But at the end of the last one that day she looks like a broken woman and sounds as exhausted as us.

But the visits continue. We send her mountains of clothes, a couple of washing airers, stationery that could fill a branch of WHSmith, and all kinds of kitchen bits. Even after we've consigned all of the chipped mugs to the tip, there are still more for charity than we can carry in one journey. It gets to the point where she doesn't even look up when the bell on the door rings any more, and we don't need to hang around to be shown where to leave things.

We move on to the smaller tasks as the bulk of the big ones are completed. Pauline saves a bundle of Dad's shirts because she wants to use them to make a quilt. I spend quite a long time polishing all the furniture because, one way or another, I've been sharing poky Zone Five flats for the past decade or so and it's been a long time since I encountered furniture that didn't arrive flat-packed. I want to savour the feeling.

We occasionally nip to the beach for a quick dip in the sea to punctuate the housework. The weather has returned to hazy sunshine and a light breeze, bar the occasional squally autumn shower. I start to wear a swimming costume underneath my clothes all the time and think nothing of not showering after being in the sea, because there's always a chance I might go again later anyway.

The last job to be done on the house is to remove all but one of the knockers from the front door. A couple are so rusted you can't even really tell what they are any more, so those go. One actually explodes in a shower of rusty flakes when James tries to lever it away. I finally conceded that he could help since none of us had used a crowbar before. And what a lucky man he is because the exploding knocker leaves us covered in a fine red dust. I can taste metal. When we remove the rest more successfully, Pauline takes her favourite, as does Lowenna because she's lived next door to them all for so long, and I keep one too. I don't know if I'll ever have my own front door to attach it to, but I want to live in hope. My chosen one is brass and depicts a ship about to be hit by a massive wave. The water curls down to become the knocker itself. It'll look completely out of place in a block of flats in London, and I don't care.

One evening, Pauline takes Lowenna and me to the Bolster & Saint. She makes me sit on one of the stools at the bar, but Lowenna gets special dispensation to find an actual chair.

'Look up,' Pauline tells me, busying herself with a cloth.

Above my head is a shiny brass plaque. I squint to make out the words.

> In loving memory of Martin Trewin. A beloved father, husband, and partner, and keeper of memories.

I stare at it for a minute or so, because it keeps going blurry as my eyes well up. When my attention returns to the pub, Pauline is holding out two glasses of gin and neat orange squash.

'What do you think?'

'It's perfect.'

She pushes one of the glasses towards me.

'Here. It's absolutely rank.'

I laugh. I reach up and brush the plaque lightly with my fingertips, and then I take a sip from the glass Pauline handed me.

'Jeez, Dad. How did you drink this?' I wonder aloud.

'She showed you, then?' Lowenna asks when I ditch the stool and join her instead. Pauline is busy with a sudden rush.

'You've seen it?'

'Got a special sneak peek before it went up. Nobody over eighty should be clambering on bar stools.'

'Hi, Grandma.' Adam appears out of nowhere and kisses Lowenna on the cheek, and the flush that comes over me in that moment is so sudden I'm half tempted to dive behind the sofa. It's a bit late for that, though. He nods. 'Charlie.'

'Hi.' I'm about to say more but then *James* shows up because apparently I live in some kind of farce now.

'There you are.' He flops into the sofa next to me and puts a proprietary hand on my knee. 'I couldn't find you.'

For a second that feels like an age I catch Adam's eye, and he stares back, and his shoulders drop the slightest bit. And then the room snaps back into real time and he extends a hand towards James. I pretend I can't see Lowenna frowning at me.

'Alright, mate?'

'Yeah – good, thanks.' James puts on his mockney 'talking to other men' voice.

'Does anybody need a refill? Grandma?'

'No, love, you're alright.'

That night James and I walk home, and I feel like I'm in a warm, melancholic calm – I don't even know – a *weird* haze, that's not even down to the gin and squash (which I ended up having about two sips of before I had to pour it away and get a house white instead).

I've always dreamed about having a night like I just did. Where it's spontaneous, and you just know people, and you chat, and it's not some big production that's been weeks in the planning, and everybody's comfortable. Even *I* am comfortable. I didn't think that really happened. And to think it happened here.

I pause on the cobbles in the middle of the high street for a moment. There's some distant, thumping bass coming from a car somewhere, and the occasional cry of a seagull because there always is. I had forgotten just how many stars you can see in a sky that doesn't constantly glow orange. I used to be able to name some of them, back before I left. Maybe I will again one day. Dotted above the shops are windows filled with flickering light from TVs. And I think I feel like part of it.

'Are you coming?' James asks from down the street. He's got miles ahead of me, but it's so quiet he doesn't even have to raise his voice.

'Sorry.' I trot to catch up. It was nice but now it's over. It just has to be.

◆ ◆ ◆

We've reached the end of the clean-up operation, really. Most of the rooms look – dare I say it? – like rooms in a house. Like, in a nice, normal house where nothing terrible has ever happened.

With the house pretty much back to how it used to be in The Good Old Days, it's like I can feel Mum there again. I can see her in the kitchen wiping up crumbs and scrambling eggs. She's in the living room reading magazines and arguing with oblivious politicians on the news. She's in the garden showing me an empty bird's nest she found under a hedge.

Pauline's taken the opportunity to nip out for an early lunch. Even James has gone out. He said he wanted to enjoy the sunshine, although it wouldn't surprise me if he wanted to call Magdalena in peace to try to come up with a game plan to get me back to the office. I'm not worried, because I don't think it would work. She's got better things to be doing than chasing mediocre employees who don't even want to work for her. There goes that certainty again. It's wonderful.

The sound of heels distracts me from where I'm sorting through one last seemingly-never-ending heap of papers. I glance out of the window and am startled to see a woman in a proper business suit and heels standing halfway up the garden path, staring at the house.

'Charlotte Trewin?' she asks when I open the door.

'Yeah.'

'My name's Jenny Angove, I'm a solicitor. I'm from Jackson's.' She holds out a card.

'Oh. OK.'

We stand awkwardly at the front door until I remember I'm the adult of the house now and I probably have to act accordingly.

'Do you want to come in?'

'If that's OK.'

I usher her into the hall. In that moment I feel a glow of pride. It just looks like an unremarkable hallway now. The woman in the suit doesn't even blink. But nor does she look afraid that something might fall on her head. And that lack of reaction has always been the aim. 'Can I get you a cup of tea?'

'Actually, would you mind if we just sat down together?'

'Sure . . .' I usher her through to the kitchen and we both sit at the table. I'm trying to ignore the prickle of worry at my hairline.

'I'm actually here to talk about something quite difficult.'

She takes a manila folder out of her bag and I lose the battle with that prickle of concern. Oh my God. I'm being sued. They could definitely get me for breach of contract at work. I bet that's what it is. Or I've accidentally stolen something they need and now I have to pay them back. Or maybe there's some kind of charge you're meant to pay at the hospital? Was I supposed to pay to get Dad's body out? Do you technically *buy* the body? Maybe it's the bank, because of all the funeral stuff on my credit card. Maybe . . .

Oh shit, she's been talking to me. For once in your life pay attention, Charlie. And she's still talking, and I'm still doing this. Stop. Stop, stop, stop.

'I'm sorry, I didn't catch what you said.'

'From which part?'

'The beginning. Sorry.'

She leans forward. She makes very intense eye contact this time, like she's trying to hypnotise me into paying attention. It works.

'I was just saying, I think you know my Uncle Reg?'

I nod, my eyes watering from trying not to blink.

'Well, he thought it might be helpful if I came by and talked you through your options. Your dad didn't have a will, Charlotte.'

'Charlie, please. What does that mean?'

'Well, the short answer is that everything he owned goes to you, as his only surviving relative. He didn't have a spouse—'

'He had Pauline.'

'But he wasn't married. And as his wife has been deceased for some time, everything passes to you. I have some paperwork for you to sign which will put you in charge of his estate, and then I'm afraid there'll be some admin for you to do.'

She flips through the folder, pulling out documents here and there, with those little sticky tabs where things need signing. My ears are ringing. There must surely be a grown-up who's coming to take care of this kind of stuff. If she thinks that's me, she's sadly mistaken. There are *limits* to what I should be left in charge of. She places a hand on top of mine and I jump.

'Charlotte. Sorry, Charlie. This really isn't something to worry about, OK? A million people have done it before, and they've managed.'

'Uh-huh.'

'And the house is all paid off – you could move in if you wanted to. Or you could sell it, or rent it out. Anyway, I'll leave you with all of the paperwork. Let me know if you have any questions.'

She puts a sheaf of forms down on the table.

'Don't freak out,' she tells me as she takes my hand and shakes it. I don't even bother doing the proper grip like you're supposed to. It must feel like she's shaking a massive spaghetti. She leaves the kitchen, and the front door opens and closes again.

I walk into the living room, where I sink into the sofa, but that doesn't feel right, so I stand straight back up again. I don't . . . I mean . . . This is . . . *mine*? The ringing in my ears is back in a big way, and I've also got pins and needles in my fingers. I try to shake them away but it doesn't work.

I wander through the house, staring into rooms like I'm seeing them for the first time. Or maybe not the *first* time, but at least as if I've forgotten the back-breaking work we've put into them over the last couple of weeks.

That's where Mum and Dad used to sit and play cards together while I watched cartoons. And there's the step Mum used to sit on as I got ready to leave for school, where she told me she loved me and handed me my book bag. Out the front is where she sat in one of those red-and-yellow plastic cars that time, because I'd demanded it while she was having one of her good days. She stuck a leg out of each side and gamely propelled herself around the garden while I rolled about in the grass laughing my head off. Dad watched, smiling benevolently.

It should go without saying that if I could swap this place for the chance of a do-over with Dad, I'd do it in a heartbeat. So, at first it feels weird, but I do start to wonder idly about the kind of life I could have if I lived here. I could get the kind of job I've always really fancied – behind a bar, or making espressos, or selling books. I'd pass the time of day with people and pay my bills, but I wouldn't need to pretend to give a shit about the Monday numbers or the EBITDA. I wouldn't need to Google what 'EBITDA' meant before every meeting. I could just smile, and say 'Hello' and 'How can I help you?', and have room in my brain for other things. Better things. The thought is so intoxicating I need to sit down again.

I have to tell someone about this, and I scroll through my phone to find the right person. This is laughable for multiple reasons. For starters, that scroll takes all of about ten seconds from start to finish. And for another thing, I already know I want to call Adam, but I don't want to acknowledge that that's what I want to do. I hover over James's name but the memory of him calling me reckless stops me from making the call. So, fuck it. I phone Adam before I can change my mind. I listen to it ring, but he doesn't answer. I call again, thinking he maybe just isn't next to his phone, and there's no answer again. I'm trying for a third time when I properly realise what I'm doing and drop the phone in horror. It hits the skirting board and my screen cracks, which is no more than I deserve.

When James returns he finds me halfway up the stairs, gazing into the middle distance. In all likelihood I'm fantasising about turning part of the garden into a vegetable patch, or getting a dog I could walk on the beach every day. I'm not sure, because I'm too engrossed to notice his arrival.

'Oh shit, are you OK?' The rustling thump of dropped shopping bags is what brings me back to the here and now. James pretty much leaps up the steps to sit beside me and strokes my hair. His hand gets caught in a tangle because who has time to brush their hair, really?

'Ouch! Yeah, I'm fine.' I rub my scalp. 'I just . . .'

I don't really want to tell him. He's already shat all over my excitement at quitting my job, and it's lovely to have this little secret burning away inside me. I have to, though. This is not little.

'A solicitor was here,' I tell him.

'Oh?'

'Yeah, she said my dad didn't leave a will.'

'Oh. Oh? Uh-huh. Yep.'

He has absolutely no idea what that means, and fair play because neither did I twenty minutes ago. An hour ago? I don't even know how long it's been.

'It means everything goes to me, because I'm all that's left. I don't think he had a lot. He had the house, though. It's all paid off.'

James sits back and puffs out his cheeks. Then he stands up and walks down to the kitchen. Then I hear whooping. And then I hear running footsteps, and his face appears over the banister.

'Charlie, this is so great!'

Hang on a second . . . Are we actually *on the same page* about this? Because it really feels like we might be on the same page about this. He'll still want to work, but he's already doing that from home, so maybe he could carry on. The train up to London to see his friends isn't *that* bad. He always says he wants me to be happy; maybe he knows this might actually do the trick. He could cook all the vegetables I grow.

He comes to sit next to me again and folds me into a hug.

'We'll have such a healthy deposit now!'

'What?' I pull my head away from his shoulder.

'Yeah! Obviously, once we've sold, we'll be in such a great position.'

'To buy somewhere?'

'Yeah. Like we talked about? I know you weren't sure this place would be yours to sell, but now that we know for certain, it's amazing! People dream about stuff like this.'

'Oh. Yeah.'

My heart sinks as my brain catches up with the rest of me. We *did* mention this. We can't live in the middle of nowhere. James wants more excitement than home-grown veg can provide. I let myself get carried away.

But James's plan is exciting too. We'll still have a place of our own, and I might be able to grow something on the windowsill. Maybe we'll get a balcony. And, like, a gerbil.

He chatters happily about areas we should be looking in, and then he gets out his phone to start downloading property apps. I force myself to smile. I'm happy. Happy, happy, happy.

◆ ◆ ◆

Lowenna phones in the afternoon and asks if I can drop round and see her. I'm so used to both of us just rocking up without permission that this is immediately worrying. What if she's ill again?

'I'll be right over. Do you need me to bring anything?'

'What? No, I'm not an invalid.'

OK, fine. Then I guess I don't need to worry after all.

'I just thought it would be nice to have some tea,' she says lightly, as I perch on the edge of her sofa a few minutes later. She's up to something. We have tea every day. And, don't get me wrong, it *is* nice. It just doesn't usually require a formal invitation. I wonder if she's heard about the house. I know news travels fast around here but there must be some element of attorney/client privilege. Or something similar that I didn't just steal from American TV shows.

'Let me get us something to drink,' Lowenna says.

'No, you stay there, I'll go.' I motion to her to sit back down and she rolls her eyes.

She mutters something, but I pretend not to hear her as I tread the well-worn, slightly grubby path between the living room and the kitchen. I flick the kettle on. It's so old that I worry it might electrocute me, but it doesn't, so I rummage around in the cupboards to find mugs and teabags. I have a moment to look around while the kettle makes straining noises. I assume that means it's at least trying to heat up.

Lowenna could give Dad a run for his money, really. There are a couple of clocks on the wall, both telling me different things. There's a full set of giant wooden cutlery nailed up there too. The wallpaper is a hideous floral which clashes with the orange varnish of the cabinets. A pile of paper pharmacy bags fills a shelf at the end of one of the units. The majority of them are unopened, and I make a mental note to scold her when she stops being weird.

The kettle reaches its death throes and makes a final spluttering sound which I gather means it's ready. I bring the mugs through to the living room and stop short as I discover that Lowenna has laid two glasses of neat whisky on the coffee table.

'How did you—'

'Keep the things you love close to your heart,' she tells me as she pulls open the collar of her blouse just enough to reveal a little flask tucked into her bra.

'Lowenna!'

'Hello?' Pauline calls.

She's upstairs, which is unexpected. I narrow my eyes at Lowenna but she's suddenly very intent on what's happening outside. Which is nothing. So that's also suspicious.

'Hi,' I say, as Pauline materialises in the doorway.

'Are we all good for teas?'

'You can have mine, love, I've gone for something a little bit stronger.' Lowenna raises her glass, and Pauline raises an eyebrow.

'Come on, Lowenna, surely the doctors gave you rules about spirits before dinner time.'

'Do you know what? They didn't mention it. Fair game as far as I'm concerned. Anyway, I might need it.'

'Why?'

I *knew* something wasn't right. Nothing about this seems normal.

'Don't get all jumpy, Charlie, you've needed some sense talking into you for ages.'

'What do you—'

'This is an intervention, love.' Pauline sits next to me and picks up the cup of tea Lowenna won't be drinking.

'Why?'

'Look, Charlie. I know that it was everything with your dad that originally brought you down here, and I know you haven't known me very long.'

'Although you've known *me* for a bloody age and you know I know what I'm talking about,' Lowenna interrupts.

'Yes, thank you!' Pauline says, shooting Lowenna a look. 'Anyway, I like to think that I could have been like a stepmother to you given half a chance, and obviously your dad loved you so much, and . . .'

Her eyes fill with tears and she chokes up as she says it. I scoot closer to her and take her hand, despite my misgivings about where this is going.

'We all miss him.' Lowenna nods, also tearing up a little. I look to the heavens to try to stop my eyes from brimming over. We all, by unspoken agreement, take a moment to collect ourselves.

'So, anyway, Charlie. What are you doing about that boyfriend of yours?' Lowenna asks.

'Fiancé,' I correct her.

'Yes. Him.'

'What about him?'

'Jesus Christ, Charlie, you're not a teenager!' Pauline interjects, making me jump. 'Are you seriously marrying him?'

Lowenna looks at Pauline with raised eyebrows.

'So much for buttering her up first.'

'Well, I'm sorry. Except I'm not because I don't like seeing her like this. I know we've all been through a lot – Charlie, you especially – but I don't like seeing you follow him around like he's marching you to some kind of punishment. He's not a bad guy. He's actually quite nice. But any fool can see you don't want to spend your life with him.'

I open my mouth because I feel like I should probably say something but I have no idea what that is.

'Charlie? You with us?'

'Sorry, yes,' I say, shaking my head to clear it. I turn to Pauline. 'And yes, I'm still getting married. Obviously.'

Pauline holds her hands up.

'It's just really clear that you're not *happy*, Charl—'

'That word again!' I slam my mug down. 'Not everybody is *happy* all the time, OK? Ask anyone.'

'But we're not talking about anyone, we're talking about *you*. And we're not talking about "all the time". Would you say you're *ever* happy?'

'Yes!'

'Can you give us an example of when? Just one.'

I wrack my brains, but in the heat of the moment I can't think of one, no. I'm wracking my brains, but nothing's coming. But that's not because I'm '*not ever* happy'. It's because I'm under pressure. And I've had a very confusing day. An image of Adam and me in the alleyway behind Razz crosses my mind, but I wouldn't say I was *happy* then. I had just switched my brain off for the evening. I felt lighter, which is different.

'I'm not going to dignify that with a response,' is the answer I settle for in the end. 'But, honestly. I'm happy.'

'You could've fooled me, love,' tuts Lowenna. 'You seem to forget that I've seen all of this before. If I thought you were going the way of your mother, I really don't know what I'd do.'

'I've just . . . A lot's happened.' I shrug. Understatement of the century.

'People die, Charlie. You can't make up for it by being miserable forever,' Pauline says. 'Who does that help? God love them, I don't think your parents set the standard for healthy relationships, so that hasn't helped. And maybe James feels like a safe option, and maybe that's what you think you need, but I can assure you that's not a good enough reason to be with somebody. We're talking about your whole life here.'

'And besides,' Lowenna interjects, 'if you're so happily engaged, what were you playing at canoodling with Adam?'

'I—'

'And don't think I didn't see you making eyes at him yesterday at the pub.'

I look at Pauline as if she's going to back me up, but there's no point. She's blowing across the top of her mug even though it must be cool enough to drink by now. She does *not* look surprised. So, great. They've already talked about it. The idea of Adam showing up and telling Lowenna about how I behaved at the bar makes me want to crawl under the sofa and never come out. My face begins to burn.

'I made a mistake,' I say, quietly.

'Well, if you're going to make mistakes it would be nice if you could consider other people's feelings first.'

I open my mouth to argue, but Pauline cuts across us both.

'Alright! We've voiced our concerns. That's all we can do. It's obviously up to Charlie what she decides.'

'Thank you.'

I sound like a sullen teenager but I can't help it.

'It's been nice to see you both,' I lie, and then I show myself out.

◆ ◆ ◆

I'm not ready to go home. My thoughts are beginning to fly and I can't pin any of them down long enough to work out how I really feel, even if the rest of the world constantly seems to have an opinion. I walk out to the road and begin stomping.

I stop into Karnkarrow Konveniences and pick up a gin in a tin (OK, fine, three) because it just feels like that kind of evening.

'You alright, love?' Mrs Rowe asks, peering at me.

'Yes, thanks,' I smile.

'You know, we do those Mooncups now.'

'Thank you, Mrs Rowe, I'm good.'

'I never doubted that for a second, love,' Mrs Rowe calls as I pull open the door. I pause, but I don't look back. And then I leave.

I take my tinnies and climb down the steps to the beach, ducking under the railings to walk along the wall. The sun is going down and the water reflects the pink of the sky. I sit down near my initials and dangle my legs over the side.

Mum was the first person to ever show me this place. She'd lift me over the handrail and then sit on the wall with me. We'd throw stones and look out for pirate ships. The stone-throwing was definitely ill-advised, and the pirate ships were non-existent. But I still loved it. Sometimes we'd see a seal or a dolphin, and it was nice just to sit there and have Mum tell me stories.

I wish Mum was here now. I wish Dad was here now. I wish I hadn't made things weird with Adam. I down the first tinny without even tasting it. I crush the can against the concrete wall, and it hurts my hand, but that feels like a welcome distraction. I give myself five minutes where everything is allowed to bubble over. I can just feel everything at once. Or, in other words, I cry like a baby: out loud and ugly.

After that, I dry my eyes and take a few hiccupy breaths. I just need to sort out my feelings. After a while of staring across the water, and downing the best part of another G&T, I have them narrowed down into two main issues:

A) Pauline, Lowenna, Adam sometimes . . . I mean, *everybody* questioning whether I'm happy all the time has made me feel like I'm doing something wrong if I'm not happy *all* the time. Which, as we all know, is ludicrous. It's unattainable. I am not falling for it. Happiness doesn't *mean* anything. Not really.

And anyway, I *am* happy. I just am. *So* happy. I have everything under control. Because I've seen what happens when people don't, and I am *not* turning into Mum.

I drain the rest of my can. Problem solved. Next. Next problem, next gin.

B) This nagging feeling that I don't want to sell the house. Which is, like, insane.

I stare across the bay. It's a clear sea day again and I can make out the shapes of the reef below the surface. There's barely a cloud in the sky. There's a definite hint of autumn in the air, but it's still warm enough not to need a jacket.

Oh, but soon. Soon the storms will roll in, one after the other after the other. It'll blow gales for months on end. It'll rain upwards, somehow, and sideways. It'll be so loud it keeps me awake at night. I have to remember it's not always sunny and charming like this. It gets bleak.

And sure, I've felt the pull of this place ever since I came back. But it's not like it's practical to *stay* here. There're no career prospects. The fantasies about pottering around part-time and living in the house I grew up in are nice, but that's all they really are: fantasies. That is not a life real people live. It's a lifestyle for characters in gentle Sunday-evening TV dramas. My parents were stuck, and I refuse to be because, again, I don't want to end up like Mum. So I should just sell the place, buy a maisonette out in Zone Nine and start my suburban marriage. And that's all there is to it.

And, look, fine. There's secret problem 'C' as well: Adam. I've been such an idiot. I made a mistake, yes. But I can never, *ever* make that mistake again. If I tell James what happened I'm sure he'd dump me. And then what happens? I stay here and become my mum? Again: no, thank you.

My phone buzzes in my pocket and makes me jump. I realise how high up I am, how many G&Ts I've drunk. I shuffle back from the edge before I wrestle my phone out of my pocket. It's Adam.

I know he's only returning my call because he's an all-round nice man and an old friend and, fine, because of the kiss-that-shall-no-longer-be-thought-about, but it still spooks me that he would call *right now*. It's like he's read my mind, like he knows I've sat in our special place and decided it's over.

God, it all feels so final. I suppose it has to be. Final is good. I know where I am with final. I drain my last tinny and grip my 'Joy' necklace as if it might transfer some to me if I hold it tight enough. My chest has stopped hurting now, and my panic sweat has dried. Sometimes all you need to do is sit on the edge of a cliff and give yourself a proper talking-to.

Life plan firmly back in place, I return along the wall to the steps. I pause to curl my toes as far over the edge as I dare. I wonder what it would be like to jump. Not that I would.

I walk back home feeling peaceful. Or, at least, calmer. When I get inside I stand at the bottom of the stairs. I'm frozen to the spot by the realisation that my time here has come to an end. Our work is done. The house is ready for somebody to come and take pictures, post them all over the internet, and find a new family to live here. They'll inhabit this once-buried part of my life which contains everything that made me 'me'. Every heartbreak and every celebration, and the darkest moments I've ever known. All ingrained in the walls and the floors and the colour of the paint in the hallway.

'Have you seen my jumper?'

I knew exactly where my jumper was. Ish. It was definitely in my room – I knew that much. But Mum kept doing this thing where she'd just sit in the living room for hours on end, staring, and it scared me. But I didn't like to admit that it scared me because she probably just needed someone to snap her out of it. I was sure I could do that. So I stood in the hallway, just outside the living room door, asking inane questions, trying to keep the worry out of my voice, and hoping to finally inspire a response.

'Can I get a biscuit?' I tried, after a while.

Silence. Still silence. Think. Think of something better.

'Shall we go to the beach?'

'Please just leave me alone, Charlie.'

I looked up to see my dad emerging from the kitchen with a couple of mugs. He shifted the mugs so he was carrying both in one hand (skills) and squeezed my shoulder with the other one as he reached me.

'It's alright, kiddo. You go out and play. I'm here.'

'I made you a tea.' James jolts me back to myself.

'OK.' I nod. 'Be there in a second.'

'It looks really good in here,' James says as if he's reading my mind.

'Yeah.' I sigh. I know what's coming next. I'm ready to talk about it.

'So when do you want to head back?'

CHAPTER TWENTY-TWO

We agree we'll go back in two days. It's enough time to do the rounds and say goodbye to everybody I've only just got reacquainted with, as well as to get packed and allow myself to get used to the idea all over again.

The first time I left I didn't really know I was never coming back. I threatened it enough, and I daydreamed about it. But teenagers are full of shit. So when Dad and I shoved a couple of battered, mismatched duffel bags into the boot of the car, I didn't know I was saying a permanent goodbye. We got to the station forty minutes too early because I didn't want to be late, even though there is nothing there, not even a ticket machine, to kill the time. Dad sat down next to me on the platform's only bench and sighed.

He'd pooh-poohed the idea of my catching the train up on my own when he wasn't going to see me again for months, but I'd worn him down. I told him there wouldn't be any parking, or that I'd have to drop my bags and immediately go to some welcome event or other. I said nobody else would be being dropped off by their parents and I didn't want to look out of place. I knew he'd have no choice but to believe me.

Neither of us knew the first thing about how universities worked, so he wouldn't have any evidence to the contrary.

'You know you can come home any time you want to, Charlie, you never have to ask. Just tell me you're on the train and I'll come and pick you up,' Dad told me as we sat together. It was just starting to rain, so he'd pulled his hood up and tightened it around his face, obscuring the few wisps of hair he still had left.

Anger flared in my chest when he said it. We'd disagreed before about whether or not I was doing the right thing. He thought I was being rash, moving so far away. I thought he was trying to hold me back from my ultimate goal of being anywhere but where I was.

'All that noise, Charlie. You're not used to it,' Dad would warn. 'It gets to you after a while. You remember Annie Trevail? Your mum's friend? She went up to London, and she had a breakdown.'

Her best friend's suicide probably had something to do with Annie Trevail's breakdown, but I didn't say that. Instead, I said nothing and clenched my fists until I left little half-moons in the palms of my hands.

'Honestly,' Dad continued as we both watched a seagull pacing up and down the platform, looking for all the world like it wanted to catch the 08.49 to Paddington as well. 'You never have to be embarrassed if you feel like you've made the wrong choice.'

I said nothing, choosing instead to kick at a piece of chewing gum in the crack between two paving slabs. The silence stretched out between us until Dad felt like he had to fill it, which he usually did.

'Of course, that's not to say that you'll regret anything. You might love it up there. People do. That's why it's so crowded. But there's just no shame if you don't.'

I said nothing and watched the seagull make his way down the platform.

'You'll have to send me lots of postcards,' he added, his voice brightening up, 'and you'll have to let me know when's a good time to come and visit you. We'll do all the touristy stuff together, Buckingham Palace and that.'

I still didn't answer.

Eventually we heard the electric swooping noises that meant the train was about to appear around the corner, and I jumped up. With one bag slung over my shoulder and the other clenched in my fist, I stepped forward to exactly where I knew the carriage doors were going to stop. Dad hovered somewhere behind me.

'Well, Charlie,' he said, gently touching my shoulder, 'let me know if you need anything, anything at all, and I'll make sure you get it. You know where I am.'

The lock on the door gave a 'thunk', and I pulled it open with my one free hand.

'See you soon,' Dad said.

I stopped on the first step up to the carriage and turned to face him. I felt breathless like I always did just before I jumped off the cliffs on the headland.

Dad pulled me into a hug as soon as he sensed my moment of weakness. I was the same height as him because I was on the step, so I could fit my chin on his shoulder. His coat smelled like the pub and the bonfire he'd lit in the garden last night to burn some of the dead plants. Like home.

'Love you,' he practically growled.

'Love you too.'

'On or off, love?' the train guard called.

We broke apart and Dad looked at me. He gave me a smile, and the tiniest of nods.

'On!' I called back, surprised at the confidence in my own voice.

I slammed the door shut behind me and stood at the window as the train pulled away, like someone in an old movie. Dad didn't wave, he just stood there and watched the train disappear around the corner.

He got smaller, and smaller. Once he'd disappeared from view I went to find my seat.

I layer the few things I brought with me when I rushed down in a panic into a suitcase, along with all kinds of bits and bobs I want to preserve from my childhood. I'm not doing the full Martin Trewin, but I do suddenly see the value in keepsakes. And the fact that there was a stash of spare suitcases in the house was actually very handy. Along with the brass crab I adopted, I fill my new case with the books I used to take to the beach with me after school, some still wavy at the edges from where I was occasionally caught out by the tide. I've included some bits from the kitchen, purely because they're nicer than anything James and I currently own. And, zipped safely away from everything else in their own net compartment, are a couple of Mum's old blouses that Pauline found right at the back of Dad's wardrobe.

I take one out now, sit down at the edge of the bed, and inhale it. At first Pauline and I had idly wondered whether they were actually Mum's or just something else Dad had picked up somewhere and consigned to the cupboard, but one breath told me all I needed to. They smell unmistakably like her. Her perfume, the occasional cigarette when she thought Dad wasn't looking, her shampoo. Sitting next to the suitcase with the fabric held to my face, I can feel my misgivings ease a little bit. I touch my necklace.

'How're you getting on?' James comes into the room with a cup of tea. His packing lasted all of about five minutes. He never really *un*packed.

'Not bad,' I tell him, taking care to keep my face neutral.

'God, Charlie, do we really need all this stuff?'

'*I* do,' I tell him, sticking my chin out defiantly. 'I'm not leaving it all behind.'

'No, I understand that, but—'

'Only me! I just came to see how you were getting on.' Pauline sticks her head through the door and I immediately wind my neck in.

'I'll leave you to it.' James ducks out of the room.

'Oh, you know. Fine.' I sit down on the bed. A spring complains somewhere in the mattress.

'Do you want to come and see Lowenna with me?'

'I probably shouldn't. I have loads to do here and' – I don't like the thought, but it's in the back of my mind nonetheless – 'well, I suppose we both need to get used to not seeing each other any more. I'm not going to be around to help. She can't rely on me.'

Pauline laughs at this and I look up, confused.

'Well, I'm sorry, love, but you weren't exactly *helping* her before, were you? Eating all her biscuits, mainly' – I open my mouth to protest but she continues before I can – 'which is fine, obviously. Don't leave thinking that people are only going to miss you because you were useful to them. We'll miss you for *you*, Charlie.'

Well, I'm definitely going to cry now. I stare into my case. Pauline follows my eyeline and takes in my bag full of a couple of items of clothing, a knife block, some plates, all crammed in with an entire series of Beatrix Potters and my old pink fluffy diaries.

'Bloody hell, how much are you taking?'

I giggle, tearfully.

'You're a chip off the old block after all.'

Pauline produces a crumpled tissue out of her sleeve and hands it to me. 'It's clean, I promise.'

I sniff and dab at my eyes. I can feel Pauline gearing herself up to ask something else. I don't have to wait long.

'Are you definitely sure, Charlie? About selling the place? About all of this? I don't want to pry.'

I take a moment before I answer. Because the truth is that I'm still really having to force myself to believe I'm making the right choice, but I do it. Maybe James isn't the man of my dreams, but he's been there and he's willing, and I know where I stand with him. My life with him will be stable. Which is what I want. If I know anything about Carncarrow it's that it cannot offer me that. And sure, I get a kind of . . . feeling . . . in my stomach when I think about it too hard, and it doesn't feel *great*, but that might be butterflies for all I know. That might be what excitement feels like. Maybe I just got broken a long time ago and I don't even recognise the signs any more.

'Yes, I'm sure.'

'OK. Well, come and see Lowenna, then.'

'Pauline?' I say, and she stops in the doorway. 'What *did* Dad tell you about Mum?'

She sighs and sits next to me on the bed.

'He said he eventually realised that what she did wasn't his fault, but he couldn't see it for a really long time. He tore himself up about it for years. He didn't think there was any one thing that made her do it in the end. And he liked to think that she didn't want to leave you both *forever*, she just wanted to stop being in pain in that moment, y'know?'

I nod, looking at my hands in my lap.

On the night before we leave, I step over the flower bed between Dad's house and Lowenna's and open her door.

'Lowenna!' I call, 'We're going!'

Lowenna's head pops out from the living room.

'Just give me five minutes.'

Twenty minutes later, we're ready to leave. I can feel James getting restless beside me. He keeps shifting from foot to foot and pointedly sighing. I choose to ignore him, not wanting to invite another argument. I don't know why he's even that bothered, it's not like he's especially worried about this event that isn't really for him. He shouldn't care if we're late. And nobody'll be on time anyway. He offers Lowenna an arm and a tight smile when she's finally ready.

'What a gent! I take back everything I've said about you,' she laughs, her eyes twinkling as she jokes. But it doesn't land right with James and he looks at me with hurt in his eyes. I shake my head and hope he'll brush it off.

The dinner is being held at the beach, and as we round the corner I can see lights twinkling on the shingle. They're mirrored by a couple of stars, which have already started to come out even though it's not quite dark yet. The moon is waxing full.

'Beware of deciding anything big while there's a full moon,' Lowenna told me once when I was little. 'It makes people do crazy things.'

I'm inclined to agree with her now.

When we reach the beach a couple of people are still laying out candles on the sand. Closer inspection tells me they're fake, which is fair enough. Mae is trying to light a fire on the stones – she's convinced a couple of branches to catch but now doesn't seem totally sure what to do with them. The glow illuminates the confusion on her face until Reg ambles over to help her.

'Come 'ere, you dozy mare,' he admonishes, holding out a hand for one of the smoking branches.

Somebody's set up a wallpaper table, digging it into the sand for stability, and it's already groaning with food. There are more dishes than there are people scrabbling around trying to get ready.

'Lots of people brought stuff early and went back for more,' Pauline explains, coming over to kiss me on the cheek. She pulls me into a tight hug and I wonder if I'm going to lose the battle with tears. I thought I had it under control. OK, come on. Pull it together. I'm fine, I'm fine, I'm fine.

To distract from my sudden hit of emotion I turn my attention back to the table. The whole thing is outlined with fairy lights, and it's so bright you can't help but look. There are huge mixing bowls full of salads – one normal, one rice, one chickpea. Somebody's made a couple of trays of sandwiches (triangular quarters, because it's a party). There are bowls of crisps, plates of cakes, and cheese on sticks. You can't tell from this spread whether I'm leaving or turning seven, and I love it.

'Any falafel?' James appears at my shoulder and I am immediately fuming. Calm down, calm down, calm down.

'I don't know,' I shrug, because I don't know, and he also has eyes and could just look for himself.

I join Pauline, ready to greet people as they arrive, generally laden with yet more food, or with crates full of clinking bottles. I resist the urge to look back at James, instead concentrating on making sure everybody has a drink and dishing out hugs as people arrive.

After ten or twenty minutes the beach looks like a different place. The dusk has given way to full-on darkness, and the lights dotted everywhere look beautiful. You can barely hear the sea over the chatter of everybody gathered on the shingle.

◆ ◆ ◆

'Charlie, can I speak to you?'

Adam appears behind me and I don't turn around, because if I turn around I might lose my resolve. But I nod. He walks past me, and I follow him to the other side of the beach cafe, where they're probably not supposed to leave bags of rubbish, but they definitely do. It doesn't *not* smell of fish.

'I've been calling you,' he says, so I guess we're just getting right to it.

'I know.'

'Because you called me.'

'I know.'

'I didn't think you'd really leave.'

'Well, what else am I going to do?'

He reaches over and kind of strokes the back of my hand with his fingertips. It's annoying in its own special way because then *I* want to grab *his* hand, just to make him hold mine properly, and *that* is how they get you. But I am determined not to be swayed. Or, at least, I'm pretty sure I've made up my mind? OK, look, I'm doing my best.

'You could stay.'

'You were the one who basically said you didn't want me to.'

'Yeah, but . . . Look, that was before. I thought you'd figure out that you belong here. I didn't think it'd get this far. You do what you want, but I'm just saying. It's kind of embarrassing that you haven't worked that out by now.'

'I guess I'm just a bit thick.' I try to smile, but it doesn't work, and he grimaces back.

'Probably.'

I don't know what else to say, and I don't think he does either. I can't figure out how to let him down once and for all without hurting him, deep down maybe I don't even *want* to, and I guess all of this is just a long-winded way of saying that I basically throw myself at him again. Look, it's just a very confusing time.

He kisses me back, properly this time, winding his hand into my hair to pull me closer, and I'm grateful because it's chilly on the beach since it got dark. Which is not a justification, obviously, but like I said, it's just all very confusing.

He eventually breaks away from me. 'You're really going to leave, aren't you?'

'I'm sorry.'

'Just take care of yourself.'

I take a couple of steps back, and then I turn around and head back towards the lights of the party.

'Charlie, wait.'

Something stops me in my tracks for a moment because am I doing the right thing? I guess maybe not, but I've decided what I've decided, and what I've decided *is* what I've decided. It really is fine. I keep walking.

◆ ◆ ◆

'Where have you been?' James is quick to accost me as I get back to the table with all the food. I am *starving*.

'Nowhere.'

I reach for a vol-au-vent. I glance up just in time to see Adam returning to the party. I catch his eye, and then we both look away. It's only for a split second, but it's long enough for James to clock it.

'Were you with him?'

'Please just leave it, OK?' And I guess there's something about the tremor in my voice that means he actually does.

I take my plate off to the edges of the party, sitting down on an upturned plastic drum and watching all of the people. All of the people who are here for *me*. If I'm not careful I'll start wondering if it's really true that nothing good has ever happened here, and we can't have that.

'I can't believe you're going back upcountry!' Mae squeals, sitting next to me and throwing an arm around me. She's clutching the neck of a Prosecco bottle. 'It's like you only just got here again.'

'I mean, I did.' I shrug. The memory of our night out comes screaming back to me and I suddenly want to cringe myself inside out. I have to sort it.

'You can't be ready to leave already, not after all this time!'

'I've got a wedding to plan,' I smile, even though that's not really an answer and we both know it. 'Actually, are the others here?'

'Yeah!' Mae stands up and points into the darkness. I squint in the same direction and see Claire and Rosenwyn picking their way over the stones towards us. Claire has a stack of plastic cups and Rosenwyn has far too much food piled onto one paper plate, which I respect so much it makes me hate myself all over again for my behaviour at the bar. Claire hands me a plastic cup and then pulls me into a hug, and Mae leans over to pour me some Prosecco.

'Billie and Emma are sorry they couldn't come,' Rosenwyn says, holding out her plate. I take a cocktail sausage gratefully.

'Are they really?'

'Of course! Why wouldn't they be?'

I don't really want to be eating a cocktail sausage while I make a heartfelt apology so I hold on to it and kind of regret taking it in the first place. I wonder if I can slip it into my pocket. I wonder how many weeks it would be before I remembered I'd done that. I let it drop to the floor.

'Oh God,' I groan. 'Because I was such a twat that night we all went out, and I'm so sorry, and I want *them* to know that too.'

Claire laughs. Mae looks like she's suppressing a smile too.

'What?'

'Charlie, it's fine.' Claire puts a hand on my arm. 'For starters it didn't end that well for anybody. You don't go to Razz if you have plans for the next morning, y'know?'

'I didn't.'

'And Jesus Christ,' Rosenwyn chimes in, 'you get a pass. I don't want to patronise you, I'm sure people do that enough, but you just do.'

'It was a really bad idea.' Mae shakes her head. 'I don't know what I was thinking doing it so soon after your dad . . . It's just been so long since somebody who moved away came back, I got excited.'

'It was a lovely idea,' I tell her. 'I'll come down again. I really will this time. We'll do it again. I'll eat something before. I'll get myself in training.' And to prove my point, I down my plastic cup of Prosecco.

'Oh, Charlie,' Mae squeals. She pulls me into a full hug, there are suddenly more arms as Claire and Rosenwyn join in, and I can't believe I ever wanted to run away from this place forever. But no. It's fine. Onwards and upwards, right?

'You all have to come to my wedding, OK?' I say into the middle of the crush. It's the first time I've invited anybody.

'Charlie' – Pauline interrupts our group hug, which is probably a good thing for oxygen reasons – 'do you need another drink?'

I look down at my squashed cup.

'I think so.'

I follow her over to the table and she grabs us two bottles of cider, removing the caps on the side of the table.

'You're going to have to teach me how to do that,' I tell her.

She holds up her bottle, and I clink mine against it. I'm careful to maintain eye contact, like they say you're supposed to, but I know I'm telling her more than I mean to in the process.

'You'll be OK, you know. I've been hard on you but it's out of love.'

I lower my gaze to the neck of my bottle, suddenly unable to look at her. Pauline grabs my wrist.

'Look at me, Charlie. Look at *this*. People love you, you know? You act like you're totally alone; I think sometimes you actually *believe* that you're totally alone. But you have so many friends.'

'But not—'

'And I know you don't have much in the way of family. But you have me now.' I look up at her, not able to quite take in what she's saying. 'You have me. If your father were still alive I would basically be your stepmother and I still can be, if you'll have me. I promise you'll always have somebody in your corner. No ulterior motive. A family.'

I look at her through a film of tears, which I'm trying my best not to let fall in this most public of settings, but it's difficult. I nod wordlessly, feeling like I'm about five years old, and Pauline scoops me into a tight hug. She smells familiar now too. My family.

'Speech!' someone shouts from somewhere, and people from all over the beach take up the call.

'Speech! Make a speech, Charlie!'

This is accompanied by the sound of plastic forks clacking against plastic glasses, because expectations never *quite* live up to reality. Pauline's eyes twinkle and I'm gripped by a sudden nervousness that makes me giggle. I stumble up the beach to get a better vantage point over everybody standing around holding mini pasties and plates of chickpea salad.

When I get into position and hold up my hand, a hush falls over the crowd. I can see James making his way towards me out of the corner of my eye, but he stops short when I shake my head at him. Looking out further I just see human shapes, and it's difficult to know who's who now that the night has well and truly set in. I can just about make out the shape of Lowenna. She's perched on a rock and one of the children seems to be waiting on her. The rest of the children are playing at the water's edge. I can hear them rather than see them.

'Go on, Charlie!' somebody calls from the crowd, mistaking my hesitation for nerves. But I'm not scared this time.

'I'm sorry,' I eventually begin. But it's not the same as at the funeral. The last murmur of chatter dies down. 'I am so sorry that I missed so much time getting to know all of you. When I left here all I wanted was to get out of Carncarrow, but I didn't honestly realise I wouldn't see it again. But that's how stubborn I was' – someone in the crowd cheers, I think it might be Pauline – 'and that was what happened. My biggest regret will always be losing touch with Dad.'

Here, my breath catches in my throat and I have to take a pause. Pauline has moved closer to the front so I can see her right there, welling up too.

'But now that I've been able to come back and get to know so many of you all over again, my second biggest regret will be losing touch with home altogether. You're such fantastic people, and I'm sorry that I forgot that for a while. Wherever I end up and whatever my life looks like in the future, I promise, from now on, I'm not going to hide you all away.'

Everybody erupts into applause. Which seems like a very self-important way to describe it but they really, really do. Somebody – Loic, maybe? – even chants my name. I feel like a conquering hero. I hold up a hand in thanks.

I hear footsteps on the shingle next to me, and James appears at my side. He takes my hand and holds it aloft, as if I've just won a boxing match. Which is nice. So I'm happy. I'm happy. He's supportive. And I'm happy.

'And I just want to say, on behalf of Charlie and myself,' James adds, trying to keep the same energy going, 'a massive thank you for the welcome you've given us while we've been here. We've really enjoyed our time. It'll be nice to get back to normality, but we won't forget you all in a hurry!'

I smile benignly beside him because I don't know what else to do. The crowd in front of us is completely silent, until somebody clears their throat. I swear, if crickets lived on the beach you would hear them chirping. It is suddenly my dearest wish for the ground to turn out to be quicksand.

'Woohoo!' James screams, still waving my hand in the air. I want no part of this and have let my arm go limp like a ragdoll's. I realise, with horror (or, more accurately, total humiliation), that he's trying to force the same reaction I got to my speech, and I cannot for one minute fathom why.

And I suppose I'm happy, I'm happy, I'm happy, I'm happy. But I'm really, really not.

◆ ◆ ◆

'What the *hell* was that about?' I demand as soon as I've closed the front door on the winding stream of villagers still making their way up from the beach and down the high street. Most carry fake candles, which illuminate Tupperware containers full of leftovers. They're probably all chatting about the spectacle Charlie's fiancé just made of himself in front of everybody.

'I dunno,' James replies. His tone of voice suggests a nonchalance which I can see, from the bright-red tips of his ears, he doesn't actually feel. 'I just wanted to say thank you to everybody. They've been . . . sound.'

He sighs and walks through to the kitchen. I can hear clinking as he pours us both a glass of wine. He hands mine to me in the hallway and then sinks into the sofa with a sigh.

I stand in the doorway and stare at him. I just . . . I mean, I've never seen anything like it.

'You're going to have to help me out here. You butted in because they're "sound"? That's not a thing! And you *don't* think that. You've made that very clear.' Ahead of me, James gets up to switch on the TV, then returns to his seat and scowls at it. He refuses to look in my direction. 'I don't understand why you have to take every situation and make it about you. There was tonight, the hospital, Dad's funeral. Help me understand.'

For a while, James says nothing, choosing instead to watch the TV with an expression of mild interest on his face. I know he doesn't feel as indifferent as he's making out. There goes that bright-red flush again, up his neck to the tops of his ears. He's keeping a tight grip on the edge of the sofa too. His knuckles are turning white. If he squeezes his glass much harder, it'll shatter.

'Because everything's always about you,' he says eventually, in a strained voice.

'That's not a reason!'

'It fucking is. Ever since I got down here everything's been about you. And people are, like, welcoming and everything, but then I get left standing on the sidelines, whether it's pub quizzes I'm not invited to, or tonight, or . . . I'm not just here to hold your handbag and look pretty, Charlie. We're *partners*. Or at least I thought we were.'

'But people don't know you down here. You can't blame them for—'

'Then introduce me to them! Honestly, Charlie, it's bad enough finding out that you have this whole past that you didn't respect me enough to tell me about, but then I come down here and you seem happy as Larry, living this other life that I don't seem to have any place in. Do I still have a place?'

I swerve his question. Anger courses through me, overwhelming any effort I've made over the past few days to think positively.

'You know, you haven't exactly made it easy to want to introduce you to people. You had a fucking fight with one of my friends within about ten minutes of meeting him. In a hospital!'

'Because he was clearly more than a friend, and my fiancée – you know, the woman I want to marry and spend the rest of my *life* with – had disappeared for literally days on end without telling me where she'd gone. And then I find her down here, happy as Larry, cuddled up with someone who isn't me. I was so *worried*, Charlie. I don't think you understand.'

I move around the sofa and stand in front of the TV because he will *not* stop staring at it.

'You keep saying that, you know? That I'm "happy as Larry". I don't think you understand that my *dad* died. That's the only reason I came down here. Because I had to say goodbye and sort things out. I didn't just run away to go on holiday.'

'Yeah, but you didn't even talk to your dad, so who cares?'

An ugly sob escapes me and James looks up, alarmed.

'*I* care, James! It's been eating me up. Even before all of this. I feel like the worst person in the world.'

James stands up, and I wonder if he's going to fold me into his arms and hold me until I finish crying.

Instead, he moves around the sofa, leaving it in between us like a saggy terracotta barrier.

'That's not what this is about, Charlie! I'm sorry that happened, you know I am. But not everything is about that. I'm pissed off that you've been leaving me out and making me feel like you don't want me to be here. I came all this way *for you*, and you act like you don't even want me.'

I open my mouth, breath still unsteady from my crying jag. And then I close it again. Because, I mean, I *didn't* want him to be here, and I didn't handle the surprise very well, so . . . could he be right? I didn't ask him to follow me here, but I also didn't make him very welcome when he did, so . . . *is* this my fault? It doesn't feel like that's correct, but my head is spinning and nothing he's said is technically wrong, so . . . maybe it's true?

'You know what,' he continues, 'maybe I should just face facts. You don't want me any more. I wasted my time. This is over.'

He moves toward the door. Blind panic takes hold of me. I feel like I've been punched in the gut.

'No,' I say, heart thumping. I really don't know what I want apart from needing to buy myself time until I can think clearly. My head is scrambled. 'I don't . . . I don't know.'

'And I don't know what you *want*, Charlie. I don't know how you expect me to understand you if you won't talk to me.' He approaches me with his arms wide, and this time he does fold me into them, before holding me at arm's length and looking intently into my eyes. 'You need to be clear with me. Do you want to stay together?'

And in that moment, I do. I can't be on my own. I can't throw away everything we have. So, I nod, still sniffling. He leans forward and kisses me, and really it's just quite nice to find a moment of silence in amongst all the yelling, so I let him carry on. When we break apart he looks at me again.

I don't want to have sex right now. I really don't. James kisses me again, harder this time. He tries to link his fingers through mine, but I keep my hands limp, so he settles for holding on to my wrists. His lips move from mine to my cheek, then my earlobe, and then down to my neck. I can't help but tense up. He senses my body stiffening and grips my shoulders. His eyes search my face, his nose a maximum of an inch from my own.

'Please,' he says.

I don't know what would happen to us if I said no again. I've worked so hard over the past week or so to get myself back into a positive place. Or, at least, a place that I hope I'll one day recognise as the beginnings of a positive place. Do I really want to jeopardise all of that now for the sake of not doing something we've done a thousand times before and will probably do a thousand times again? His eyes continue to search my face. I nod.

He pulls me into him, hands on my chest, and then up my top. He never did waste any time. I'm conscious that the curtains are still open, the occasional person still walking past. I don't want to be seen.

'Let's go upstairs,' I whisper as he kisses my shoulder.

He breaks away from me and nods, taking my hand.

He sweats and strains on top of me and I feel like I might as well not be there. As he pants into the pillow next to where my neck becomes my shoulder, I'm fully aware that I could be any woman. As a teenager I used to sneak glances at magazines that promised to teach you how to 'drive him wild in bed' and similar intellectual achievements, and I imagined that adults across the land were doing all kinds of gymnastic things every night. Adam and I, on the rare occasion that we did anything more than snog up against a tree, mostly did it in ridiculous places, hoping against hope that nobody would walk past and catch us in the act. There wasn't time for creativity. I always imagined things would be different when I was a glamorous city girl, but it turned out that my imagination wasn't required. All James has ever wanted from me is to be physically present and to let him get on with it.

Which he does now. His breathing gets faster and more ragged, so I know I only have to grit my teeth for another minute at the most.

I do realise, by the way, that I could have sat down and talked about this with him. We could have had the frank and honest discussion that agony aunts are always recommending in magazines. I did try, once.

I figured the best time to talk about it would be when the subject was fresh in our minds, so just afterwards seemed perfect. So as we lay in bed on Saturday morning (you know it's the weekend before payday for us when sex happens on a Saturday morning – it fills twenty minutes of an otherwise quiet day spent at home because we can't afford to do much else) and James got his breath back, I decided to go for it.

'Do you ever think we could, you know, improve things?' I shifted onto my side, just in time to see him jolt back to wakefulness, surprised by my question.

'Improve what?'

'This.' I loosely gestured around the room and then realised it might look like I was suggesting DIY, so I clarified. 'Sex.'

He sat up and pulled the covers up to his chin. I immediately knew I'd approached it wrong. My heart sank. I sat up as well.

'Don't you like it?'

'No, no, that's not it,' I back-pedalled, inwardly kicking myself for letting the agony aunts convince me that anyone could have a frank and honest discussion about anything. 'I just . . . I didn't know if there was anything you wanted me to do differently, or if you wanted to try anything new, or . . .'

He looked at me with a slight frown. I tried to make my face look reassuring and put a hand on his arm.

'But you're not unhappy?' he asked, after the silence seemed to go on for an age.

'No! No, not unhappy, just wondering if maybe we could be putting in more, y'know, effort?'

'Because I'm happy.'

'Good!'

'And you're happy?'

'I'm happy.'

'So then, if we're both happy, what would we change?' He laughed, as if I'd said something foolish, and settled back onto the mattress, pulling me into him as he did so.

'I don't know,' I laughed back, even though I didn't feel like laughing. My brain twisted itself into knots trying to figure out how that could have gone so spectacularly wrong. Meanwhile, James planted a kiss on my head and rearranged the duvet with a happy little sigh.

I've never forgiven those agony aunts, if I'm totally honest.

So now I lie quietly, pressed against the mattress. Try to think of nice things. Palm trees on a tropical beach. Winning the lottery. Raindrops on roses and whiskers on kittens. It'll be over soon.

All the while James slams into me over and over again, his arms tense as he holds himself up, his face buried in my neck. It's a small mercy that I won't have to see the face he pulls when he finishes.

One shuddering breath, then another, and a small sound that I can only describe as a whinny, and it's all over. He collapses on top of me, winded. After a couple of minutes panting directly into my collarbone, he climbs off and cuddles up to me, resting his head on my shoulder and sighing.

It doesn't take long for his breathing to slow down. He begins to twitch as he drifts off to sleep and I can relax. But then his arm snakes its way across my stomach and I tense up again. Except that's not very positive of me, and I have to remember that I'm happy. I'm happy, I'm happy, I'm happy.

The landing light is still on and it's shining right in my eyes. I don't want to get up, because I'll have to climb over James, and there's very little room for manoeuvre in this bed. I turn to face the wall and squeeze my eyes shut to try to block out the light. It doesn't work. I give up.

I roll onto my back and stare up at the ceiling. James has started snoring softly beside me. I used to think it was sweet. Actually, I used to think it was incredible. Every little snuffle to my left-hand side was a reminder that somebody actually wanted to fall asleep in the same room as me. I'd practically given up on the idea of connecting with anybody. The loneliness had been crushing, even as I'd chatted idly to people at work about how I preferred my own company, or thought boyfriends might get in the way.

I was so relieved when James asked me out. Not because it was James, particularly, just because *somebody* had. Even more so when he asked me to stay the night after the requisite three-date wait. It meant that I wasn't actually the monstrous outcast I was worrying I might become. I had to have something going for me.

I turn onto my other side and examine James's sleeping face. I wonder if, deep down inside, he also feels like he's strapped into a fairground ride he thought would be fun, but now isn't so sure about.

I can't ask him. Too risky. What if I thought I was articulating something we both felt, only to find out that it had never even occurred to him? I don't think I could smooth my way out of that if I tried.

But surely, if we're having a problem we should be able to work through it together. I should at least feel like I can talk about it. Ever since James arrived at the crematorium there's been a low-level sinking feeling in my stomach, but now it drops away completely and I gasp.

This isn't right.

I can tell Lowenna's just switched her bedroom light off because a slice of brightness on the ceiling suddenly disappears. What would she think?

Who am I kidding? She already knows. Pauline does too. Or else, what was that intervention all about? And everybody who was at the dinner tonight could see it, I bet. My toes curl at the idea that people have been feeling sorry for me again, watching me tie myself into something they know isn't right for me.

And what about Adam? He disappeared after we . . . Well, he disappeared. So I think he missed James's moment of madness, but someone will tell him. What will he think? And why do I still care what he thinks?

I draw my knees up to my chest. Behind me, James shifts in his sleep, murmuring something.

I just need to acknowledge that the positive mindset I've built up for myself over the past few days has slipped a bit. It happens. I can get it back. I take a few of those mindfulness breaths. I'd bet a ton of money this wasn't the situation work had in mind when they arranged that seminar.

In for four, hold for four, out for eight. And again. And again. And again. I find a more comfortable position to lie in and wait for the panic to subside.

It doesn't matter what anybody else thinks, I tell myself, yet again. It's unrealistic to expect to be wild with joy every single day. I will settle for having somebody around who cares when I don't come home, and who makes it affordable to live without nine flatmates. And who sometimes brings home a curry on his way back from the station. Anything above that is unrealistic. At the moment I'm mainly comfortable. And 'mainly comfortable' is a damn sight better than it could be.

I ignore the little voice somewhere right at the back of my brain yelling at me about everything I've just decided being bullshit. I roll over onto my side again, huddle under the duvet, and stare at the wall until the sun starts to make the entire room go pink.

I'm happy. I'm happy. I'm happy. I'm happy. I'm happy. I'm happy. I'm happy.

CHAPTER TWENTY-THREE

'Dad.'

He looked so small when I finally found him. Curled up on his side, his skin grey against the pink of the hospital blanket. The curtains around his bed were closed. A couple of families arranged around beds further down the ward glanced up as I arrived, but then returned their attention to their own patients with sympathetic smiles. We were all in this together but, at the same time, not at all. Dad tried to lift his head when I spoke but I could see the effort of doing so written across his face.

'Don't, please.'

Having felt hesitant all the way here, absolutely certain that he wouldn't want to see me and there'd been an admin error, I dashed the last couple of steps and took Dad's hand. He placed his free one over the top of mine. They were cold.

'You're here,' he whispered, a little smile spreading across his face. My heart folded in on itself as I tried to keep my face bright. I guess I wanted to be encouraging. I'm not sure exactly why. We both knew why I was there.

'Oh my God, Dad.'

'It's OK, Charlie.'

'No, it's—'

'Charlie.'

He tried to cut across me forcefully, but he was so weak it came out a whisper.

After it was over I leaned against the wall in the smoking area and took deep, second-hand-smoky breaths.

'You OK?' a man in a hospital gown asked me as he stubbed out his cigarette. I nodded. It seemed easier than telling him that I didn't want to leave the grounds. The world outside the car park barrier was suddenly one that I wasn't prepared for.

'Here.' He proffered his cigarette packet.

I shook my head.

'Suit yourself.'

'Do you really need all this stuff?' James asks. I know it's a joke (I hope it's a joke. I choose to believe it's a joke) but, running on no sleep and high anxiety, I don't find it funny.

'I have to go and check something,' I say, after a minute of watching him throw himself against a bag that clearly won't fit in the available space. It comes out sounding strangled – I can't get the words cleanly past the lump forming in my throat.

We started packing up the car twenty minutes ago, but I have to leave James to it. His elaborate game of Tetris is shaking my readjusted positive mindset to its core, and I really don't want to lose it over some suitcases that don't quite fit into an economy hire car.

I stomp back up the front garden and throw myself onto the ground, hugging my knees. It takes less than ten seconds for the dew on the grass to soak into my jeans and I jump back up, instead kicking the first few brown leaves where they've landed on the grass. I stand on the front lawn staring out at the tiny triangle of sea it's just possible to make out between the trees. As soon as they lose their leaves in the autumn, this house has a full sea view.

I can hear James swearing at the luggage, but he's obscured by the oak tree at the end of the garden. It's becoming something of a monster, really, stealing water from all of the other plants, casting shade over ours and Lowenna's garden and, if you park under it, providing the perfect perch for the seagulls to—

'For crying out loud, there's bird shit all over the window!'

James's anguished shout causes a couple of starlings on the roof to take flight in alarm. It's only seven o'clock.

'Would you be quiet?' I hiss in a stage whisper as I walk back down to the road, slipping in the dewy grass. 'People are asleep.'

'Look at it, though.' He indicates the windscreen, which is, indeed, a Jackson Pollock of excrement. I nod, not quite sure what he wants me to say.

'Honestly,' he continues, 'the sooner we get out of this shithole the better.'

He storms back up the garden path and leaves me staring at the Pollock, waiting for the flare of anger about the 'shithole' comment to subside. As I blink away angry tears, Pauline and Lowenna walk into view. Behind them, Mae holds the upper arms of a couple of the children I remember from last night, and Loic and Reg bring up the rear.

'What are you doing here?'

'Just out for our regular seven a.m. group constitutional.' Lowenna winks. 'What do you *think* we're doing here?'

'We came to say goodbye.' Mae pushes forward.

Lowenna rolls her eyes. 'Yes, thank you, Mae. I think she might have worked that one out, don't you?'

One of Mae's children (I wish I could be more specific but, honestly, they all look the same to me) throws himself at my legs, wrapping his arms around them and resting his head on my thigh. I reach down and touch his head in surprise. Rationally, I know that his mother has told him he has to hug me when he sees me.

He doesn't know who the hell I am, he's just following orders. But still. It's cute?

I wonder what his life is going to be like here. I wonder if he likes the same things I used to when I was his age. I wonder if he'll let himself get so bitter and twisted inside that he can no longer work out what he needs to do with his life to feel normal.

'You're not like me,' I tell him, quietly. He looks up at me and smiles, and then runs in the direction of the beach.

'Not in the sea!' Mae yells after him. 'Here,' she adds, pulling a posy out of a canvas bag. 'Put them in water when you get back and they should be OK.'

I look down at the flowers and back up at Mae. Her hand touches mine as I take the posy, and I grasp it and pull her into a hug.

'Here you go, young lady.' Loic places a hand on my shoulder, and I break away from Mae. He thrusts a plastic Coke bottle into my hand, half-filled with something brown and unctuous. 'Little sharpener for when you get back. Or before. No judgement here.'

'Loic, that better not have come from the Bolster,' Pauline scolds.

'No comment.' He winks at me.

'Alright, well, that means it definitely has, so you owe the pub the exact cost of whatever's in there, don't you?'

Loic deflates. He reaches over and takes the bottle back from me.

'It's the thought that counts, Loic, thank you,' I smile.

'Here you go, young 'un.' Lowenna steps forward, proffering possibly the world's largest plastic bag of sandwiches. I make a mental note to remove the egg mayonnaise ones before we embark on our five-hour journey in an enclosed space, and then I pull her into a hug. Her voice is muffled by my shoulder as she adds, 'It's a three-lunch journey at least.'

As we break apart, Lowenna touches my cheek.

'You go careful, you hear me? Look after yourself.'

She steps towards Mae, who puts an arm around her.

'You've done a good job here, young Charlie,' Reg says. I hug him extra-hard, still grateful that he showed up when he did on my very first day.

Reg joins the others. It's beginning to feel a little bit like a receiving line at a wedding. Which is good practice, I suppose. And then Pauline stands alone next to the car.

'Found a shit bucket!' James shouts in triumph as he reappears at the garden gate, clutching a bucket in one hand and a sponge in the other. He catches sight of Lowenna's scowl. 'Oh. Sorry.'

He hesitates for a minute, staring at the little crowd. Steam rises lazily off the bucket. Lowenna starts tapping her foot.

'Here, let me.' I eventually give in, reaching for the bucket and sponge and proffering the bag full of sandwiches in exchange.

'No, no, no, that's OK.' James seems to be jolted back into the present moment and snaps into action. He reaches the car in about three paces and starts slopping soapy water all over the windscreen.

Pauline comes to stand next to me and puts a gentle hand on my shoulder. For a while we simply watch James wash seagull droppings off the windscreen.

'Take care of yourself, OK?' Pauline eventually says. I turn to face her, and her eyes are full of concern. I feel a flash of annoyance at myself for not hiding my misgivings better when I briefly had them. Now she's worried about me. And she needn't be.

'I'll be fine,' I tell her, summoning all the brightness I can muster. The very act of doing that makes my stomach sink even further inside my body. 'I promise.'

'You know that I'm here. We're *all* here.'

'Well, we'll probably have to be in touch anyway, about the house, the estate, that kind of stuff.'

'Of course. But outside of that' – we watch James walk away and pour soapy, shitty water onto the roots of the oak tree – 'I don't want to lose touch, Charlie, OK? You're all I have left of him. I'm not going to let you get away with it so easily.'

I nod. I don't want to repeat old mistakes.

'Here, I want you to have this.' Pauline hands me something small and square, and I look down to see Dad in a little gold frame. It's not Dad how I remember him, and nor is it how he looked the last time I ever saw him, but it's him. He's completely bald, and the skin on his face looks looser, but not in a bad way. It creases around his eyes as he smiles for the camera. He looks happy. I stroke the glass.

The ability to form words briefly eludes me so I can't do anything but nod, clutch the frame to my chest for a moment, and then slide it into my pocket. Pauline pulls me into a hug and we squeeze each other so tight it's as if each of us is trying to leave a permanent impression on the other.

'You're OK,' Pauline says as she lets go. I'm not sure if she's saying it to herself or to me. But as she joins Lowenna in the gaggle of people on the pavement, I choose to believe it was to me. Because I am. I am, I am, I am.

'You'll be OK, you know.'

I jumped. I was sitting with my back against a rock, watching the water advancing and retreating, trying to focus on the sound they made against the shingle rather than my thoughts. It was a week since Mum had killed herself and I was torn between never wanting to be in the house again and not wanting to be out of it in case people spoke to me. So, I'd taken to tucking myself away into tiny, uncomfortable spaces wherever I could find them, and was surprised to hear Lowenna's voice. It took me a while to realise she was perched on top of the rock I was leaning against.

'Charlie.'

I still didn't answer and that's when she started tapping me on the shoulder. I put up with it for a little while but then—

'What?'

If she was taken aback by the ferocity of my response she didn't show it.

'Will you come back to the house, please?'

'I can't.'

'Come back to mine, then.'

'Why?'

'So that somebody knows where you are, Charlie. You can't just wander off when you're in a state. Anything could happen.'

'I'm not in a state!' I shouted, exactly how somebody who was in a bit of a state might.

Lowenna sighed and pressed her lips together. I stared back out to sea. The sky was getting dark, the sea shining bright, glassy blue. We sat there for a couple of minutes, staring towards the horizon, locked in a game of chicken I would not back down from. Lowenna eventually shifted with a groan.

'Charlie, please. I'm too old for this. Come back with me. The tide's coming in, it'll be dark soon, and the last thing we need is for something bad to happen to you too.'

I muttered and played with a piece of seaweed with the toe of my trainer.

'What was that?'

I gave a very dramatic, very teenage sigh.

'I said I wish it would.'

And then a hand closed around my upper arm and I was hoisted to my feet.

'Ow!'

'Charlotte Elizabeth Trewin, don't you ever say that again.'

I glanced around me for an escape route but my only options were the sea, a patch of exceptionally slippery seaweed, or shoving my way past Lowenna, and I wasn't brave enough for any of them. So I stared at my feet.

'Do you think your father doesn't have enough to deal with without you running around putting yourself in harm's way too? He already blames himself for what happened to your mum – what do you think he'd do if something happened to you now?'

'Yeah, but—'

'No "buts", young lady.'

'I just—'

'You "just" what?'

I bit the inside of my cheek to stop myself from saying anything and my eyes brimmed. It came out anyway.

'It's my fault. I should have done something. I should have been better, worth sticking around for.'

'Charlie,' Lowenna said, but her voice sounded different. She looked kind of . . . I wasn't even sure. Lost? She grabbed my hand and yanked my arm again. I ended up in a hug this time.

I walk back up the path to the front door. The house feels different now. It's not a place I need to run from, and it isn't stuffed to the rafters with bad memories. Or junk.

The single knocker we left on the door has had a scrub, and now shines in the sunlight that's just starting to peek through the clouds. I look up at Lowenna's window, which has been thrown open to greet the day while she says goodbye to me.

I step into the hallway and it's like a different place. It's bright, airy, and nothing is covered in dust. I still hate cleaning with a passion, but I have to admit I've done a good job here. My last bag sits on the carpet under the window, and I grasp the handles, taking a deep breath as I pick it up. This is it.

It's funny, I have the urge to run around the place saying good-bye to all of the rooms and hugging the walls. I've never experienced that before, here or anywhere else. I'm happy. I'm happy, I'm happy, I'm happy. This is fine, and I am happy.

'You ready to go?' James interrupts my swirl of thoughts. I nod. 'I can't wait to get back. Fancy an Indian tonight? You don't get good international food out in the sticks.'

I make an indeterminate noise and James takes me by the hand. He leads me out of the front door, not noticing that I trail one arm behind me to brush it as we pull it shut behind us. The keys have been surrendered to Pauline, which is probably for the best because I think the act of locking up might be more symbolism than I can deal with right now.

I pause halfway down the path and turn to look back at the house. It looks a little bit like a smiling face – upstairs windows for eyes, with part-closed curtains that look like they're half closed with laughter. The thatch on the roof could be hair, and the bright-red door is a mouth.

I feel a tug on my arm.

'Come on,' James says gently. But when I don't move immediately the tugging gets more insistent. 'Charlie, please.'

There's panic in his voice.

Our goodbye committee is still waiting by the car. They give us a little cheer as we emerge from the gate. I sling my last bag onto the back seat and put one hand on the passenger-side door. This is fine. I'm happy. It's fine.

I take a big breath, pull open the door, climb in, and shut it, all in one motion. Like ripping off a plaster. A plaster which was covering up my bright, shiny future, obviously.

James starts the engine and a chorus of goodbyes start up outside. They grow louder as we pull away from the kerb. I wave like a lunatic, in stark contrast to James's casual hand in the air. When I look back,

283

Loic is holding the bottle of unspecified contraband alcohol aloft in a cheers. As they all diminish into nothing, I swivel back in my seat to watch Carncarrow pass us by. There goes the library, and the florist. I see Mrs Rowe opening up Karnkarrow Konveniences and she waves. I lift a hand, and then she's gone. We head past the Bolster, all locked up at this time of the morning, the bright-yellow shutters clashing perfectly with the blue walls. The only life to be seen is a couple of seagulls scrapping over cigarette butts under a picnic table out the front. The flowers still look gorgeous.

The road gets steeper as you climb out of town. Dad always told me I should go out on my bike more and I categorically refused because of this ridiculous hill. The engine of the tiny car starts to struggle. The huge amount of luggage and the need for it to carry more than one person probably isn't helping. It whines and James floors it.

'Come on, you piece of shit,' he pleads.

I roll my eyes and gaze out of the window. I've been trying not to think that this might be the last time I see any of these places. But, I mean, if history has taught me anything it's that I leave Carncarrow and tend not to return for over a decade.

I haven't really come up to this end of town while I've been back. I suppose because it's more for the tourists. The food is pricier, and there are galleries and antiques shops. The buildings are the oldest ones in town, and so warped that they lean into the road, their top floors practically touching. I stare through the window of Bailie's Burgers as James jams on the handbrake. Inside, actual Bailie herself wipes down tables in preparation for opening.

I remember sitting there with Mum when I was a child. I was colouring in one of the menus, which had a beach scene on it, specifically designed to keep the children of frazzled holidaymakers quiet for ten minutes. Except there was no blue pencil in the little pot the waitress

gave me when we sat down. My heart started to flutter. My lip wob-
bled. Mum stopped rubbing her temples and put a hand over mine.

'What's wrong?'

'There's no blue.'

'So, use another colour.'

'But it's for the sky!'

'And?'

'And the sea!'

'No, not . . .' She sighed and rubbed her eyes. Looking back, I
suppose the signs were there, but I do at least recognise that I was too
young to know. See? I'm learning. 'Just do them another colour and
don't whine.'

'But it's not right!'

She looked down at me then. Really looked. It felt a bit like she was
staring straight into my soul. Her eyes were . . . They weren't angry. I didn't
think I was in trouble. But they were fierce. I shrank back in my chair.

'Charlie Trewin, I never want to hear you worrying about some-
thing not being right ever again.'

'But—'

'OK. Let's back up. Don't murder people, and don't steal from
them. Don't copy people at school, and don't start bullying anybody.
But. If nobody's getting hurt, then there's no such thing as "wrong". So
what if you colour the sea in yellow and the sky in red? This is your
picture – you can do what you like.'

I tentatively picked up the green pencil and lightly coloured in a
corner of the sky, careful not to go over the lines. A lightning bolt did
not strike me dead, so it seemed like she might actually be right.

'Can I join in?' Mum asked.

I nodded, and she picked up the purple pencil and started doodling
patterns in all of the clouds. Some of the patterns went over the lines
and everything. My jaw dropped.

'What?' She grinned at me.

'Nothing,' I told her, unable to contain a bubble of mirth. I kicked my legs happily and started colouring in earnest.

Our food finally arrived. Some kind of salad for Mum, because adulthood was (and is) nothing if not tiresome, and turkey dinosaurs for me, because every food outlet in a ten-mile radius knew that they were all I'd eat and had them in stock just in case. The waitress looked over my shoulder at the picture.

'That's beautiful.'

'Mummy said I could do what I liked.'

'Your mum's a very wise woman, isn't she?'

Mum tugged the picture out of the way of my plateful of beige. There were also a few peas on there, but we're talking very few because everybody knew I wasn't going to eat them. Mum smiled at me.

'Do you mind if we keep this?' the waitress asked. 'I think it would look super-cool on the wall, don't you?'

I looked at Mum for reassurance, but she just gave me a neutral smile.

'What did we talk about, Charlie? You do what you like.'

I couldn't believe it was up to me to make all of these decisions. First I could pick the colour of the sky, and now I could choose to be an actual artist with my picture on display?

'Yes,' I told the waitress, emphatically.

'Amazing!' She genuinely looked delighted and reached for the picture. 'I can't wait to put it up.'

'Did that feel good?' Mum asked me when she'd left us to our meal.

I nodded, suddenly more preoccupied with the curly fries on my plate, but happy to allow Mum to continue speaking if she needed to.

'That's what being in control feels like,' she said. 'You always get to be in control. Don't you forget it.'

I flicked a couple of peas off my plate and grinned.

'Excuse me, young lady, you get to be in control, you don't get to be cheeky.' Mum stole a chip from my plate and laughed.

James turns the key once, twice, and the engine shudders into life. He slowly releases the handbrake, and we move, painfully, forward. Mum's words from another lifetime ring in my ears as the cafe finally slips past the window.

I don't know what it is about this moment, but it *is* something about this moment. It hits me like so many waves on the beach in a storm: powerful and unavoidable. At first I think it's straightforward nausea. Because of the hill, or the fumes from the engine, or my lack of breakfast, or . . . I don't know. James slams the brake on again, then tries another hill start. And suddenly I know that I'm just not leaving. Everything about this is wrong. Who am I helping by making myself miserable forever?

'Stop!' I place a hand on James's arm, which distracts him. He takes his foot off the accelerator and we roll backwards. We both scream, and James pulls the handbrake on, leaving us straddling both lanes.

'What the *fuck*?'

'Sorry.'

'You can't just make people jump when they're trying to drive.'

'Sorry, I know, I just . . . I can't do this.'

'Well, neither can I if you keep pulling stunts like that.'

'No, James.' I put my hand back on his arm and he begrudgingly turns to meet my eye. There's resignation in his, and I know he knows what I'm about to say. 'I mean, I can't do this. I can't go back. I can't get married. I can't do any of it.'

He opens his mouth and closes it a couple of times. His eyes move from left to right as he tries to think what to say. The colour drains out of his face, and then the signature red flush rises up his neck. He draws himself up, straightening his spine and pushing his shoulders back. He's gearing up for something, but what? To argue? To shout? To cry? I hold my breath as I wait for whatever's next. I'm not sure I'll be able to hang on to this newfound resolve. And then he just exhales and shrinks back into the driver's seat.

'I know,' he sighs, quietly, as all of the fight drains out of him.

We sit in the car for a minute, in silence, absorbing it all. The engine makes some metallic clicks and pings as it cools down.

'You . . . You *know?*'

'Yeah. Something's been off. Ever since I got down here and you weren't wearing your ring.'

I nod, chewing my lip. I could correct him about how long things have been off for, but why?

'Alright, well,' James says, eventually, 'no sense in sitting here all day.'

He climbs out, opens the boot, and starts removing my luggage.

'I knew I couldn't compete with this place. As soon as I arrived.' He gives a bitter laugh. 'I fucking knew it. You belong here.'

'Sorry.'

We stand awkwardly on the hill, neither of us quite knowing what to do, or how to really draw a line under this thing permanently. I pile my bags against a bench out of the way of the road, and then I look back at him. He's just staring at me, sadly. He opens his arms and I walk into them without hesitation. He feels so familiar that for a second I have misgivings. Am I being an idiot to give up the only person who's ever loved me? But I know the answer is 'no'. Because he's not that. There are lots of people who love me. I just forgot about them. For once in I don't know how long, I feel . . . fine, I suppose. There's no flutter of panic in my tummy or sinking feeling in my heart. I just feel normal.

I step away from the hug and walk a couple of paces back to my bags.

'Oh, James' – he's just about to climb into the car when he turns around – 'it's not about you having to compete with here. I feel like I was in it for the wrong reasons, y'know?'

'I suppose.' He sighs. It seems to come from his toes. 'But you do belong here.'

'I really am sorry.' I can't stop the smile spreading across my face, even as my eyes burn with tears. It's like something I've been suppressing has finally had room to expand. I'm breathing as deep as I can for the first time in a long time and it smells like the sea, and chips, and home.

I hold up a hand as James pulls away. The car protests less now, and actually makes it up the hill without the extra person and the extra person-worth of luggage. It feels like a sign. I know I'm right about this. There's that certainty again.

My eyes fall to my bags resting against the bench at the top of the quay and then rise to the harbour beyond. The tide is about as in as it can be and the water sparkles in the early sunlight. A few little boats bob there, looking like an illustration from a children's book. It's another one of those 'over-saturated photo' kind of days, and I can't resist it. I take a step and then my body takes over (would it be wanky to say it's my heart? Because I actually think it might be my heart) and I break into a run. When I reach the end of the quay, I fling myself off.

The moment I cannonball into the water I know I've done the right thing. This is home. The fact that I'm still wearing clothes and shoes prevents me from swimming properly, but in this moment I simply couldn't care less. I let out the cry of joy that's been building in my chest since James drove off. A couple of seagulls who've drifted over to suss out if I have any food take flight, disgruntled. I roll over onto my back and gaze at that bright-blue sky.

CHAPTER TWENTY-FOUR

One Year Later

Lowenna and Pauline often talk with glee about the time I jumped into the harbour with all my clothes on. I've tried to explain the logic behind it, but they've never quite understood. Which is fair enough because I suppose there wasn't a huge amount of logic involved to begin with.

'Seems like a good way to catch your death, if you ask me,' Lowenna always laughs.

That was also the view of Pamela Bateman, the Coastwatch officer on duty that morning, who assumed I was trying to throw myself to my death and scrambled a lifeboat. I don't think she's ever quite forgiven me, no matter how many times I explain that I did it because I was having an epiphany. I still buy her a drink out of fear every time I see her at the Bolster & Saint. It's actually costing me quite a lot of money at this point. Not ideal on a coffee-shop wage.

On the anniversary of the day I jumped into the harbour, I stretch myself out long enough to reach past each corner of my bed, in full starfish fashion. I look at the clock. Ten a.m. I suppose I should grace the world with my presence eventually. But stretching myself out in bed with nobody to get in my way, and no one there to judge me for the lateness of the hour, is one of life's true pleasures.

When I do finally emerge, I make myself a coffee and sit at the kitchen table. I ponder where I would be if I'd let things carry on as they were. Only just starting to calm down and retract my elbows from another fight across London, I imagine. Maybe the sweat on the back of my blouse would have just dried. More generally, I suppose I'd be a wife. I often wonder if I would have changed my name. I think not, but it's easy to say that now, when I have nobody's opinion in the mix but my own. James and I would probably have given each other the silent treatment until one of us cracked, and that 'one of us' would have been me. My therapist says I have an avoidant personality, which is a bit rich considering I see her every week without fail, even when I don't want to. But she has a ton of certificates on the wall, so I suppose she's the boss.

I've painted the kitchen a bright yellow, which, Lowenna always says, makes it look like you're eating breakfast inside an egg yolk.

The house is mine now. It still smells like the home I grew up in, but I spent an exhausting couple of weeks painting every single room, unable to tell my arse from my elbow in a haze of dust sheets and out-of-place furniture. And now it's so much more than that place I spent years wanting to run away from.

It's incredible how much a life can change in a year. I never believed it before. I didn't dare to, because where there was hope there was the possibility of disappointment. My phone buzzes as I'm getting all misty-eyed looking at my egg-yolk-yellow walls.

See you later? Adam's text reads. I shoot back a thumbs-up.

I wouldn't want anybody to think that I broke it off with James and immediately jumped into bed with Adam. Because, first and foremost, I have never 'jumped into bed' with anybody in my life. Far too athletic. And I had things I needed to figure out. I don't like to think about anything in my life as 'traumatic', exactly. But I did have, like, proper, wanky 'working on myself' kind of work to do.

And he didn't hang around waiting for me either. And nor should he have, because maybe I'd never have been in the right place, y'know? He dated a depressingly hot surfer girl for a month or two while she was in Cornwall this summer. I was very mature and supportive, while also trying to avoid ever sitting next to her because I didn't think my self-esteem could take it.

'It's OK,' Lowenna once said to me while I may or may not have been grinding my teeth and staring at them in the Bolster. 'She's a looker, but I don't think he'd settle down with a supermodel.'

Which might have been rude? But, anyway, I'd done lots of proper, wanky 'working on myself' kind of work already by then so I could take it, and life went on.

And maybe now I'm ready, and maybe now he's single, and maybe we'll see what happens. I chew my lip and play with my coffee cup.

My phone buzzes again, making me jump. So popular this morning. I roll my eyes but secretly feel a little thrill. OK, a big thrill. My phone is still ringing. Pay attention.

'Hello?'

'Lowenna says to get your arse out here now, please,' Pauline tells me curtly. 'I mean, she didn't phrase it quite like that but that's the summary.'

'Just give me a minute,' I laugh. I can hear Pauline relaying that back.

'You've had about a hundred already!' Lowenna shouts in the background.

I grab my bag and head for the door. Pauline and Lowenna wait on the bench I added to the front lawn. I love sitting here and staring down at the sea once the leaves have disappeared from the trees. I'll only get a couple of days each winter where the weather's nice enough to do it, but that's good enough for me.

'Are you ready?' Pauline asks gently.

'I should bloody hope so – she's had more than enough time,' Lowenna grumbles.

I shoulder my bag and there's a metallic clanking sound as I follow Pauline down to the beach. Lowenna brings up the rear, but any time I try to help her she swats me away.

When we're all arranged on the shingle near the water's edge, I remove two brass urns from my backpack and place them next to each other on the sand. I can't believe we're doing this. But it's time. Pauline puts an arm around my shoulders, and Lowenna loops hers around my elbow on the other side.

After a moment I hand one of the urns to Pauline and hug the other one tight. Pauline looks at me, and I give her a nod. Then we take off the lids, wade up to our knees, and empty the contents together.

We stay there for a little while, watching the shadows of Mum and Dad being pulled away by the retreating tide. Pauline sniffs and I hand her a tissue, then we join Lowenna back on the beach. She's poured us all a gin and neat orange squash, which remains utterly disgusting. Especially, it turns out, when you have it before you've even had lunch.

I fight with the barbecue for a really long time before I manage to get the bloody thing lit. Then Pauline takes over. I sit on the blanket, by Lowenna's feet, like I used to do years and years ago before everything went wrong.

'Room for one more?'

Adam strides towards us, swinging a Tesco bag in one hand and one from the chip shop in the other. He hands them to Lowenna, who begins digging through, and then he sits next to me on the blanket and nudges me with his shoulder. I smile and nudge him back.

I don't know if I'll stay here forever. I don't know when I'll totally forgive myself for the way things ended with Dad. I don't know what Mum would think of the woman I've become. I don't know how to have a serious conversation. I don't really know how to organise a funeral. I don't even know what I'm having for breakfast tomorrow.

But.

But.

I do know that in this moment I am happy, happy, happy.

ACKNOWLEDGEMENTS

I used to imagine the day I got to write the acknowledgements for a book that I had actually written and, as it turns out, it's nerve-wracking! For one thing, the word 'acknowledgements' really stops looking like a word once you've stared at it for too long. I'm also paranoid that I'll miss somebody out. There are lots of people without whom *Happy Happy Happy* wouldn't exist.

I'm very grateful to everyone at ACM UK and especially Sara O'Keeffe, for being the first person to see something in my manuscript. Thank you for your belief in me, and for helping me to mould this story into something that more people might want to read.

I am also hugely grateful to everybody at Lake Union. Thank you to Victoria Oundjian and Celine Kelly, who gave me fantastic feedback and editorial guidance that helped me to get even further under Charlie Trewin's skin. It's been lovely having you both in my corner. Thanks also to Jill Sawyer for her meticulous copy-editing, and to Silvia Crompton for her very thorough (and educational) proofread.

A big thank you to Laura Barnett for her teaching and feedback while I was still working on my first draft; I might not have made it to the end otherwise.

I have some fantastic writer friends who have all been kind enough to read chunks and/or entire drafts of my manuscript and give much-appreciated feedback. So, huge thanks to Kerry Harden, Rebecca Hilton, Susie Lovelock, Todd Minchinton, Linda O'Sullivan, Zoe Rankin, Rosie Whitaker, and Helen Yarnall. I love our little-yet-globe-spanning group. Long may it continue!

Massive thanks to Mel Leung, who very nicely agreed to read what I thought was my final draft with fresh eyes and then let me bombard her with questions when she'd finished. I can only apologise that the version you read actually turned out to be very unfinished after all.

The biggest thank you goes to my family; especially Mum, Dad, and Lisa for your non-stop support. Thank you for being there through the blogging years, the comedy phase, The Miserables, and everything else that somehow led me here. It means the world.

ABOUT THE AUTHOR

Photo © 2021 Claire Wilson

Nicola Masters grew up on the outskirts of London and studied English and drama at Goldsmiths. She had several jobs before becoming a novelist, including as a receptionist, an HR adviser and an admin assistant. She now lives on the north coast of Cornwall, where she enjoys swimming in the sea and spending time at the beach. *Happy Happy Happy* is her first novel.